Escape with us into the worlds of fantasy, where good must triumph, where evil must get its comeuppance, and where the grim, drab reality of the everyday world with its care and woes can be forgotten.

THE YEAR'S BEST FANTASY STORIES is another great DAW institution, side by side with DAW's "bests" in science fiction, horror tales, and overseas SF. Originally edited by Lin Carter, it is now being continued with the same care and selectivity by Arthur W. Saha.

Now read the best of the year by Tanith Lee, Michael Bishop, C. J. Cherryh, Roger Zelazny, and many more....

DAW Anthologies include:

THE ANNUAL WORLD'S BEST SF
Edited by Donald A. Wollheim with
  Arthur W. Saha

THE YEAR'S BEST HORROR STORIES
Edited by Karl Edward Wagner

THE YEAR'S BEST FANTASY STORIES
Edited by Arthur W. Saha

THE GREAT SF STORIES (1939 . . .)
Edited by Isaac Asimov and Martin H. Greenberg

TERRA SF: The Best from Western Europe
Edited by Richard W. Nolane

HECATE'S CAULDRON
Edited by Susan Shwartz

AMAZONS
Edited by J. A. Salmonson

THE YEAR'S BEST FANTASY STORIES: 8

Edited by
Arthur W. Saha

DAW Books, Inc.
DONALD A. WOLLHEIM, PUBLISHER

1633 Broadway, New York, NY 10019

PUBLISHED BY
THE NEW AMERICAN LIBRARY
OF CANADA LIMITED

COPYRIGHT ©, 1982, BY DAW BOOKS, INC.

ALL RIGHTS RESERVED.

COVER ART, *Talena*, BY OLIVIERO BERNI.

DEDICATION

For Matthew

With love from a proud father.

FIRST PRINTING, OCTOBER 1982

2 3 4 5 6 7 8 9

DAW TRADEMARK REGISTERED
U.S. PAT. OFF. MARCA REGISTRADA.
HECHO EN WINNIPEG, CANADA

PRINTED IN CANADA
COVER PRINTED IN U.S.A.

ACKNOWLEDGMENTS

"When the Clock Strikes" by Tanith Lee first appeared in *Weird Tales #1*. Copyright © 1980 by Tanith Lee. Reprinted by permission of the author.

"Midas Night" by Sam Wilson first appeared in *Rod Serling's The Twilight Zone Magazine*, August 1981. Copyright © 1981 by TZ Publications, Inc. Reprinted by permission of the author.

"Unicorn Variation" by Roger Zelazny first appeared in *Isaac Asimov's Science Fiction Magazine*, April 13, 1981. Copyright © 1981 by Davis Publications, Inc. Reprinted by permission of the author.

"The Only Death in the City" by C. J. Cherryh first appeared in *Sunfall*. Copyright © 1981 by C. J. Cherryh. Reprinted by permission of the author.

"The Quickening" by Michael Bishop first appeared in Universe 11. Copyright © 1981 by Terry Carr. Reprinted by permission of the author.

"The River Maid" by Jane Yolen first appeared in *The Magazine of Fantasy & Science Fiction*, January 1981. Copyright © 1980 by Mercury Press, Inc. Reprinted by permission of the author and her agent, Curtis Brown, Ltd.

"Skirmish on Bastable Street" by Bob Leman first appeared in *The Magazine of Fantasy & Science Fiction*, June 1981. Copyright © 1981 by Mercury Press, Inc. Reprinted by permission of the author.

"A Pattern of Silver Strings" by Charles de Lint first appeared as a limited edition chapbook from Triskell Press. Copyright © 1981 by Charles de Lint. Reprinted by permission of the author.

"A Friend in Need" by Lisa Tuttle first appeared in *Rod Serling's The Twilight Zone Magazine*, August 1981. Copyright © 1981 by TZ Publications, Inc. Reprinted by permission of the author and her agent, Howard Morhaim Literary Agency.

"Pooka's Bridge" by Gillian FitzGerald first appeared in *Elsewhere*. Copyright © 1981 by Gil FitzGerald. Reprinted by permission of the author.

"The Belonging Kind" by John Shirley and William Gibson first appeared in Shadows 4. Copyright © 1981 by John Shirley and William Gibson. Reprinted by permission of the authors.

Table of Contents

Introduction	7
WHEN THE CLOCK STRIKES By Tanith Lee	9
MIDAS NIGHT By Sam Wilson	26
UNICORN VARIATION By Roger Zelazny	35
THE ONLY DEATH IN THE CITY By C.J. Cherryh	60
THE QUICKENING By Michael Bishop	78
THE RIVER MAID By Jane Yolen	107
SKIRMISH ON BASTABLE STREET By Bob Leman	113
A PATTERN OF SILVER STRINGS By Charles de Lint	129
A FRIEND IN NEED By Lisa Tuttle	151
POOKA'S BRIDGE By Gillian FitzGerald	164
THE BELONGING KIND By John Shirley and William Gibson	178

INTRODUCTION

Fantasy is alive and well and flourishing. That is a fact that became very obvious to me while reading short fiction for this year's anthology and from observation of other events during 1981.

The main sources for short fantasy fiction remain the genre magazines, anthologies and collections, and the small press. However, whereas in 1980 there was only one genre magazine even partially devoted to fantasy, *The Magazine of Fantasy & Science Fiction*, last year two new titles, *Rod Serling's The Twilight Zone Magazine* and *Fantasy Book*, appeared along with the revival of a third, *Weird Tales*, in book-magazine format. *Twilight Zone*, which was inspired by the very popular old television series of the same name, appears to be a newsstand success. *Fantasy Book* is available only by subscription and in specialty shops, and I wish it well. Fantasy tales are also appearing occasionally in the regular science fiction magazines, and the men's magazines seem to have increased their fantasy content as well.

Many excellent fantasy novels were published during the year. Some of them, primarily supernatural horror, made the best-seller lists.

Not only has the World Fantasy Convention become a permanent fixture, but other conventions wholly devoted to fantasy have also appeared on the scene. Whereas regular science fiction conventions might have devoted one or two panels to fantasy in the past, now much of the program is centered around fantasy, with panels and speeches based on almost every branch of the subject. Many conventions are even scheduling midnight panels with emphasis on spooks and haunts and other creatures that only come out at night.

The film industry, not to be outdone and having noticed the popularity of fantasy, presented for the public's enjoyment a variety of movies last year. They covered everything from sword and sorcery to fantastic adventure to myth to, of course, horror. Once again a fantasy film, *Raiders of the Lost Ark,* was the top box office draw. Several other fantasy films also made the top ten at the box office.

I don't purport to know why there has been such a rise in interest in fiction about worlds that never were and never could be. Even a fictional world, no matter how familiar, that contains even one supernatural or mythical being is not the real world we know. Some authors have said that they write fantasy in order to examine reality. Perhaps many readers, too, are finding that fantasy is a way to examine or cope with or even escape from reality. On the other hand, perhaps they are simply finding that fantasy can be a highly entertaining form of relaxation.

Whatever the reasons may be I'll leave to others to hypothesize about, and I'm sure we'll be seeing many articles on the subject. I do know that much superb fantasy fiction is being written, and here are eleven of the very best pieces of short fiction published in 1981.

Let us embark now on a voyage to fantasyland. It's a voyage that will take us to places that are in many ways very familiar as well as to places that are totally removed from us in space and time. I'm sure the journey will by richly rewarding and enjoyable.

ARTHUR W. SAHA
Cooperstown, NY

Tanith Lee

WHEN THE CLOCK STRIKES

Here is the latest of Tanith Lee's retellings of classic fairy tales. The heroine of the original story has been celebrated in opera, the ballet, movies and song. The tale that follows, however, presents a much darker, and perhaps grimmer, version of that well-known young woman's story than the one with which most of us are familiar.

Yes, the grand ballroom is filled only with dust now. The slender columns of white marble and the slender columns of rose-red marble are woven together by cobwebs. The vivid frescoes, on which the Duke's treasury spent so much, are dimmed by the dust; the faces of the painted goddesses look grey. And the velvet curtains—touch them, they will crumble. Two hundred years now, since anyone danced in this place on the sea-green floor in the candle-gleam. Two hundred years since the wonderful clock struck for the very last time.

I thought you might care to examine the clock. It was considered exceptional in its day. The pedestal is ebony and the face fine porcelain. And these figures, which are of silver, would pass slowly about the circlet of the face. Each figure represents, you understand, an hour. And as the appropriate hours came level with this golden bell, they would strike it the correct number of times. All the figures are unique, as you see. Beginning at the first hour, they are, in this order, a girl-child, a dwarf, a maiden, a youth, a lady and a knight. And here, notice, the figures grow older as the day declines: a queen and king for the seventh and eighth hours, and after these, an abbess and a magician, and next to last, a hag. But the very last is the strangest of all. The twelfth figure; do you recognize him? It is Death. Yes, a most curious clock. It was reckoned a marvelous thing then. But it has not struck for two hundred years. Possibly you have been told the story? No? Oh, but I am certain that you have heard it, in another form, perhaps.

However, as you have some while to wait for your carriage, I will recount the tale, if you wish.

I will start with what was said of the clock. In those years, this city was prosperous, a stronghold—not as you see it today. Much was made in the city that was ornamental and unusual. But the clock, on which the twelfth hour was Death, caused something of a stir. It was thought unlucky, foolhardy, to have such a clock. It began to be murmured, jokingly by some, by others in earnest, that one night when the clock struck the twelfth hour, Death would truly strike with it.

Now life has always been a chancy business, and more so then. The Great Plague had come but twenty years before and was not yet forgotten. Besides, in the Duke's court there was much intrigue, while enemies might be supposed to plot beyond the city walls, as happens even in our present age. But there was another thing.

It was rumored that the Duke had obtained both his title and the city treacherously. Rumor declared that he had systematically destroyed those who had stood in line before him, the members of the princely house that formerly ruled here. He had accomplished the task slyly, hiring assassins talented with poisons and daggers. But rumor also declared that the Duke had not been sufficiently thorough. For though he had meant to rid himself of all that rival house, a single descendant remained, so obscure he had not traced her—for it was a woman.

Of course, such matters were not spoken of openly. Like the prophecy of the clock, it was a subject for the dark.

Nevertheless, I will tell you at once, there was such a descendant he had missed in his bloody work. And she was a woman. Royal and proud she was, and seething with bitter spite and hunger for vengeance, and as bloody as the Duke, had he known it, in her own way.

For her safety and disguise, she had long ago wed a wealthy merchant in the city, and presently bore the man a daughter. The merchant, a dealer in silks, was respected, a good fellow but not wise. He rejoiced in his handsome and aristocratic wife. He never dreamed what she might be about when he was not with her. In fact, she had sworn allegiance to Satanas. In the dead of night she would go up into an old tower adjoining the merchant's house, and there she would say portions of the Black Mass, offer sacrifice, and thereafter practice witchcraft against the Duke. This witchery took a common form, the creation of a wax image and the maiming of the image that, by sympathy, the injuries inflicted on the wax be passed on to the living body of the victim. The woman was capable in what she did. The Duke fell sick. He lost the use of his limbs and was racked by excruciating pains from which he could get no relief. Thinking himself on the brink of death, the Duke named his sixteen year old son his heir. This son was dear to the Duke, as everyone knew, and be sure the woman knew it too. She intended sorcerously to murder the young man in his turn, preferably in his father's sight. Thus, she let the Duke linger in his agony, and commenced planning the fate of the prince.

Now all this while she had not been toiling alone. She had one helper. It was her own daughter, a maid of fourteen, that she had recruited to her service nearly as soon as the infant could walk. At six or seven, the child had been lisping the satanic rite along with her mother. At fourteen, you may imagine, the girl was well versed in the Black Arts, though she did not have her mother's natural genius for them.

Pehaps you would like me to describe the daughter at this point. It has a bearing on the story, for the girl was astonishingly beautiful. Her hair was the rich dark red of antique burnished copper, her eyes were the hue of the reddish-golden amber that traders bring from the East. When she walked, you would say she was dancing. But when she danced, a gate seemed to open in the world, and bright fire spangled inside it, but she was the fire.

The girl and her mother were close as gloves in a box. Their games in the old tower bound them closer. No doubt the woman believed herself clever to have got such a helpmate, but it proved her undoing.

It was in this manner. The silk merchant, who had never suspected his wife for an instant of anything, began to mistrust the daughter. She was not like other girls. Despite her great beauty, she professed no interest in marriage, and none in clothes or jewels. She preferred to read in the garden at the foot of the tower. Her mother had taught the girl her letters, though the merchant himself could read but poorly. And often the father peered at the books his daughter read, unable to make head or tail of them, yet somehow not liking them. One night very late, the silk merchant came home from a guild dinner in the city, and he saw a slim pale shadow gliding up the steps of the old tower, and he knew it for his child. On impulse, he followed her, but quietly. He had not considered any evil so far, and did not want to alarm her. At an angle of the stair, the lighted room above, he paused to spy and listen. He had something of a shock when he heard his wife's voice rise up in glad welcome. But what came next drained the blood from his heart. He crept away and went to his cellar for wine to stay himself. After the third glass he ran for neighbors and for the watch.

The woman and her daughter heard the shouts below and saw the torches in the garden. It was no use dissembling. The tower was littered with evidence of vile deeds, besides what the woman kept in a chest beneath her unknowing husband's bed. She understood it was all up with her, and she understood too how witchcraft was punished hereabouts. She snatched a knife from the altar.

The girl shrieked when she realized what her mother was at. The woman caught the girl by her red hair and shook her.

"Listen to me, my daughter," she cried, "and listen carefully, for the minutes are short. If you do as I tell you, you can escape their wrath and only I need die. And if you live I am satisfied, for you can carry on my labor after me. My vengeance I shall leave you, and my witchcraft to exact it by. Indeed, I promise you stronger powers than mine. I will beg my lord Satanas for it and he will not deny me, for he is just, in his fashion, and I have served him well. Now, will you attend?"

"I will," said the girl.

So the woman advised her, and swore her to the fellowship

of hell. And then the woman forced the knife into her own heart and dropped dead on the floor of the tower.

When the men burst in with their swords and staves and their torches and their madness, the girl was ready for them.

She stood blank-faced, blank-eyed, with her arms hanging at her sides. When one touched her, she dropped down at his feet.

"Surely she is innocent," this man said. She was lovely enough that it was hard to accuse her. Then her father went to her and took her hand and lifted her. At that the girl opened her eyes and she said, as if terrified: "How did I come here? I was in my chamber sleeping—"

"The woman has bewitched her," the father said.

He desired very much that this be so. And when the girl clung to his hand and wept, he was certain of it. They showed her the body with the knife in it. The girl screamed and seemed to lose her senses totally.

She was put to bed. In the morning, a priest came and questioned her. She answered steadfastly. She remembered nothing, not even of the great books she had been observed reading. When they told her what was in them, she screamed again and apparently would have thrown herself from the narrow window, only the priest stopped her.

Finally, they brought her the holy cross in order that she might kiss it and prove herself blameless.

Then she knelt, and whispered softly, that nobody should hear but one—"Lord Satanas, protect thy handmaid." And either that gentleman has more power than he is credited with, or else the symbols of God are only as holy as the men who deal in them, for she embraced the cross and it left her unscathed.

At that, the whole household thanked God. The whole household saving, of course, the woman's daughter. She had another to thank.

The woman's body was burnt, and the ashes put into unconsecrated ground beyond the city gates. Though they had discovered her to be a witch, they had not discovered the direction her witchcraft had selected. Nor did they find the wax image with its limbs all twisted and stuck through with needles. The girl had taken that up and concealed it. The Duke continued in his distress, but he did not die. Sometimes, in the dead of night, the girl would unearth the image from under a loose brick by the hearth, and gloat over it, but she did nothing else. Not yet. She was fourteen and the cloud of her mother's acts still hovered over her. She knew what she must do next.

The period of mourning ended.

"Daughter," said the silk merchant to her, "why do you not remove your black? The woman was malign and led you into wickedness. How long will you mourn her, who deserves no mourning?"

"Oh my father," she said, "never think I regret my wretched mother. It is my own unwitting sin I mourn." And she grasped his hand and spilled her tears on it. "I would rather live in a convent," said she, "than mingle with proper folk. And I would seek a convent too, if it were not that I cannot bear to be parted from you."

Do you suppose she smiled secretly as she said this? One might suppose it. Presently she donned a robe of sackcloth and poured ashes over her red-copper hair. "It is my penance," she said. "I am glad to atone for my sins."

People forgot her beauty. She was at pains to obscure it. She slunk about like an aged woman, a rag pulled over her head, dirt smeared on her cheeks and brow. She elected to sleep in a cold cramped attic and sat all day by a smoky hearth in the kitchens. When someone came to her and begged her to wash her face and put on suitable clothes and sit in the rooms of the house, she smiled modestly, drawing the rag or a piece of hair over her face. "I swear," she said, "I am glad to be humble before God and men."

They reckoned her pious and they reckoned her simple. Two years passed. They mislaid her beauty altogether, and reckoned her ugly. They found it hard to call to mind who she was exactly, as she sat in the ashes or shuffled unattended about the streets like a crone.

At the end of the second year, the silk merchant married again. It was inevitable, for he was not a man who liked to live alone.

On this occasion, his choice was a harmless widow. She already had two daughters, pretty in an unremarkable style. Perhaps the merchant hoped they would comfort him for what had gone before, this normal cheery wife and the two sweet, rather silly daughters, whose chief interests were clothes and weddings. Perhaps he hoped also that his

When the Clock Strikes

deranged child might be drawn out by company. But that hope foundered. Not that the new mother did not try to be pleasant to the girl. And the new sisters, their hearts grieved by her condition, went to great lengths to enlist her friendship. They begged her to come from the kitchens or the attic. Failing in that, they sometimes ventured to join her, their fine silk dresses trailing on the greasy floor. They combed her hair, exclaiming, when some of the ash and dirt were removed, on its color. But no sooner had they turned away, than the girl gathered up handfuls of soot and ash and rubbed them into her hair again. Now and then, the sisters attempted to interest their bizarre relative in a bracelet or a gown or a current song. They spoke to her of the young men they had seen at the suppers or the balls which were then given regularly by the rich families of the city. The girl ignored it all. If she ever said anything it was to do with penance and humility. At last, as must happen, the sisters wearied of her, and left her alone. They had no cares and did not want to share in hers. They came to resent her moping greyness, as indeed the merchant's second wife had already done.

"Can you do nothing with the girl?" she demanded of her husband. "People will say that I and my daughters are responsible for her condition, and that I ill-treat the maid from jealousy of her dead mother."

"Now how could anyone say that?" protested the merhant, "when you are famous as the epitome of generosity and kindness."

Another year passed, and saw no huge difference in the household.

A difference there was, but not visible.

The girl who slouched in the corner of the hearth was seventeen. Under the filth and grime she was, impossibly, more beautiful, although no one could see it.

And there was one other invisible item—her powers, (which all this time she had nurtured, saying her prayers to Satanas in the black of midnight), her powers were rising like a dark moon in her soul.

Three days after her seventeenth birthday, the girl straggled about the streets as she frequently did. A few noted her and muttered it was the merchant's ugly simple daughter and paid no more attention. Most did not know her at all.

She had made herself appear one with the scores of impoverished flotsam which constantly roamed the city, beggars and starvelings. Just outside the city gates, these persons congregated in large numbers, slumped around fires of burning refuse or else wandering to and fro in search of edible weeds, scraps, the miracle of a dropped coin. Here the girl now came, and began to wander about as they did. Dusk gathered and the shadows thickened. The girl sank to her knees in a patch of earth as if she had found something. Two or three of the beggars sneaked over to see if it were worth snatching from her—but the girl was only scrabbling in the empty soil. The beggars, making signs to each other that she was touched by God—mad—left her alone. But, very far from mad, the girl presently dug up a stoppered clay urn. In this urn were the ashes and charred bones of her mother. She had got a clue as to the location of the urn by devious questionings here and there. Her occult power had helped her to be sure of it.

In the twilight, padding along through the narrow streets and alleys of the city, the girl brought the urn homewards. In the garden at the foot of the old tower, gloom-wrapped, unwitnessed, she unstoppered the urn and buried the ashes freshly. She muttered certain unholy magics over the grave. Then she snapped off the sprig of a young hazel tree, and planted it in the newly-turned ground.

I hazard you have begun to recognize the story by now. I know you suppose I tell it wrongly. Believe me, this is the truth of the matter. But if you would rather I left off the tale . . . No doubt your carriage will soon be here—No? Very well. I shall continue.

I think I should speak of the Duke's son at this juncture. The prince was nineteen, able, intelligent and of noble bearing. He was of that rather swarthy type of looks one finds here in the north, but tall and slim and clear-eyed. There is an ancient square where you may see a statue of him, but much eroded by two centuries, and the elements. After the city was sacked, no care was lavished on it.

The Duke treasured his son. He had constant delight in the sight of the young man and what he said and did. It was the only happiness the invalid had.

Then, one night, the Duke screamed out in his bed. Servants came running with candles. The Duke moaned that a sword was transfixing his heart, an inch at a time. The prince hurried into the chamber, but in that instant the Duke spasmed horribly and died. No mark was on his body. There had never been a mark to show what ailed him.

The prince wept. They were genuine tears. He had nothing to reproach his father with, everything to thank him for. Nevertheless, they brought the young man the seal-ring of the city, and he put it on.

It was winter, a cold, blue-white weather with snow in the streets and countryside and a hard wizened sun that drove thin sharp blades of light through the sky, but gave no warmth. The Duke's funeral cortege passed slowly across the snow, the broad open chariots draped with black and silver, the black-plumed horses, the chanting priests with their glittering robes, their jeweled crucifixes and golden censers. Crowds lined the roadways to watch the spectacle. Among the beggar women stood a girl. No one noticed her. They did not glimpse the expression she veiled in her ragged scarf. She gazed at the bier pitilessly. As the young prince rode by in his sables, the seal-ring on his hand, the eyes of the girl burned through her ashy hair, like a red fox through grasses.

The Duke was buried in the mausoleum you can visit to this day, on the east side of the city. Several months elapsed. The prince put his grief from him, and took up the business of the city competently. Wise and courteous he was, but he rarely smiled. At nineteen his spirit was worn. You might think he guessed the destiny that hung over him.

The winter was a hard one, too. The snow had come, and having come was loath to withdraw. When at last the spring returned, flushing the hills with color, it was no longer sensible to be sad.

The prince's name day fell about this time. A great banquet was planned, a ball. There had been neither in the palace for nigh on three years, not since the Duke's fatal illness first claimed him. Now the royal doors were to be thrown open to all men of influence and their families. The prince was liberal, charming and clever even in this. Aristocrat and rich trader were to mingle in the beautiful dining room, and in this very chamber, among the frescoes, the marbles and the candelabra. Even a merchant's daughter, if the merchant were notable in the city, would get to dance on the sea-green floor, under the white eye of the fearful clock.

The clock. There was some renewed controversy about the clock. They did not dare speak to the young prince. He was a skeptic, as his father had been. But had not a death already occurred? Was the clock not flying in the jaws of fate? For those disturbed by it, there was a dim writing in their minds, in the dust of the street or the pattern of blossoms. *When the clock strikes*—But people did not positively heed these warnings. Man is afraid of his fears. He ignores the shadow of the wolf thrown on the paving before him, saying: "It is only a shadow."

The silk merchant received his invitation to the palace, and to be sure, thought nothing of the clock. His house had been thrown into uproar. The most luscious silks of his workshops were carried into the house and laid before the wife and her two daughters who chirruped and squealed with excitement. The merchant stood smugly by, above it all yet pleased at being appreciated. "Oh, father!" cried the two sisters, "may I have this one with the gold piping?" "Oh, father, this one with the design of pineapples?" Later, a jeweler arrived and set out his trays. The merchant was generous. He wanted his women to look their best. It might be the night of their lives. Yet all the while, at the back of his mind, a little dark spot, itching, aching. He tried to ignore the spot, not scratch at it. His true daughter, the mad one. Nobody had bothered to tell her about the invitation to the palace. They knew how she would react, mumbling in her hair about her sin and her penance, paddling her hands in the greasy ash to smear her face. Even the servants avoided her as if she were just the cat seated by the fire. Less than the cat, for the cat saw to the mice—Just a block of stone. And yet, how fair she might have looked, decked in the pick of the merchant's wares, jewels at her throat. The prince himself could not have been unaware of her. And though marriage was impossible, other less holy, though equally honorable contracts might have been arranged to the benefit of all concerned. The merchant sighed. He had scratched the darkness after all. He attempted to comfort himself by watching the two sisters exult over their apparel. He refused to admit that the finery would somehow make them seem but more ordinary than they were by contrast.

When the Clock Strikes

The evening of the banquet arrived. The family set off. Most of the servants sidled after. The prince had distributed largesse throughout the city; oxen roasted in the squares and the wine was free by royal order.

The house grew somber. In the deserted kitchen the fire went out.

By the hearth, a segment of the gloom rose up.

The girl glanced around her, and she laughed softly and shook out her filthy hair. Of course, she knew as much as anyone, and more than most. This was to be her night, too.

A few minutes later she was in the garden beneath the old tower, standing over the young hazel tree which thrust up from the earth. It had become strong, the tree, despite the harsh winter. Now the girl nodded to it. She chanted under her breath. At length a pale light began to glow, far down near where the roots of the tree held to the ground. Out of the pale glow flew a thin black bird, which perched on the girl's shoulder. Together, the girl and the bird passed into the old tower. High up, a fire blazed that no one had lit. A tub steamed with scented water that no one had drawn. Shapes that were not real and barely seen flitted about. Rare perfumes, the rustle of garments, the glint of gems as yet invisible filled and did not fill the restless air.

Need I describe further? No. You will have seen paintings which depict the attendance upon a witch of her familiar demons. How one bathes her, another anoints her, another brings clothes and ornaments. Perhaps you do not credit such things in any case. Never mind that. I will tell you what happened in the courtyard before the palace.

Many carriages and chariots had driven through the square, avoiding the roasting oxen, the barrels of wine, the cheering drunken citizens, and so through the gates into the courtyard. Just before ten o'clock (the hour, if you recall the clock, of the magician) a solitary carriage drove through the square and into the court. The people in the square gawped at the carriage and pressed forward to see who would step out of it, this latecomer. It was a remarkable vehicle that looked to be fashioned of solid gold, all but the domed roof that was transparent flashing crystal. Six black horses drew it. The coachman and postillion were clad in crimson, and strangely masked as curious beasts and reptiles. One of these beast-men now hopped down and opened the door of the carriage. Out came a woman's figure in a cloak of white fur, and glided up the palace stair and in at the doors.

There was dancing in the ballroom. The whole chamber was bright and clamorous with music and the voices of men and women. There, between these two pillars, the prince sat in his chair, dark, courteous, seldom smiling. Here the musicians played, the deep-throated viol, the lively mandolin. And there the dancers moved up and down on the sea-green floor. But the music and the dancers had just paused. The figures on the clock were themselves in motion. The hour of the magician was about to strike.

As it struck, through the doorway came the figure in the fur cloak. And, as if they must, every eye turned to her.

For an instant she stood there, all white, as though she had brought the winter snow back with her. And then she loosed the cloak from her shoulders, it slipped away, and she was all fire.

She wore a gown of apricot brocade embroidered thickly with gold. Her sleeves and the bodice of her gown were slashed over ivory satin sewn with large rosy pearls. Pearls, too, were wound in her hair that was the shade of antique burnished copper. She was so beautiful that when the clock was still, nobody spoke. She was so beautiful it was hard to look at her for very long.

The prince had got up from his chair. He did not know he had. Now he started out across the floor, between the dancers, who parted silently to let him through. He went toward the girl in the doorway as if she drew him by a chain.

The prince had hardly ever acted without considering first what he did. Now he did not consider. He bowed to the girl

"Madam," he said, "you are welcome. Madam," he said, "tell me who you are."

She smiled.

"My rank," she said. "Would you know that, my lord? It is similar to yours, or would be were I now mistress in my dead mother's palace. But unfortunately, an unscrupulous man caused the downfall of our house."

"Misfortune indeed," said the prince. "Tell me your name. Let me right the wrong done you."

"You shall," said the girl. "Trust me, you shall. For my name, I would rather keep it secret for the present. But you may call me, if you will, a pet name I have given myself—Ashella."

"Ashella . . . But I see no ash about you," said the prince, dazzled by her gleam, laughing a little stiffly, for laughter was not his habit.

"Ash and cinders from a cold and bitter hearth," said she. But she smiled again. "Now everyone is staring at us, my lord, and the musicians are impatient to begin again. Out of all these ladies, can it be you will lead me in the dance?"

"As long as you will dance," he said, "you shall dance with me."

And that is how it was.

There were many dances, slow and fast, whirling measures and gentle ones. And here and there, the prince and the maiden were parted. Always then he looked eagerly after her, sparing no regard for the other girls whose hands lay in his. It was not like him, he was usually so careful. But the other young men who danced on that floor, who clasped her fingers or her narrow waist in the dance, also gazed after her when she was gone. She danced, as she appeared, like fire. Though if you had asked those young men whether they would rather tie her to themselves, as the prince did, they would have been at a loss. For it is not easy to keep pace with fire.

The hour of the hag struck on the clock.

The prince grew weary of dancing with the girl and losing her in the dance to others and refinding her and losing her again.

Behind the curtains there is a tall window in the east wall that opens on the terrace above the garden. He drew her out there, into the spring night. He gave an order, and small tables were brought with delicacies and sweets and wine. He sat by her, watching every gesture she made, as if he would paint her portrait afterwards.

In the ballroom, here, under the clock, the people murmured. But it was not quite the murmur you would expect, the scandalous murmur about a woman come from nowhere that the prince had made so much of. At the periphery of the ballroom, the silk merchant sat, pale as a ghost, thinking of a ghost, the living ghost of his true daughter. No one else recognized her. Only he. Some trick of the heart had enabled him to know her. He said nothing of it. As the step-sisters and wife gossiped with other wives and sisters, an awful foreboding weighed him down, sent him cold and dumb.

And now it is almost midnight, the moment when the page of the night turns over into day. Almost midnight, the hour when the figure of Death strikes the golden bell of the clock. And what will happen when the clock strikes? Your face announces that you know. Be patient; let us see if you do.

"I am being foolish," said the prince to Ashella on the terrace. "But perhaps I am entitled to be foolish, just once in my life. What are you saying?" For the girl was speaking low beside him, and he could not catch her words.

"I am saying a spell to bind you to me," she said.

"But I am already bound."

"Be bound then. Never go free."

"I do not wish it," he said. He kissed her hands and he said, "I do not know you, but I will wed you. Is that proof your spell has worked? I will wed you, and get back for you the rights you have lost."

"If it were only so simple," said Ashella, smiling, "but the debt is too cruel. Justice requires a harsher payment."

And then in the ballroom, Death struck the first note on the golden bell.

The girl smiled and she said, "I curse you in my mother's name."

The second stroke.

"I curse you in my own name."

The third stroke.

"And in the name of those that your father slew."

The fourth stroke.

"And in the name of my Master, who rules the world."

As the fifth, the sixth, the seventh strokes pealed out, the prince stood nonplussed. At the eighth and the ninth strokes, the strength of the malediction seemed to curdle his blood. He shivered and his brain writhed. At the tenth stroke, he saw a change in the loveliness before him. She grew thinner, taller. At the eleventh stroke, he beheld a thing in a ragged black cowl and robe. It grinned at him. It was all grin below a triangle of sockets of nose and eyes. At the twelfth stroke, the prince saw Death and knew him.

In the ballroom, a hideous grinding noise, as the gears of the clock failed. Followed by a hollow booming, as the mechanism stopped entirely.

When the Clock Strikes

The conjuration of Death vanished from the terrace.

Only one thing was left behind. A woman's shoe. A shoe no woman could ever have danced in. It was made of glass.

Did you intent to protest about the shoe? Shall I finish the story, or would you rather I did not? It is not the ending you are familiar with. Yes, I perceive you understand that, now.

I will go quickly, then, for your carriage must soon be here. And there is not a great deal more to relate.

The prince lost his mind. Partly from what he had seen, partly from the spells the young witch had netted him in. He could think of nothing but the girl who had named herself Ashella. He raved that Death had borne her away but he would recover her from Death. She had left the glass shoe as token of her love. He must discover her with the aid of the shoe. Whomsoever the shoe fitted would be Ashella. For there was this added complication, that Death might hide her actual appearance. None had seen the girl before. She had disappeared like smoke. The one infallible test was the shoe. That was why she had left it for him.

His ministers would have reasoned with the prince, but he was past reason. His intellect had collapsed as totally as only a profound intellect can. A lunatic, he rode about the city. He struck out at those who argued with him. On a particular occasion, drawing a dagger, he killed not apparently noticing what he did. His demand was explicit. Every woman, young or old, maid or married, must come forth from her home, must put her foot into the shoe of glass. They came. They had no choice. Some approached in terror, some weeping. Even the aged beggar women obliged, and they cackled, enjoying the sight of royalty gone mad. One alone did not come.

Now it is not illogical that out of the hundreds of women who's feet were put into the shoe, a single woman might have been found that the shoe fitted. But this did not happen. Nor did the situation alter, despite a lurid fable that some, tickled by the idea of wedding the prince, cut off their toes that the shoe might fit them. And if they did, it was to no avail, for still the shoe did not.

Is it really surprising? The shoe was sorcerous. It constantly changed itself, its shape, its size, in order that no foot, save one, could ever be got into it.

Summer spread across the land. The city took on its golden summer glaze, its fetid summer smell.

What had been a whisper of intrigue, swelled into a steady distant thunder. Plots were being hatched.

One day, the silk merchant was brought, trembling, and grey of face, to the prince. The merchant's dumbness had broken. He had unburdened himself of his fear at confession, but the priest had not proved honest. In the dawn, men had knocked on the door of the merchant's house. Now he stumbled to the chair of the prince.

Both looked twice their years, but if anything, the prince looked the elder. He did not lift his eyes. Over and over in his hands he turned the glass shoe.

The merchant, stumbling too in his speech, told the tale of his first wife and his daughter. He told everything, leaving out no detail. He did not even omit the end: that since the night of the banquet the girl had been absent from his house, taking nothing with her—save a young hazel from the garden beneath the tower.

The prince leapt from his chair.

His clothes were filthy and unkempt. His face was smeared with sweat and dust . . . it resembled, momentarily, another face.

Without guard or attendant, the prince ran through the city toward the merchant's house, and on the road, the intriguers waylaid and slew him. As he fell, the glass shoe dropped from his hands, and shattered in a thousand fragments.

There is little else worth mentioning.

Those who usurped the city were villains and not merely that, but fools. Within a year, external enemies were at the gates. A year more, and the city had been sacked, half burned out, ruined. The manner in which you find it now, it is somewhat better than it was then. And it is not now anything for a man to be proud of. As you were quick to note, many here earn a miserable existence by conducting visitors about the streets, the palace, showing them the dregs of the city's past.

Which was not a request, in fact, for you to give me money. Throw some from your carriage window if your conscience bothers you. My own wants are few.

No, I have no further news of the girl, Ashella, the witch. A devotee of Satanas, she has doubtless worked plentiful woe in the world. And a witch is long-lived. Even so, she will die eventually. None escape Death. Then you may pity her, if you like. Those who serve the gentleman below—who can guess what their final lot will be? But I am very sorry the story did not please you. It is not, maybe, a happy choice before a journey.

And there is your carriage at last.

What? Ah, no, I shall stay here in the ballroom where you came on me. I have often paused here through the years. It is the clock. It has a certain—what shall I call it—power, to draw me back.

I am not trying to unnerve you. Why should you suppose that? Because of my knowledge of the city, of the story? You think that I am implying that I myself am Death? Now you laugh. Yes, it is absurd. Observe the twelfth figure on the clock. Is he not as you have always heard Death described? And am I in the least like that twelfth figure?

Although, of course, the story was not as you had heard it, either.

Sam Wilson

MIDAS NIGHT

Chance meetings in greasy diners can sometimes lead to unexpected results. At least such is the case with the protagonist of "Midas Night." Who really does own the world?

For Muriel

Life, in its usual magnanimous fashion, was offering him a chance to face the limits of his courage. Eric Carew had no desire to be beaten or stabbed to death, so he stayed inside the seedy little diner.

He had never been in a fight in his twenty years; or at least he'd never *won* any of the few unpleasant physical encounters he had not managed to avoid. But even these, he knew, in the safety of retrospective reflection, had been minor affairs, brief attacks by bullies, compared to this. This would cost him much more.

He sat in the back at a stained table, trying to distract himself from his mounting fear by sketching, on a large pad, a portrait of the old man who sat at a window booth in the front of the diner. Next to the sketch pad sat a half-finished cup of coffee, dead as the moon. It had been delivered black by the surly waitress ("Cook went home sick," she'd told him. "I can give you soup and coffee—or you can go some-

Midas Night

where else"), and subsequent attempts to resurrect it with cream and then sugar had failed miserably. But there it was. If he ate better, he didn't pay the rent.

Starving artists, he frequently mused, were romantic figures only to *very* low-grade morons.

His mind wasn't on the lifeless substance in the cup, though. Across the street he saw three figures cloaked in the shadows of this cold, snowless January night. They had been there for a very long time.

He wouldn't look at them anymore...

The diner held only the three of them: Carew—a frightened art student seeking refuge; an ill-tempered middle-aged waitress who read a newspaper behind the counter next to the cash register; and the old man.

The old man might have been nine thousand years old. His long white beard tumbled from his parchmentlike face in knots and webs, spilling onto the otherwise empty table before him. He was lost in a large knee-length coat that had apparently entered the final stages of leprosy long ago. It was buttoned, top to bottom. His eyes—

His eyes were wild.

The old man had been dozing—for centuries, perhaps. Now his eyes swept the diner, back and forth and back again. He fixed his stare on Carew.

Uncomfortable, Carew looked down at his attempt to capture that strange face with pencil strokes. It was all wrong. *This* face had to be created outward from the eyes, where the ages-old soul still burned.

Despite himself, Carew smiled. Funny how terror can fuel the imagination. This was just an old bum, seeking shelter from the cold. Apparently the waitress didn't care who came in here.

He tore the sheet from the pad.

He was in trouble. He had to do something while he still could. But what? The police...?

It had been a stupid move, and he'd known it at the time. But things weren't going well for him at this point in his life. Jodi had left him, his studies were suffering as a result, and he'd needed a psychological lift. At least he'd thought so. He had cashed the student assistance check at a currency exchange instead of depositing it as usual in his minuscule savings account.

And for a few brief minutes he'd actually felt better, full of endless possibilities, carrying close to four hundred dollars in cash in his very pockets. To Carew, that amount of money to spend freely was a fortune. He had gone with the feeling. New York had been his! Fantastic meals in elegant restaurants! New, sharp-looking clothes! Broadway musicals! Perhaps—yes, this was it—a daredevil trip over to Atlantic City, where he would win untold riches! Then he would bombard Jodi with flowers, truckloads of them, gifts, promises of a secure future that couldn't fail to bring her back. Then, of course, she would marry him, and . . .

And . . . He had seen himself reflected in the glass of a barbershop window, fragmented through the crisscross protective iron gate, and had been aware of a fool staring back at him. The glorious feeling had vanished into the freezing air

Meeting Jodi had been the most wonderful event of his life—at the time. Even now she flashed into his mind, golden hair sailing on the wind behind her, smile to turn his insides to sweet mud. Her image was always vivid, real. She had meant everything to him.

But now he realized that he had been no more than a hobby to her, an ego boost while she hunted for a man who could afford her. It was hopeless. She was gone for good. Maybe—if he withdrew every cent and sold what little he had—maybe he would have enough for a one-way ticket to a South Pacific Island, to start a new life . . .

The hell with it, he thought. Fantasy time was over. He had to live in the real world. One that included an empty apartment.

And the footsteps behind him . . .

He'd seen them when he'd cashed the check, standing outside the currency exchange, three guys about his age, watching. And now here he was, seven o'clock at night, trapped in an almost empty diner miles from home, waiting to be assaulted by hoodlums. The three had made no direct threats, but they had followed him for six blocks, all the way to this diner.

Well, he'd never pretended to be a hero. If they weren't

gone in ten minutes, he would definitely call the police. He looked at his wristwatch.

"Good evening, sir."

The old man was standing at his table. Startled, Carew quickly turned the sketch over.

The old man slid into the seat opposite him.

"Yes?" Carew asked.

"They're after me you know." The words came fast, but with perfect clarity.

"Pardon me?"

"They're after me. I got away."

"Who's after you?"

"*They* are."

Carew felt embarrassed, uneasy. He had never felt comfortable in situations like this. This derelict was obviously off in his own dream world.

"I own the world, you know."

"Oh?"

"They want to put me away."

"Yes, that is a problem."

"But they won't get me again."

Behind the counter the waitress turned a page of her newspaper.

Across the street, the burning ends of three cigarettes moved forward in the darkness.

"Let me have your coffee."

Carew felt the walls closing in on him; panic was squeezing his chest. *Hello, police department? I seem to have a problem—*

"Your coffee," said the old man.

"What? Yes, yes, take it!"

The other reached across the table with hands that, to Carew, looked as if they'd been young before Babylon. With both hands he grasped the cup, brought it to his lips, and drank down the rest of the coffee without a sound.

Now I know you're immortal, if you can drink that, thought Carew. He looked around. *I can't stay in here all night. They can very easily come in here and get me. At any second.*

Taking a deep breath, he rose from the table, trying to collect his thoughts. He'd never called the police for help in his life. What actual *proof* did he have that he was in danger? How should he word it?

The old man reached over, grabbed him by the sleeve of his jacket, and pulled him back down.

"Where are you going?"

"I—I have to make a phone call."

The old man kept his grip locked on Carew's sleeve. "They're after me. *You've got to help me.*"

Carew pulled free, gently, but didn't get back up. Something in the man's voice, something in the man's eyes, held him.

"Why would anybody be after you?"

The old man leaned forward. His face might have been an abstract impression of Hiroshima at a certain point in its history.

"I own the world," he whispered. "They keep me locked up so I can't be in charge."

It was all so ridiculous, Carew told himself. But he felt himself drawn by the old man's passion.

"If you own the world, why are you asking for my coffee? I mean, you're not exactly dressed like—"

"Only a few people know. They say I'm crazy, too old, that I forget things. They say they have to take care of me. They give me drugs, hide me in strange places, make me look like this so nobody will believe me if I get away from them. They tricked me!"

"How did you get to own the world, anyway?"

"I made a deal!"

Carew was fascinated, but he didn't have the time. A thought occurred to him.

"Are those the guys who are after you, across the street?"

The old man turned quickly and looked, then turned back and shook his head.

"Not them."

"Well, I think they're after *me.*"

"They try to control me. But the world, everything, belongs to me!"

And just then the three of them walked beneath a streetlight and across the street, moving toward the diner. Their hands were pushed forward in the pockets of their jackets. One had a large chain draped over his shoulder.

"I'm going to call the police."

Midas Night

Behind the counter the waitress was oblivious to the coming violence. She turned another page.

The three of them didn't come into the diner, but split up just outside it, two to the left, the one with the chain to the right, all out of sight.

Now he was sure. He got up and went to the telephone, picked up the receiver, and tapped out the emergency number. *Life*, he thought. An hour ago he'd welcomed death, his one and only great love gone away. Now, faced with its very real possibility: *I guess I'm having second thoughts about the whole thing.*

Right. Go out and tell the big guy with the chain a few good jokes.

He remembered that he didn't know exactly where he was; he turned to ask the waitress the address.

He saw that the old man was not there.

The phone buzzed briefly, then went dead.

He hung up, picked up the receiver, dialed again. This time he was greeted with silence. Icy claws began to tear down his spine. He tried it once more. Nothing. Silence. Nothing.

"Excuse me," Carew said to the waitress. Tears were about to explode from his eyes; he fought to hold back the flood.

The waitress looked up at him.

"Your phone is out of order."

She shrugged and went back to the newspaper.

He was in trouble. He was trapped, trapped. He resisted an impulse to curl up into a ball, resisted falling into the dark pit of hopelessness. There had to be knives behind the counter. Perhaps he could grab one, bluff his way—

Then, as in a nightmare, things began to happen quickly.

Outside, someone was shouting, sending loud, sharp barks hammering through the air. It was enough to bring the waitress to the window.

"My God," she said.

He never knew what made him move across the diner, out into the cold night, but suddenly he was there.

Apparently they'd gotten bored waiting for him; the three of them were beating up the old man, punching him, throwing him back and forth. He was alone with them on the street.

Carew stood frozen, watching. An impulse to run surged

up from deep within him. He could get away now; they weren't looking at him. Run, call the cops for the old man.

They slammed the old man against the side of a building next to the diner.

"Let him go," Carew said.

Now it was too late to run; he was committed to this new course of action.

They dropped the old man on the sidewalk, advanced on Carew, two with steel pipes, one with his chain.

Carew rushed forward, smashed the tallest of the three in the mouth with his fist before he could swing the chain from his shoulder. For this act of daring he was rewarded with the sight of a pipe coming down on his head from the left; he raised his arm, warded off the blow, felt the pipe slam against his fingers. The pain fueled his mad courage; he smashed his opponent a right to the stomach. The one with the chain was holding his face with both hands. The old man was crawling away. The third of the group stood there, momentarily confused.

A small black car was approaching, slowing, coming to a halt in the street beside them. Carew had no idea who they were; he had no desire to discover if they were friends of these three. The one who had hit him with the pipe was coming at him, one hand clutching his stomach.

Carew knew he'd had luck and the element of surprise on his side to last this long; he turned and ran from the scene. As he ran, sucking icy air into his lungs, both hands in pain, the right one bleeding from a cut caused by scraping the tall one's teeth when he'd punched him, Carew felt fear no longer, but a sense of exhilaration. He'd been tested, he'd proven himself. It made a big difference to him.

He heard the car door shut behind him; he turned to look.

Two men were standing on the sidewalk. The three youths hadn't chased him, but stood looking at the two men, pulled back, ready, it seemed, to take flight themselves.

Carew stood and watched. One man made directly for the diner. The other reached into his pocket and withdrew small box of some kind. He pulled from this what looked like an antenna, and pointed it at the three youths. At first, Carew mistook it for a walkie-talkie.

What happened next stunned him, defied belief.

The man didn't hold the box to his mouth. He kept it waist

Midas Night

high. The three youths started to back away, bumping into each other. No longer predators. Prey—to something unbelievable.

Without a sound, with no fuss at all, the three of them slumped to the ground. And didn't move.

The man retracted the antenna, put the box back into his coat pocket.

Carew felt the familiar sensations of fear again.

He watched as the old man was helped into the back seat of the car. He watched as the man's partner came out of the diner and got into the front seat of the car, not even glancing at the fallen bodies on the sidewalk. As the car came down the street toward him, Carew was never more aware that he was alone, by himself on the sidewalk six or seven doors from the diner, by himself in the universe. He couldn't move.

The car stopped next to him and the man in the driver's seat got out. He was nondescript; later, Carew would remember nothing at all about him. He could have been a ghost.

He placed a very real hand on Carew's right shoulder.

"We want to thank you for your help." The man's voice was warm, yet commanding. "Please forget everything you've seen here tonight."

"What—what's going on?"

"You're very lucky the old guy likes you. We won't . . . can't touch your mind. Because he really likes you. When he is specific and definite about something, it is carried out. It has to be. *Be nice to him,* he said."

"Who were those three guys? And who is *he?*"

"They were three street punks. He is just a senile old man who is grateful to you for giving him your coffee. Your life is going to be much more . . . pleasant from now on. You're a very lucky man, Mr. Carew."

"I don't understand . . ."

"Don't try to." The grip on his shoulder tightened, but not painfully. "World economics is very complicated, Mr. Carew. Just say, simply, that *somebody* has to be the owner; and this somebody has to be watched. We strive for balance. Or everything falls apart. But don't question. Go back to the diner. Enjoy the rest of your long, happy life."

"The diner?"

"Please . . . It will explain more than I can now."

The man got back into the car, behind the wheel. In the

rear the old man was asleep next to the man with the black box. The man in front leaned out the window.

"One piece of advice," he said. "Don't get greedy."

The car pulled away. When it was gone, Carew walked back to the diner. Slowly, very slowly. He wouldn't question now. Maybe later. Maybe. At this moment all he felt was a not-unpleasant sense of anticipation.

He ignored the bodies, went inside. The waitress was still behind the counter with her newspaper. But—

It was not the same woman.

This one was young, pretty. A strange sensation engulfed him; she reminded him of his first girlfriend, junior year of high school.

Isn't that remarkable. I haven't thought of her in years.

She looked up and smiled at him.

Still not questioning, he walked over to his booth. The sketch of the old man was gone. Next to the sketch pad was a full cup of steaming hot coffee.

He sat down and turned to look at the phone. It was all still very much like a dream, yet he knew he could probably pick it up now and connect himself to a lifetime with Jodi. He might do it. He might not.

Right now he felt as he had as a child, on those delicious Christmas mornings when it was still real. Or before taking the first downward plunge on a roller coaster.

"It's fresh and good, if I do say so myself," the waitress said, smiling again. Carew smiled back at her. He sat there for a while, just staring at the cup, feeling his body tingle.

It was probably a perfect cup of coffee. He had no reason to doubt that. No reason in the world.

Roger Zelazny

UNICORN VARIATION

> *Many species of wildlife have become extinct during the recorded history of mankind, and many more species are on the lists of endangered or vanishing animals and plants kept by wildlife conservation groups. Will the ecological niches left vacant by these species be replaced by other forms of life? Maybe their replacements are already known to us but only in bestiaries and other writings about mythical creatures.*

A bizarrerie of fires, cunabulum of light, it moved with a deft, almost dainty deliberation, phasing into and out of existence like a storm-shot piece of evening; or perhaps the darkness between the flares was more akin to its truest nature—swirl of black ashes assembled in prancing cadence to the lowing note of desert wind down the arroyo behind buildings as empty yet filled as the pages of unread books or stillnesses between the notes of a song.

Gone again. Back again. Again.

Power, you said? Yes, It takes considerable force of identity to manifest before or after one's time. Or both.

As it faded and gained it also advanced, moving through the warm afternoon, its tracks erased by the wind. That is, on those occasions when there were tracks.

A reason. There should always be a reason. Or reasons.

It knew why it was there—but not why it was *there*, in that particular locale.

It anticipated learning this shortly, as it approached the desolation-bound line of the old street. However, it knew that the reason may also come before, or after. Yet again, the pull was there and the force of its being was such that it had to be close to something.

The buildings were worn and decayed and some of them fallen and all of them drafty and dusty and empty. Weeds grew among floorboards. Birds nested upon rafters. The droppings of wild things were everywhere; and it knew them all as they would have known it, were they to meet face to face.

It froze, for there had come the tiniest unanticipated sound from somewhere ahead and to the left. At that moment, it was again phasing into existence and it released its outline which faded as quickly as a rainbow in hell, but the naked presence remained beyond subtraction.

Invisible, yet existing, strong, it moved again. The clue. The cue. Ahead. A *gauche*. Beyond the faded word SALOON on weathered board above. Through the swinging doors. (One of them pinned alop.)

Pause and assess.

Bar to the right, dusty. Cracked mirror behind it. Empty bottles. Broken bottles. Brass rail, black, encrusted. Tables to the left and rear. In various states of repair.

Man seated at the best of the lot. His back to the door. Levis. Hiking boots. Faded blue shirt. Green backpack leaning against the wall to his left.

Before him, on the tabletop, is the faint, painted outline of a chessboard, stained, scratched, amost obliterated.

The drawer in which he had found the chessmen is still partly open.

He could no more have passed up a chess set without working out a problem or replaying one of his better games than he could have gone without breathing, circulating his blood or maintaining a relatively stable body temperature.

It moved nearer, and perhaps there were fresh prints in the dust behind it, but none noted them.

It too, played chess.

It watched as the man replayed what had perhaps been his finest game, from the world preliminaries of seven years past. He had blown up after that—surprised to have gotten even as far as he had—for he never could perform well under pressure. But he had always been proud of that one game, and he relived it as all sensitive beings do certain turning points in their lives. For perhaps twenty minutes, no one could have touched him. He had been shining and pure and hard and clear. He had felt like the best.

It took up a position across the board from him and stared. The man completed the game, smiling. Then he set up the board again, rose and fetched a can of beer from his pack. He popped the top.

When he returned, he discovered that White's King's Pawn had been advanced to K4. His brow furrowed. He turned his head, searching the bar, meeting his own puzzled gaze in the grimy mirror. He looked under the table. He took a drink of beer and seated himself.

He reached out and moved his Pawn to K4. A moment later, he saw White's King's Knight rise slowly into the air and drift forward to settle upon KB3. He stared for a long while into the emptiness across the table before he advanced his own Knight to his KB3.

White's Knight moved to take his Pawn. He dismissed the novelty of the situation and moved his Pawn to Q3. He all but forgot the absence of a tangible opponent as the White Knight dropped back to its KB3. He paused to take a sip of beer, but no sooner had he placed the can upon the tabletop than it rose again, passed across the board and was upended. A gurgling noise followed. Then the can fell to the floor, bouncing, ringing with an empty sound.

"I'm sorry," he said, rising and returning to his pack. "I'd have offered you one if I'd thought you were something that might like it."

He opened two more cans, returned with them, placed one near the far edge of the table, one at his own right hand.

"Thank you," came a soft, precise voice from a point beyond it.

The can was raised, tilted slightly, returned to the tabletop.

"My name is Martin," the man said.

"Call me Tlingel," said the other. "I had thought that perhaps your kind was extinct. I am pleased that you at least have survived to afford me this game."

"Huh?" Martin said. "We were all still around the last time that I looked—a couple of days ago."

"No matter. I can take care of that later," Tlingel replied. "I was misled by the appearance of this place."

"Oh. It's a ghost town. I backpack a lot."

"Not important. I am near the proper point in your career as a species. I can feel that much."

"I am afraid that I do not follow you."

"I am not at all certain that you would wish to. I assume that you intend to capture that cawn?"

"Perhaps. Yes, I do wish to. What are you talking about?"

The beer can rose. The invisible entity took another drink.

"Well," said Tlingel, "to put it simply, your—successors—grow anxious. Your place in the scheme of things being such an important one, I had sufficient power to come and check things out."

" 'Successors'? I do not understand."

"Have you seen any griffins recently?"

Martin chuckled.

"I've heard the stories," he said, "seen the photos of the one supposedly shot in the Rockies. A hoax, of course."

"Of course it must seem so. That is the way with mythical beasts."

"You're trying to say that it was real?"

"Certainly. Your world is in bad shape. When the last grizzly bear died recently, the way was opened for the griffins—just as the death of the last aepyornis brought in the yeti, the dodo the Loch Ness creature, the passenger pigeon the sasquatch, the blue whale, the kraken, the American eagle, the cockatrice—"

"You can't prove it by me."

"Have another drink."

Martin began to reach for the can, halted his hand and stared.

A creature approximately two inches in length, with a human face, a lion-like body and feathered wings was crouched next to the beer can.

"A mini-sphinx," the voice continued. "They came when you killed off the last smallpox virus."

"Are you trying to say that whenever a natural species dies out a mythical one takes its place?" he asked.

"In a word—yes. Now. It was not always so, but you have

destroyed the mechanisms of evolution. The balance is now redressed by those others of us from the morning land—we, who have never truly been endangered. We return, in our time."

"And you—whatever you are, Tlingel—you say that humanity is now endangered?"

"Very much so. But there is nothing that you can do about it, is there? Let us get on with the game."

The sphinx flew off. Martin took a sip of beer and captured the Pawn.

"Who," he asked then, "are to be our successors?"

"Modesty almost forbids," Tlingel replied. "In the case of a species as prominent as your own, it naturally has to be the loveliest, most intelligent, most important of us all."

"And what are you? Is there any way that I can have a look?"

"Well—yes. If I exert myself a trifle."

The beer can rose, was drained, fell to the floor. There followed a series of rapid rattling sounds retreating from the table. The air began to flicker over a large area opposite Martin, darkening within the growing flamework. The outline continued to brighten, its interior growing jet black. The form moved, prancing about the saloon, multitudes of tiny, cloven hoof-prints scoring and cracking the floorboards. With a final, near-blinding flash it came into full view and Martin gasped to behold it.

A black unicorn with mocking, yellow eyes sported before him, rising for a moment onto its hind legs to strike a heraldic pose. The fires flared about it a second longer, then vanished.

Martin had drawn back, raising one hand defensively.

"Regard me!" Tlingel announced. "Ancient symbol of wisdom, valor, and beauty, I stand before you!"

"I thought your typical unicorn was white," Martin finally said.

"I am archetypical," Tlingel responded, dropping to all fours, "and possessed of virtues beyond the ordinary."

"Such as?"

"Let us continue our game."

"What about the fate of the human race? You said—"

". . . And save the small talk for later."

"I hardly consider the destruction of humanity to be small talk."

"And if you've any more beer . . ."

"All right," Martin said, retreating to his pack as the creature advanced, its eyes like a pair of pale suns. "There's some lager."

Something had gone out of the game. As Martin sat before the ebon horn on Tlingel's bowed head, like an insect about to be pinned, he realized that his playing was off. He had felt the pressure the moment he had seen the beast—and there was all that talk about an imminent doomsday. Any run-of-the-mill pessimist could say it without troubling him, but coming from a source as peculiar as this . . .

His earlier elation had fled. He was no longer in top form. And Tlingel was good. Very good. Martin found himself wondering whether he could manage a stalemate.

After a time, he saw that he could not and resigned.

The unicorn looked at him and smiled.

"You don't really play badly—for a human," it said.

"I've done a lot better."

"It is no shame to lose to me, mortal. Even among mythical creatures there are very few who can give a unicorn a good game."

"I am pleased that you were not wholly bored," Martin said. "Now will you tell me what you were talking about concerning the destruction of my species?"

"Oh, that," Tlingel replied. "In the morning land where those such as I dwell, I felt the possibility of your passing come like a gentle wind to my nostrils, with the promise of clearing the way for us—"

"How is it supposed to happen?"

Tlingel shrugged, horn writing on the air with a toss of the head.

"I really couldn't say. Premonitions are seldom specific. In fact, that is what I came to discover. I should have been about it already, but you diverted me with beer and good sport."

"Could you be wrong about this?"

"I doubt it. That is the other reason I am here."

"Please explain."

"Are there any beers left?"

"Two, I think."
"Please."
Martin rose and fetched them.
"Damn! The tab broke off this one," he said.
"Place it upon the table and hold it firmly."
"All right."
Tlingel's horn dipped forward quickly, piercing the can's top.
". . . Useful for all sorts of things," Tlingel observed, withdrawing it.
"The other reason you're here . . ." Martin prompted.
"It is just that I am special. I can do things that the others cannot."
"Such as?"
"Find your weak spot and influence events to exploit it, to—hasten matters. To turn the possibility into a probability, and then—"
"*You* are going to destroy us? Personally?"
"That is the wrong way to look at it. It is more like a game of chess. It is as much a matter of exploiting your opponent's weaknesses as of exercising your own strengths. If you had not already laid the groundwork I would be powerless. I can only influence that which already exists."
"So what will it be? World War III? An ecological disaster? A mutated disease?"
"I do not really know yet, so I wish you wouldn't ask me in that fashion. I repeat that at the moment I am only observing. I am only an agent—"
"It doesn't sound that way to me."
Tlingel was silent. Martin began gathering up the chessmen.
"Aren't you going to set up the board again?"
"To amuse my destroyer a little more? No thanks."
"That's hardly the way to look at it—"
"Besides, those are the last beers."
"Oh." Tlingel stared wistfully at the vanishing pieces, then remarked, "I would be willing to play you again without additional refreshment . . ."
"No thanks."
"You are angry."
"Wouldn't you be, if our situations were reversed?"
"You are anthropomorphizing."

"Well?"

"Oh, I suppose I would."

"You could give us a break, you know—at least, let us make our own mistakes."

"You've hardly done that yourself, though, with all the creatures my fellows have succeeded."

Martin reddened.

"Okay. You just scored one. But I don't have to like it."

"You are a good player. I know that. . . ."

"Tlingel, if I were capable of playing at my best again, I think I could beat you."

The unicorn snorted two tiny wisps of smoke.

"Not *that* good," Tlingel said.

"I guess you'll never know."

"Do I detect a proposal?"

"Possibly. What's another game worth to you?"

Tlingel made a chuckling noise.

"Let me guess: You are going to say that if you beat me you want my promise not to lay my will upon the weakest link in mankind's existence and shatter it."

"Of course."

"And what do I get for winning?"

"The pleasure of the game. That's what you want, isn't it?"

"The terms sound a little lopsided."

"Not if you are going to win anyway. You keep insisting that you will."

"All right. Set up the board."

"There is something else that you have to know about me first."

"Yes?"

"I don't play well under pressure, and this game is going to be a terrific strain. You want my best game, don't you?"

"Yes, but I'm afraid I've no way of adjusting your own reactions to the play."

"I believe I could do that myself if I had more than the usual amount of time between moves."

"Agreed."

"I mean a lot of time."

"Just what do you have in mind?"

"I'll need time to get my mind off it, to relax, to come back to the positions as if they were only problems . . ."

"You mean to go away from here between moves?"

"Yes."

"All right. How long?"

"I don't know. A few weeks, maybe."

"Take a month. Consult your experts, put your computers onto it. It may make for a slightly more interesting game."

"I really didn't have that in mind."

"Then it's time that you're trying to buy."

"I can't deny that. On the other hand, I will need it."

"In that case, I have some terms. I'd like this place cleaned up, fixed up, more lively. It's a mess. I also want beer on tap."

"Okay. I'll see to that."

"Then I agree. Let's see who goes first."

Martin switched a black and a white pawn from hand to hand beneath the table. He raised his fists then and extended them. Tlingel leaned forward and tapped. The black horn's tip touched Martin's left hand.

"Well, it matches my sleek and glossy hide," the unicorn announced.

Martin smiled, setting up the white for himself, the black pieces for his opponent. As soon as he had finished, he pushed his Pawn to K4.

Tlingel's delicate, ebon hoof moved to advance the Black King's Pawn to K4.

"I take it that you want a month now, to consider your next move?"

Martin did not reply but moved his Knight to KB3. Tlingel immediately moved a Knight to QB3.

Martin took a swallow of beer and then moved his Bishop to N5. The unicorn moved the other Knight to B3. Martin immediately castled and Tlingel moved the Knight to take his Pawn.

"I think we'll make it," Martin said suddenly, "If you'll just let us alone. We do learn from our mistakes, in time."

"Mythical beings do not exactly exist in time. Your world is a special case."

"Don't you people ever make mistakes?"

"Whenever we do they're sort of poetic."

Martin snarled and advanced his Pawn to Q4. Tlingel immediately countered by moving the Knight to Q3.

"I've got to stop," Martin said, standing. "I'm getting mad, and it will affect my game."

"You will be going, then?"
"Yes."
He moved to fetch his pack.
"I will see you here in one month's time?"
"Yes."
"Very well."

The unicorn rose and stamped upon the floor and lights began to play across its dark coat. Suddenly, they blazed and shot outward in all directions like a silent explosion. A wave of blackness followed.

Martin found himself leaning against the wall, shaking. When he lowered his hand from his eyes, he saw that he was alone, save for the knights, the bishops, the kings, the queens, their castles and both the kings' men.

He went away.

Three days later Martin returned in a small truck, with a generator, lumber, windows, power tools, paint, stain, cleaning compounds, wax. He dusted and vacuumed and replaced rotted wood. He installed the windows. He polished the old brass until it shone. He stained and rubbed. He waxed the floors and buffed them. He plugged holes and washed glass. He hauled all the trash away.

It took him the better part of a week to turn the old place from a wreck back into a saloon in appearance. Then he drove off, returned all of the equipment he had rented and bought a ticket for the Northwest.

The big, damp forest was another of his favorite places for hiking, for thinking. And he was seeking a complete change of scene, a total revision of outlook. Not that his next move did not seem obvious, standard even. Yet, something nagged. . . .

He knew that it was more than just the game. Before that he had been ready to get away again, to walk drowsing among shadows, breathing clean air.

Resting, his back against the bulging root of a giant tree, he withdrew a small chess set from his pack, set it up on a rock he'd moved into position nearby. A fine, mist-like rain was settling, but the tree sheltered him, so far. He reconstructed the opening through Tlingel's withdrawal of the Knight to Q3. The simplest thing would be to take the Knight with the Bishop. But he did not move to do it.

He watched the board for a time, felt his eyelids drooping, closed them and drowsed. It may only have been for a few minutes. He was never certain afterwards.

Something aroused him. He did not know what. He blinked several times and closed his eyes again. Then he reopened them hurriedly.

In his nodded position, eyes directed downward, his gaze was fixed upon an enormous pair of hairy, unshod feet—the largest pair of feet that he had ever beheld. They stood unmoving before him, pointed toward his right.

Slowly—very slowly—he raised his eyes. Not very far, as it turned out. The creature was only about four and a half feet in height. As it was looking at the chessboard rather than at him, he took the opportunity to study it.

It was unclothed but very hairy, with a dark brown pelt, obviously masculine, possessed of low brow ridges, deep-set eyes that matched its hair, heavy shoulders, five-fingered hands that sported opposing thumbs.

It turned suddenly and regarded him, flashing a large number of shining teeth.

"White's pawn should take the pawn," it said in a soft, nasal voice.

"Huh? Come on," Martin said. "Bishop takes Knight."

"You want to give me black and play it that way? I'll walk all over you."

Martin glanced again at its feet.

". . . Or give me white and let me take that pawn. I'll still do it."

"Take white," Martin said, straightening. "Let's see if you know what you're talking about." He reached for his pack. "Have a beer?"

"What's a beer?"

"A recreational aid. Wait a minute."

Before they had finished the six-pack, the sasquatch—whose name, he had learned, was Grend—had finished Martin. Grend had quickly entered a ferocious midgame, backed him into a position of dwindling security and pushed him to the point where he had seen the end and resigned.

"That was one hell of a game," Martin declared, leaning back and considering the ape-like countenance before him.

"Yes, we Bigfeet are pretty good, if I do say it. It's our one big recreation, and we're so damned primitive we don't have much in the way of boards and chessmen. Most of the time, we just play it in our heads. There're not many can come close to us."

"How about unicorns?" Martin asked.

Grend nodded slowly.

"They're about the only ones can really give us a good game. A little dainty, but they're subtle. Awfully sure of themselves, though, I must say. Even when they're wrong. Haven't seen any since we left the morning land, of course. Too bad, Got any more of that beer left?"

"I'm afraid not. But listen, I'll be back this way in a month. I'll bring some more if you'll meet me here and play again."

"Martin, you've got a deal. Sorry. Didn't mean to step on your toes."

He cleaned the saloon again and brought in a keg of beer which he installed under the bar and packed with ice. He moved in some bar stools, chairs and tables which he had obtained at a Goodwill store. He hung red curtains. By then it was evening. He set up the board, ate a light meal, unrolled his sleeping bag behind the bar and camped there that night.

The following day passed quickly. Since Tlingel might show up at any time, he did not leave the vicinity, but took his meals there and sat about working chess problems. When it began to grow dark, he lit a number of oil lamps and candles.

He looked at his watch with increasing frequency. He began to pace. He couldn't have made a mistake. This was the proper day. He—

He heard a chuckle.

Turning about, he saw a black unicorn head floating in the air above the chessboard. As he watched, the rest of Tlingel's body materialized.

"Good evening, Martin." Tlingel turned away from the board. "The place looks a little better. Could use some music . . ."

Martin stepped behind the bar and switched on the transistor radio he had brought along. The sounds of a string quartet filled the air. Tlingel winced.

"Hardly in keeping with the atmosphere of the place."

He changed stations, located a Country & Western show.

"I think not," Tlingel said. "It loses something in transmission."

He turned it off.

"Have we a good supply of beverage?"

Martin drew a gallon stein of beer—the largest mug that he could locate, from a novelty store—and set it upon the bar. He filled a much smaller one for himself. He was determined to get the beast drunk if it were at all possible.

"Ah! Much better than those little cans," said Tlingel, whose muzzle dipped for but a moment. "Very good."

The mug was empty. Martin refilled it.

"Will you move it to the table for me?"

"Certainly."

"Have an interesting month?"

"I suppose I did."

"You've decided upon your next move?"

"Yes."

"Then let's get on with it."

Martin seated himself and captured the Pawn.

"Hm. Interesting."

Tlingel stared at the board for a long while, then raised a cloven hoof which parted in reaching for the piece.

"I'll just take that bishop with this little Knight. Now I suppose you'll be wanting another month to decide what to do next.

Tlingel leaned to the side and drained the mug.

"Let me consider it," Martin said, "while I get you a refill."

Martin sat and stared at the board through three more refills. Actually, he was not planning. He was waiting. His response to Grend had been Knight takes Bishop, and he had Grend's next move ready.

"Well?" Tlingel finally said. "What do you think?"

Martin took a small sip of beer.

"Almost ready," he said. "You hold your beer awfully well."

Tlingel laughed.

"A unicorn's horn is a detoxicant. Its possession is a universal remedy. I wait until I reach the warm-glow stage, then I use my horn to burn off any excess and keep me right there."

"Oh," said Martin. "Neat trick, that."

" . . . If you've had too much, just touch my horn for a moment and I'll put you back in business."

"No, thanks. That's all right. I'll just push this little Pawn in front of the queen's Rook two steps ahead."

"Really . . ." said Tlingel. "That's interesting. You know, what this place really needs is a piano—rinkytink, funky . . . Think you could manage it?"

"I don't play."

"Too bad."

"I suppose I could hire a piano player."

"No. I do not care to be seen by other humans."

"If he's really good, I suppose he could play blindfolded."

"Never mind."

"I'm sorry."

"You are also ingenious. I am certain that you will figure something out by next time."

Martin nodded.

"Also, didn't these old places used to have sawdust all over the floors?"

"I believe so."

"That would be nice."

"Check."

Tlingel searched the board frantically for a moment.

"Yes. I meant 'yes'. I said 'check'. It means 'yes' sometimes, too."

"Oh. Rather. Well, while we're here . . ."

Tlingel advanced the Pawn to Q3.

Martin stared. That was not what Grend had done. For a moment, he considered continuing on his own from here. He had tried to think of Grend as a coach up until this point. He had forced away the notion of crudely and crassly pitting one of them against the other. Until P–Q3. Then he recalled the game he had lost to the sasquatch.

"I'll draw the line here," he said, "and take my month."

"All right. Let's have another drink before we say good night. Okay?"

"Sure. Why not?"

They sat for a time and Tlingel told him of the morning land, of primeval forests and rolling plains, of high craggy mountains and purple seas, of magic and mythic beasts.

Martin shook his head.

"I can't quite see why you're so anxious to come here," he said, "with a place like that to call home."

Tlingel sighed.

"I suppose you'd call it keeping up with the griffins. It's the thing to do these days. Well. Till next month . . ."

Tlingel rose and turned away.

"I've got complete control now. Watch!"

The unicorn form faded, jerked out of shape, grew white, faded again, and was gone, like an afterimage.

Martin moved to the bar and drew himself another mug. It was a shame to waste what was left. In the morning, he wished the unicorn were there again. Or at least the horn.

It was a gray day in the forest and he held an umbrella over the chessboard upon the rock. The droplets fell from the leaves and made dull, plopping noises as they struck the fabric. The board was set up again through Tlingel's P–Q3. Martin wondered whether Grend had remembered, had kept proper track of the days . . .

"Hello," came the nasal voice from somewhere behind him and to the left.

He turned to see Grend moving about the tree, stepping over the massive roots with massive feet.

"You remembered," Grend said. "How good! I trust you also remembered the beer?"

"I've lugged up a whole case. We can set up the bar right here."

"What's a bar?"

"Well, it's a place where people go to drink—in out of the rain—a bit dark, for atmosphere—and they sit up on stools before a big counter, or else at little tables—and they talk to each other—and sometimes there's music—and they drink."

"We're going to have all that here?"

"No. Just the dark and the drinks. Unless you count the rain as music. I was speaking figuratively."

"Oh. It does sound like a very good place to visit, though."

"Yes. If you will hold this umbrella over the board, I'll set up the best equivalent we can have here."

"All right. Say, this looks like a version of that game we played last time."

"It is. I got to wondering what would happen if it had gone this way rather than the way that it went."

"Hmmm. Let me see . . ."

Martin removed four six-packs from his pack and opened the first.

"Here you go."

"Thanks."

Grend accepted the beer, squatted, passed the umbrella back to Martin.

"I'm still white?"

"Yeah."

"Pawn to King six."

"Really?"

"Yep."

"About the best thing for me to do would be to take this Pawn with this one."

"I'd say. Then I'll just knock off your Knight with this one."

"I guess I'll just pull this Knight back to K2."

". . . And I'll take this one over to B3. May I have another beer?"

An hour and a quarter later, Martin resigned. The rain had let up and he had folded the umbrella.

"Another game?" Grend asked.

The afternoon wore on. The pressure was off. This one was just for fun. Martin tried wild combinations, seeing ahead with great clarity, as he had that one day . . .

"Stalemate," Grend announced much later. "That was a good one, though. You picked up considerably."

"I was more relaxed. Want another?"

"Maybe in a little while. Tell me more about bars now."

So he did. Finally, "How is all that beer affecting you?" he asked.

"I'm a bit dizzy. But that's all right. I'll still cream you the third game."

And he did.

"Not bad for a human, though. Not bad at all. You coming back next month?"

"Yes."

"Good. You'll bring more beer?"

"So long as my money holds out."

"Oh. Bring some plaster of Paris then. I'll make you some nice footprints and you can take casts of them. I understand they're going for quite a bit."

Unicorn Variation

"I'll remember that."

Martin lurched to his feet and collected the chess set.

"Till then."

"Ciao."

Martin dusted and polished again, moved in the player piano and scattered sawdust upon the floor. He installed a fresh keg. He hung some reproductions of period posters and some atrocious old paintings he had located in a junk shop. He placed cuspidors in strategic locations. When he was finished, he seated himself at the bar and opened a bottle of mineral water. He listened to the New Mexico wind moaning as it passed, to grains of sand striking against the windowpanes. He wondered whether the whole world would have that dry, mournful sound to it if Tlingel found a means for doing away with humanity, or—disturbing thought—whether the successors to his own kind might turn things into something resembling the mythical morning land.

This troubled him for a time. Then he went and set up the board through Black's P–Q3. When he turned back to clear the bar he saw a line of cloven hoofprints advancing across the sawdust.

"Good evening, Tlingel," he said. "What is your pleasure?"

Suddenly, the unicorn was there, without preliminary pyrotechnics. It moved to the bar and placed one hoof upon the brass rail.

"The usual."

As Martin drew the beer, Tlingel looked about.

"The place has improved, a bit."

"Glad you think so. Would you care for some music?"

"Yes."

Martin fumbled at the back of the piano, locating the switch for the small, battery-operated computer which controlled the pumping mechanism and substituted its own memory for rolls. The keyboard immediately came to life.

"Very good," Tlingel stated. "Have you found your move?"

"I have."

"Then let us be about it."

He refilled the unicorn's mug and moved it to the table.

"Pawn to King six," he said, executing it.

"What?"

"Just that."

"Give me a minute. I want to study this."

"Take your time."

"I'll take the Pawn," Tlingel said, after a long pause and another mug.

"Then I'll take this Knight."

Later, "Knight to K2," Tlingel said.

"Knight to B3."

An extremely long pause ensued before Tlingel moved the Knight to N3.

The hell with asking Grend, Martin suddenly decided. He'd been through this part any number of times already. He moved his Knight to N5.

"Change the tune on that thing!" Tlingel snapped.

Martin rose and obliged.

"I don't like that one either. Find a better one or shut it off!"

After three more tries, Martin shut if off.

"And get me another beer!"

He refilled their mugs.

"All right."

Tlingel moved the Bishop to K2.

Keeping the unicorn from castling had to be the most important thing at the moment. So Martin moved his Queen to R5. Tlingel made a tiny, strangling noise, and when Martin looked up smoke was curling from the unicorn's nostrils.

"More beer?"

"If you please."

As he returned with it, he saw Tlingel move the Bishop to capture the Knight. There seemed no choice for him at that moment, but he studied the position for a long while anyhow.

Finally, "Bishop takes Bishop," he said.

"Of course."

"How's the warm glow?"

Tlingel chuckled.

"You'll see."

The wind rose again, began to howl. The building creaked.

"Okay," Tlingel finally said, and moved the Queen to Q2.

Martin stared. What was he doing? So far, it had gone all right, but— He listened again to the wind and thought of the risk he was taking.

"That's all, folks," he said, leaning back in his chair. "Continued next month."

Tlingel sighed.

"Don't run off. Fetch me another. Let me tell you of my wanderings in your world this past month."

"Looking for weak links?"

"You're lousy with them. How do you stand it?"

"They're harder to strengthen than you might think. Any advice?"

"Get the beer."

They talked until the sky paled in the east, and Martin found himself taking surreptitious notes. His admiration for the unicorn's analytical abilities increased as the evening advanced.

When they finally rose, Tlingel staggered.

"You all right?"

"Forgot to detox, that's all. Just a second. Then I'll be fading."

"Wait!"

"Whazzat?"

"I could use one, too."

"Oh. Grab hold, then."

Tlingel's head descended and Martin took the tip of the horn between his fingertips. Immediately, a delicious, warm sensation flowed through him. He closed his eyes to enjoy it. His head cleared. An ache which had been growing within his frontal sinus vanished. The tiredness went out of his muscles. He opened his eyes again.

"Thank—"

Tlingel had vanished. He held but a handful of air.

"—you."

"Rael here is my friend," Grend stated. "He's a griffin."

"I'd noticed."

Martin nodded at the beaked, golden-winged creature.

"Pleased to meet you, Rael."

"The same," cried the other in a high-pitched voice. "Have you got the beer?"

"Why—uh—yes."

"I've been telling him about beer," Grend explained, half-apologetically. "He can have some of mine. He won't kibitz or anything like that."

"Sure. All right. Any friend of yours—"

"The beer!" Rael cried. "Bars!"

"He's not real bright," Grend whispered. "But he's good company. I'd appreciate your humoring him."

Martin opened the first six-pack and passed the griffin and the sasquatch a beer apiece. Rael immediately punctured the can with his beak, chugged it, belched and held out his claw.

"Beer!" he shrieked. "More beer!"

Martin handed him another.

"Say, you're still into that first game, aren't you?" Grend observed, studying the board. "Now, *that* is an interesting position."

Grend drank and studied the board.

"Good thing it's not raining," Martin commented.

"Oh, it will. Just wait a while."

"More beer!" Rael screamed.

Martin passed him another without looking.

"I'll move my Pawn to N6," Grend said.

"You're kidding."

"Nope. Then you'll take that Pawn with your Bishop's Pawn. Right?"

"Yes . . ."

Martin reached out and did it.

"Okay. Now I'll just swing this Knight to Q5."

Martin took it with the Pawn.

Grend moved his Rook to K1.

"Check," he announced.

"Yes. That *is* the way to go," Martin observed.

Grend chuckled.

"I'm going to win this game another time," he said.

"I wouldn't put it past you."

"More beer?" Rael said softly.

"Sure."

As Martin passed him another, he noticed that the griffin was now leaning against the tree trunk.

After several minutes, Martin pushed his King to B1.

"Yeah, that's what I thought you'd do," Grend said. "You know something?"

"What?"

"You play a lot like a unicorn."

"Hm."

Grend moved his Rook to R3.

Later, as the rain descended gently about them and Grend beat him again, Martin realized that a prolonged period of silence had prevailed. He glanced over at the griffin. Rael had tucked his head beneath his left wing, balanced upon one leg, leaned heavily against the tree and gone to sleep.

"I told you he wouldn't be much trouble," Grend remarked.

Two games later, the beer was gone, the shadows were lengthening, and Rael was stirring.

"See you next month?"

"Yeah."

"You bring any plaster of Paris?"

"Yes, I did."

"Come on, then. I know a good place pretty far from here. We don't want people beating about *these* bushes. Let's go make you some money."

"To buy beer?" Rael said, looking out from under his wing.

"Next month," Grend said.

"You ride?"

"I don't think you could carry both of us," said Grend, "and I'm not sure I'd want to right now if you could."

"Bye-bye then," Rael shrieked, and he leaped into the air, crashing into branches and tree trunks, finally breaking through the overhead cover and vanishing.

"There goes a really decent guy," said Grend. "He sees everything and he never forgets. Knows how everything works—in the woods, in the air—even in the water. Generous, too, whenever he has anything."

"Hm," Martin observed.

"Let's make tracks," Grend said.

"Pawn to N6? Really?" Tlingel said. "All right. The Bishop's Pawn will just knock off the Pawn."

Tlingel's eyes narrowed as Martin moved the Knight to Q5.

"At least this is an interesting game," the unicorn remarked. "Pawn takes Knight."

Martin moved the Rook.

"Check."

"Yes, it is. This next one is going to be a three-flagon move. Kindly bring me the first."

Martin thought back as he watched Tlingel drink and ponder. He almost felt guilty for hitting it with a powerhouse like the sasquatch behind its back. He was convinced now that the unicorn was going to lose. In every variation of this game that he'd played with Black against Grend, he'd been beaten. Tlingel was very good, but the sasquatch was a wizard with not much else to do but mental chess. It was unfair. But it was not a matter of personal honor, he kept telling himself. He was playing to protect his species against a supernatural force which might well be able to precipitate World War III by some arcane mind-manipulation or magically induced computer foulup. He didn't dare give the creature a break.

"Flagon number two, please."

He brought it another. He studied it as it studied the board. It was beautiful, he realized for the first time. It was the loveliest living thing he had ever seen. Now that the pressure was on the verge of evaporating and he could regard it without the overlay of fear which had always been there in the past, he could pause to admire it. If something *had* to succeed the human race, he could think of worse choices...

"Number three now."

"Coming up."

Tlingel drained it and moved the King to B1.

Martin leaned forward immediately and pushed the Rook to R3.

Tlingel looked up, stared at him.

"Not bad."

Martin wanted to squirm. He was struck by the nobility of the creature. He wanted so badly to play and beat the unicorn on his own, fairly. Not this way.

Tlingel looked back at the board, then almost carelessly moved the Knight to K4.

"Go ahead. Or will it take you another month?"

Martin growled softly, advanced the Rook, and captured the Knight.

"Of course."

Tlingel captured the Rook with the Pawn. This was not the way that the last variation with Grend had run. Still...

He moved his Rook to KB3. As he did, the wind seemed to commence a peculiar shrieking, above, amid the ruined buildings.

"Check," he announced.

The hell with it! he decided. I'm good enough to manage my own endgame. Let's play this out.

He watched and waited and finally saw Tlingel move the King to N1.

He moved his Bishop to R6. Tlingel moved the Queen to K2. The shrieking came again, sounding nearer now. Martin took the Pawn with the Bishop.

The unicorn's head came up and it seemed to listen for a moment. Then Tlingel lowered it and captured the Bishop with the King.

Martin moved his Rook to KN3.

"Check."

Tlingel returned the King to B1.

Martin moved the Rook to KB3.

"Check."

Tlingel pushed the King to N2.

Martin moved the Rook back to KN3.

"Check."

Tlingel returned the King to B1, looked up and stared at him, showing teeth.

"Looks as if we've got a drawn game," the unicorn stated. "Care for another one?"

"Yes, but not for the fate of humanity."

"Forget it. I'd given up on that a long time ago. I decided that I wouldn't care to live here after all. I'm a little more discriminating than that.

"Except for this bar." Tlingel turned away as another shriek sounded just beyond the door, followed by strange voices. "What is that?"

"I don't know," Martin answered, rising.

The doors opened and a golden griffin entered.

"Martin!" it cried. "Beer! Beer!"

"Uh—Tlingel, this is Rael, and, and—"

Three more griffins followed him in. Then came Grend, and three others of his own kind.

"—and that one's Grend," Martin said lamely. "I don't know the others."

They all halted when they beheld the unicorn.

"Tlingel," one of the sasquatches said. "I thought you were still in the morning land."

"I still am, in a way. Martin, how is it that you are acquainted with my former countrymen?"

"Well—uh—Grend here is my chess coach."

"Aha! I begin to understand."

"I am not sure that you really do. But let me get everyone a drink first."

Martin turned on the piano and set everyone up.

"How did you find this place?" he asked Grend as he was doing it. "And how did you get here?"

"Well . . ." Grend looked embarrassed. "Rael followed you back."

"Followed a jet?"

"Griffins are supernaturally fast."

"Oh."

"Anyway, he told his relatives and some of my folks about it. When we saw that the griffins were determined to visit you, we decided that we had better come along to keep them out of trouble. They brought us."

"I—see. Interesting . . ."

"No wonder you played like a unicorn, that one game with all the variations."

"Uh—yes."

Martin turned away, moved to the end of the bar.

"Welcome, all of you," he said. "I have a small announcement. Tlingel, a while back you had a number of observations concerning possible ecological and urban disasters and lesser dangers. Also, some ideas as to possible safeguards against some of them."

"I recall," said the unicorn.

"I passed them along to a friend of mine in Washington who used to be a member of my old chess club. I told him that the work was not entirely my own."

"I should hope so."

"He has since suggested that I turn whatever group was involved into a think tank. He will then see about paying something for its efforts."

"I didn't come here to save the world," Tlingel said.

"No, but you've been very helpful. And Grend tells me that the griffins, even if their vocabulary is a bit limited, know almost all that there is to know about ecology."

"That is probably true."

"Since they have inherited a part of the Earth, it would be to their benefit as well to help preserve the place. Inasmuch as this many of us are already here, I can save myself some

Unicorn Variation

travel and suggest right now that we find a meeting place—say here, once a month—and that you let me have your unique viewpoints. You must know more about how species become extinct than anyone else in the business."

"Of course," said Grend, waving his mug, "but we really should ask the yeti, also. I'll do it, if you'd like. Is that stuff coming out of the big box music?"

"Yes."

"I like it. If we do this think-tank thing, you'll make enough to keep this place going?"

"I'll buy the whole town."

Grend conversed in quick gutturals with the griffins, who shrieked back at him.

"You've got a think tank," he said, "and they want more beer."

Martin turned toward Tlingel.

"They were your observations. What do you think?"

"It may be amusing," said the unicorn, "to stop by occasionally." Then, "So much for saving the world. Did you say you wanted another game?"

"I've nothing to lose."

Grend took over the tending of the bar while Tlingel and Martin returned to the table.

He beat the unicorn in thirty-one moves and touched the extended horn.

The piano keys went up and down. Tiny sphinxes buzzed about the bar, drinking the spillage.

C. J. Cherryh

THE ONLY DEATH IN THE CITY

> *C. J. Cherryh's* Sunfall *is a rich and varied collection of tales of six cities in Earth's unbelievably distant future, a future in which the sun itself is no longer the vigorous star of our time. Here from that collection is a story about Paris, The City of Lights, and its citizens who have lived through untold incarnations, all of which they remember vividly—and of a youth who is almost unique. He is a "new soul," one who has never experienced a previous life.*

It was named the City of Lights. It had known other names in the long history of Earth, in the years before the sun turned wan and plague-ridden, before the moon hung vast and lurid in the sky, before the ships from the stars grew few and the reasons for ambition grew fewer still. It stretched as far as the eye could see . . . if one saw it from the outside, as the inhabitants never did. It was so vast that a river flowed through it, named the Sin, which in the unthinkable past had flowed through a forest of primeval beauty, and then through a countless succession of cities, through ancient ages of empires. The City grew about the Sin, and enveloped it, so that, stone-channelled, it flowed now through the halls of the City, thundering from the tenth to the fourteenth level in a free fall, and flowing meekly along the channel within the fourteenth, a grand canal which supplied the City and made it self-sufficient. The Sin came from the outside, but it was so changed and channelled that no one remembered that this was so. No one remembered the outside. No one cared. The City was sealed, and had been so for thousands of years.

There *were* windows, but they were on the uppermost levels, and they were tightly shuttered. The inhabitants feared the sun, for popular rumor held that the sun was a source of vile radiations, unhealthful, a source of plagues. There were windows, but no doors, for no one would choose to leave. No one ever had, from the day the outer walls were built. When the City must build in this age, it built downward, digging a twentieth and twenty-first level for the burial of the dead .. for the dead of the City were transients, in stone coffins, which might always be shifted lower still when the living needed room.

Once, it had been a major pastime of the City to tour the lower levels, to seek out the painted sarcophagi of ancestors, to seek the resemblances of living face to dead so common in this long self-contained city. But now those levels were full of dust, and few were interested in going there save for funerals.

Once, it had been a delight to the inhabitants of the City to search the vast libraries and halls of art for histories, for the City lived much in the past, and reveled in old glories ... but now the libraries went unused save for the very lightest of fictions, and those were very abstract and full of drug-dream fancies.

More and more... the inhabitants *remembered*.

There were a few at first who were troubled with recollections and a thorough familiarity with the halls—when once it was not uncommon to spend one's time touring the vast expanse of the City, seeing new sights. These visionaries sank into ennui ... or into fear, when the recollections grew quite vivid.

There was no need to go to the lower levels seeking ancestors. They lived ... incarnate in the sealed halls of the City, in the persons of their descendants, souls so long immured within the megalopolis that they began to wake to former pasts, for dying, they were reborn, and remembered, eventually. So keenly did they recall that now mere infants did not cry, but lay patiently dreaming in their cradles, or, waking, stared out from haunted eyes, gazing into mothers' eyes with millennia of accumulated lives, *aware*, and waiting for adulthood, for body to overtake memory.

Children played . . . various games, wrought of former lives.

The people lived in a curious mixture of caution and recklessness: caution, for they surrounded themselves with the present, knowing the danger of entanglements; recklessness, for past ceased to fascinate them as an unknown and nothing had permanent meaning. There was only pleasure, and the future, which held the certainty of more lives, which would remember the ones they currently lived. For a very long time, death was absent from the halls of the City of Lights.

Until one was born to them.

Only rarely were there those born new, new souls which had not made previous journeys within the City, babes that cried, children who grew up conscious of their affliction, true children among the reborn.

Such was Alain.

He was born in one of the greatest of families—those families of associations dictated more by previous lives than by blood, for while it was true that reincarnation tended to follow lines of descendancy, this was not always the case; and sometimes there were those from outside the bloodline who drifted in as children, some even in their first unsteady steps, seeking old lives, old connections. But Alain was new. He was born to the Jade Palace Family, which occupied the tenth level nearest the stairs, although he was not *of* that family or indeed of any family, and therefore grew up less civilized.

He tried. He was horribly conscious of his lack of taste, his lack of discrimination which he could not excuse as originality: originality was for—older—minds and memories. His behavior was simply awkward, and he stayed much in the shadows in Jade Palace, enduring this life and thinking that his next would surely be better.

But Jade was neighbor to Onyx Palace, and it was inevitable that these two houses mix upon occasion of anniversaries. These times were Alain's torment when he was

The Only Death in the City

a child, when his naïve and real childhood was exposed to outsiders; they became torment of a different kind in his fourteenth year, when suddenly his newly maturing discrimination settled upon a certain face, a certain pale loveliness in the Onyx House.

"Only to be expected," his mother sighed. He had embarrassed her many times, and diffidently came to her now with this confession . . . that he had seen in this Onyx princess what others saw within their own houses; an acuteness of longing possessed him which others claimed only for old recognitions and old lovers of former lives. He was new, and it was for the first time. "Her name," his mother asked.

"Ermine," he whispered, his eyes downcast upon the patterns of the carpets, which his aunt had loomed herself in a long-past life. "Her name is Ermine."

"Boy," his mother said, "you are a droplet in the canal of *her* lives. Forget her."

It was genuine pity he heard in his mother's voice, and this was very rare. *You entertain me,* was the kindest thing she had yet said to him, high compliment, implying he might yet attain to novelty. Now her kind advice brought tears to his eyes, but he shook his head, looked up into her eyes, which he did seldom: they were very old and very wise and he sensed them forever comparing him to memories ages past.

"Does anyone," he asked, "ever forget?"

"Boy, I give you good advice. Of course I can't stop you. You'll be born a thousand times and so will she, and you'll never make up for your youth. But such longings come out again if they're not checked, in this life or the next, and they make misery. Sleep with many; make good friends, who may be born in your next life; no knowing whether you'll be man or woman or if they'll be what they are. Make many friends, that's my advice to you, so that whether some are born ahead of you and some behind, whether sexes are what they are . . . there'll be *some* who'll be glad to see you among them. That's how one makes a place for one's self. I did it ages ago before I began to remember my lives. But I've every confidence you'll remember yours at once; that's the way things are, now. And when you've a chance to choose intelligently as you do in these days, why, lad, be very glad for good advice. Don't set your affections strongly in your very first life. Make no enemies either. Think of your uncle Legran and Pertito, who kill each other in every life they live, whatever they are. Never set strong patterns. Be wise, A pattern set so early could make all your lives tragedy."

"I love her," he said with all the hopeless fervor of his fourteen unprefaced years.

"Oh my dear," his mother said, and sadly shook her head. She was about to tell him one of her lives, he knew, and he looked again at the carpet, doomed to endure it.

He did not see Onyx Ermine again that year, not the next nor the two succeeding: his mother maneuvered the matter very delicately and he was thwarted. But in his eighteenth year the quarrel Pertito had with uncle Legran broke into feud, and his mother died, stabbed in the midst of the argument.

Complications, she had warned him. He stood looking at her coffin the day of the funeral and fretted bitterly for the loss of her who had been his best and friendliest advisor, fretted also for her sake, that she had been woven into a pattern she had warned him to avoid. Pertito and Legran were both there, looking hate at one another. "You've involved Claudette," Pertito had shouted at Legran while she lay dying on the carpet between them; and the feud was more bitter between the two than it had ever been, for they had both loved Claudette, his mother. It would not be long, he thought with the limits of his experience in such matters, before Pertito and Legran would follow her. He was wise and did not hate them, wrenched himself away from the small gathering of family and wider collection of curious outside Jade Palace, for he had other things to do with his lives, and he thought that his mother would much applaud his good sense.

But while he was walking away from the gathering he saw Ermine standing there among her kin of Onyx.

And if she had been beautiful when they were both fourteen, she was more so now. He stood and stared at her, a vision of white silk and pearls from the Sin, of pale hair and pink flushed skin. It was Ermine who drew him back to his mother's funeral . . . Claudette, he must think of his mother now, by her true name, for she had stopped being his mother, and might at this moment be born far across the City, to begin her journey back to them. This mourning was only ceremony, a farewell of sorts, excuse for a party. It grew, as they walked the stairs past the thundering waters of the Sin,

The Only Death in the City

as more and more curious attached themselves and asked who had died, and how, and the tale was told and retold at other levels. But it was the kin who really knew her who did the telling; in his own low estate he kept silent and soon grew disaffected from all the empty show . . . his eyes were only for Ermine.

He moved to her side as they walked constantly down the long stairs which wrapped the chute of the Sin. "Might we meet after?" he asked, not looking at her, for shyness was the rule of his life.

He felt her look at him; at least he perceived a movement, a certain silence, and the heat crept to his face. "I think we might," she said, and his heart pounded in his breast.

Never set strong patterns, Claudette had warned him; and before her body was entombed her voice seemed far away, and her advice less wise than it had seemed. After all, *she* had passed that way, and he was about to live life on his own.

I shall be wise, he promised her ghost. Claudette would be a child of his generation, surely . . . perhaps . . . the thought stunned him, perhaps his own with Ermine's. She would be very welcome if she were. He would tell her so many things that he would have learned by then. It would be one of those rare, forever marriages, himself with Ermine; Ermine would love him . . . such a drawing could not be one-sided. The feeling soaring in him was the whole world and it was unreasonable to him that Ermine could go unmoved.

He was four years wiser than he had been, and filled with all the history he had been able to consume by reading and listening.

Pertito and Legran argued loudly near him. He paid them no heed. They reached the level of the tombs, far below the course of the Sin, and with great solemnity—all of them loved pomp when there was excuse for it—conveyed Claudette to her tomb. The populace was delighted when Pertito accused Legran of the murder; was elated when the whole funeral degenerated into a brawl, and the Pertito/Legran quarrel embroiled others. It found grand climax when knives were drawn, and uncle Legran and Pertito vowed suicide to expiate the wrong done Claudette. This was a grand new turn to the centuries-old drama, and the crowd gasped and applauded, profoundly delighted by a variation in a vendetta more than thirty centuries old. The two walked ahead of the returning crowd, and from the tenth level, leaped into the chute of the Sin, to the thunderous applause of much of the City. Everyone was cheerful, anticipating a change in the drama in their next lives. Novelty—it was so rarely achieved, and so to be savored. The souls of Pertito and Legran would be welcomed wherever they incarnated, and there would be an orgy to commemorate the day's grand events, in the fond hope of hastening the return of the three most delightsome participants in the cycles of the City.

And Jade Alain fairly skipped up the long, long stairs above the thundering flood of the Sin, to change his garments for festal clothes, his very best, and to attend on Onyx Ermine.

He decked himself in sable and the green and white stones of his name, and with a smile on his face and a lightness in his step he walked to the doors of Onyx Palace.

There were no locks, of course, nor guards. The criminals of the City were centuries adept and not so crude. He walked in quite freely as he had come in company to the great anniversaries of the houses, asked of an Onyx child where might be the princess Ermine. The wise-eyed child looked him up and down and solemnly led him through the maze of corridors, into a white and yellow hall, where Ermine sat in a cluster of young friends.

"Why, it's the Jade youth," she said delightedly.

"It's Jade Alain," another yawned. "He's very new."

"Go away," Ermine bade them all. They departed in no great haste. The bored one paused to look Alain up and down, but Alain avoided the eyes . . . looked up only when he was alone with Ermine.

"Come here," she said. He came and knelt and pressed her hand.

"I've come," he said, "to pay you court, Onyx Ermine."

"To sleep with me?"

"To pay you court," he said. "To marry you."

She gave a little laugh. "I'm not wont to marry. I have very seldom married."

"I love you," he said. "I've loved you for four years."

"Only that?" Her laugh was sweet. He looked up into her eyes and wished that he had not, for the age that was there.

"Four years," she mocked him. "But how old are you, Jade Alain?"

"It's," he said in a faint voice, "my first life. And I've never loved anyone but you."

"Charming," she said, and leaned and kissed him on the lips, took both his hands and drew them to her heart. "And shall we be lovers this afternoon?"

He accepted. It was a delirium, a dream half true. She brought him through halls of white and yellow stone and into a room with a bed of saffron satin. They made love there all the afternoon, though he was naïve and she sometimes laughed at his innocence; though sometimes he would look by mistake into her eyes and see all the ages of the City looking back at him. And at last they slept; and at last they woke.

"Come back again," she said, "when you're reborn. We shall find pleasure in it."

"Ermine," he cried. "Ermine!"

But she left the bed and shrugged into her gown, called attendants and lingered there among the maids, laughter in her aged eyes. "In Onyx Palace, newborn lover, the likes of you are servants . . . like these, even after several lifetimes. What decadences Jade tolerates to bring one up a prince! You have diverted me, put a crown on a memorable day. Now begone. I sense myself about to be bored."

He was stunned. He sat a good long moment after she had left in the company of her maids, heart-wounded and with heat flaming in his face. But then, the reborn were accustomed to speak to him and to each other with the utmost arrogance. He thought it a testing, as his mother had tested him, as Pertito and Legran had called him hopelessly young, but not without affection . . . He thought, sitting there, and thought, when he had dressed to leave . . . and concluded that he had not utterly failed to amuse. It was novelty he lacked.

He might achieve this by some flamboyance, a fourth Jade death . . . hastening into that next life . . . but he would miss Onyx Ermine by the years that she would continue to live, and he would suffer through lifetimes before they were matched in age again.

He despaired. He dressed again and walked out to seek her in the halls, found her at last in the company of Onyx friends, and the room echoing with laughter.

At him.

It died for a moment when she saw him standing there. She held out her hand to him with displeasure in her eyes, and he came to her, stood among them.

There was a soft titter from those around her.

"You should have sent him to me," a woman older than the others whispered, and there was general laughter.

"For you there *is* no novelty," Ermine laughed. She lolled carelessly upon her chair and looked up at Alain. "Do go now, before you become still more distressed. Shall I introduce you to my last husband?" She stroked the arm of the young woman nearest her. "She was. But that was very long ago. And already you are dangerously predictable. I fear I shall be bored."

"Oh, how can we be?" the woman who had been her husband laughed. "We shall be entertained at Jade's expense for years. He's very determined. Just look at him. This is the sort of fellow who can make a pattern, isn't he? Dear Ermine, he'll plague us all before he's done, create some nasty scandal and we shall all be like Legran and Pertito and poor Claudette . . . or whatever their names will be. We shall be sitting in this room cycle after cycle fending away this impertinent fellow."

"How distressing," someone yawned.

The laughter rippled round again, and Ermine rose from her chair, took his burning face in her two hands and smiled at him. "I cannot even remember being the creature you are. There is no hope for you. Don't you know that I'm one of the oldest in Onyx? You've had your education. Begone."

"*Four years*," someone laughed. "She won't look at me after thirty lifetimes."

"Good-bye," she said.

"What might I do," he asked quietly, "to convince you of novelty and persuade you, in this life or the next?"

Then she did laugh, and thought a moment. "Die the death for love of me. No one has done that."

"And will you marry me before that? It's certain there's no bargain after."

There was a shocked murmur among her friends, and the flush drained from the cheeks of Onyx Ermine.

"He's quite mad," someone said.

"Onyx offered a wager," he said. "Jade would never say

what it doesn't mean. Shall I tell this in Jade, and amuse my elders with the tale?"

"I shall give you four years," she said, "since you reckon that a very long time."

"You will marry me."

"You will die the death after that fourth year, and I shall not be bothered with you in the next life."

"No," he said. "You will not be bothered."

There was no more laughter. He had achieved novelty. The older woman clapped her hands solemnly, and the others joined the applause. Ermine inclined her head to them, and to him; he bowed to all of them in turn.

"Arrange it," she said.

It was a grand wedding, the more so because weddings were rare, on the banks of the Sin where alone in the City there was room enough to contain the crowd. Alain wore black with white stones; Ermine wore white with yellow gold. There was dancing and feasting and the dark waters of the Sin glistened with the lights of lanterns and sparkling fires, with jewel-lights and the glowing colors of the various palaces of the City.

And afterward there was long, slow lovemaking, while the celebrants outside the doors of Jade Palace drank themselves giddy and feted a thing no one had ever seen, so bizarre a bargain, with all honor to the pair which had contrived it.

In days following the wedding all the City filed into Jade to pay courtesy, and to see the wedded couple . . . to applaud politely the innovation of the youngest and most tragic prince of the City. It was the more poignant because it was real tragedy. It eclipsed that of the Grand Cyclics. It was one of the marks of the age, an event unduplicatable, and no one wished to miss it.

Even the Death came, almost the last of the visitors, and that was an event which crowned all the outré affair, an arrival which struck dumb those who were in line to pay their respects and rewarded those who happened to be there that day with the most bizarre and terrible vision of all.

She had come far, up all the many turnings of the stairs from the nether depths of the City, where she kept her solitary lair near the tombs. She came robed and veiled in black, a spot of darkness in the line. At first no one realized the nature of this guest, but all at once the oldest did, and whispered to the others.

Onyx Ermine knew, being among the oldest, and rose from her throne in sudden horror. Alain stood and held Ermine's hand, with a sinking in his heart.

Their guest came closer, swathed in her robes . . . she, rumor held it, had a right to Jade, who had been born here—not born at all, others said, but engendered of all the deaths the City never died. She drank souls and lives. She had prowled among them in the ancient past like a beast, taking the unwilling, appearing where she would in the shadows. But at last she established herself by the tombs below, for she found some who sought her, those miserable in their incarnations, those whose every life had become intolerable pain. She was the only death in the City from which there was no rebirth.

She was the one by whom the irreverent swore, lacking other terrors.

"Go away," the eldest of Jade said to her.

"But I have come to the wedding," the Death said. It was a woman's voice beneath the veils. "Am I not party to this? I was not consulted, but shall I not agree?"

"We have heard," said Onyx Ermine, who was of too many lifetimes to be set back for long, "we have heard that you are not selective."

"Ah," said the Death. "Not lately indeed; so few have come to me. But shall I not seal the bargain?"

There was silence, dread silence. And with a soft whispering of her robes the Death walked forward, held out her hands to Jade Alain, leaned forward for a kiss.

He bent, shut his eyes, for the veil was gauze, and he had no wish to see. It was hard enough to bear the eyes of the many-lived; he had no wish at all to gaze into hers, to see what rumor whispered he should find there, all the souls she had ever drunk. Her lips were warm through the gauze, touched lightly, and her hands on his were delicate and kind.

She walked away then. He felt Ermine's hand take his, cold and sweating. He settled again into the presence hall throne and Ermine tok her seat beside him. There was awe on faces around them, but no applause.

"She has come out again," someone whispered. "And she hasn't done that in ages. But I remember the old days. She may hunt again. She's *awake*, and interested."

"It's Onyx's doing," another voice whispered. And in that coldness the last of the wedding guests drifted out.

The doors of Jade Palace closed. "Bar them," the eldest said. It was for the first time in centuries.

And Ermine's hand lay very cold in Alain's.

"Madam," he said, "are you satisfied?"

She gave no answer, nor spoke of it after.

There were seasons in the City. They were marked in anniversaries of the Palaces, in exquisite entertainments, in births and deaths.

The return of Claudette was one such event, when a year-old child with wise blue eyes announced his former name, and old friends came to toast the occasion.

The return of Legran and Pertito was another, for they were twin girls in Onyx, and this complication titillated the whole City with speculations which would take years to prove.

The presence of Jade Alain at each of these events was remarked with a poignancy which satisfied everyone with sensitivity, in the remarkable realization that Onyx Ermine, who hid in disgrace, would inevitably return to them, and this most exquisite of youths would not.

One of the greatest Cycles and one of the briefest lives existed in intimate connection. It promised change.

And as for the Death, she had no need to hunt, for the lesser souls, seeking to imitate fashion in this drama, flocked to her lair in unusual number . . . some curious and some self-destructive, seeking their one great moment of passion and notoriety, when a thousand thousand years had failed to give them fame.

They failed of it, of course, for such demises were only following a fashion, not setting one; and they lacked inventiveness in their endings as in their lives.

It was for the fourth year the City waited.

And in its beginning:

"It is three-fourths gone," Onyx Ermine said. She had grown paler still in her shamed confinement within Jade

Palace. In days before this anniversary of their wedding she had received old friends from Onyx, the first time in their wedded life she had received callers. He had remarked then a change in her lovemaking, that what had been pleasantly indifferent acquired ... passion. It was perhaps the rise in her spirits. There were other possibilities, involving a former lover. He was twenty-two and saw things more clearly than once he had.

"You will be losing something," he reminded her coldly, "beyond recall and without repetition. That should enliven your long life."

"Ah," she said, "don't speak of it. I repent the bargain. I don't want this horrid thing, I don't; I don't want you to die."

"It's late for that," he said.

"I love you."

That surprised him, brought a frown to his brow and almost a warmth to his heart, but he could muster only sadness. "You don't," he said. "You love the novelty I've brought. You have never loved a living being, not in all your lifetimes. You never could have loved. That is the nature of Onyx."

"No. You don't know. Please. Jade depresses me. Please let's go and spend the year in Onyx, among my friends. I must recover them, build back my old associations. I shall be all alone otherwise. If you care anything at all for my happiness, let's go home to Onyx."

"If you wish," he said, for it was the first time that she had shown him her heart, and he imagined that it might be very fearsome for one so long incarnate in one place to spend too much time apart from it. His own attachments were ephemeral. "Will it make you content?"

"I shall be very grateful," she said, and put her arms about his neck and kissed him tenderly.

They went that day, and Onyx received them, a restrained but festive occasion as befitted Ermine's public disfavor .. but she fairly glowed with life, as if all the shadows she had dreaded in Jade were gone. "Let us make love," she said, "oh now!" And they lay all afternoon in the saffron bed, a slow and pleasant time.

"You're happy," he said to her. "You're finally happy."

"I love you," she whispered in his ear as they dressed for

dinner, she in her white and pearls and he in his black and his green jade. "Oh let us stay here and not think of other things."

"Or of year's end?" he asked, finding that thought incredibly difficult, this day, to bear.

"Hush," she said, and gave him white wine to drink.

They drank together from opposite sides of one goblet, sat down on the bed and mingled wine and kisses. He felt strangely numb, lay back, with the first intimation of betrayal. He watched her cross the room, open the door. A tear slipped from his eye, but it was anger as much as pain.

"Take him away," Onyx Ermine whispered to her friends. "Oh take him quickly and end this. *She* will not care if he comes early."

"The risk we run . . ."

"Would you have her come *here*? For three years I have lived in misery, seeing *her* in every shadow. I can't bear it longer. I can't bear touching what I'm going to lose. Take him there. Now."

He tried to speak. He could not. They wrapped him in the sheets and satin cover and carried him, a short distance at first, and then to the stairs, by many stages. He heard finally the thunder of the falls of the Sin, and the echoes of the lower levels . . . heard the murmur of spectators near him at times, and knew that none but Jade might have interfered. They were all merely spectators. That was all they wished to be, to avoid complications.

Even, perhaps, Jade itself . . . observed.

They laid him down at last in a place where feet scuffed dryly on dust, and fled, and left silence and dark. He lay long still, until a tingling in his fingers turned to pain, which traveled all his limbs and left him able again to move. He stirred, and staggered to his feet, cold in a bitter wind, chilled by the lonely dark. From before him came the dim light of lamps, and a shadow sat between them.

"You are betrayed," the Death said.

He wrapped his arms about him against the chill and stared at her.

"She doesn't love you," said the Death. "Don't you know that?"

"I knew," he said. "But then, no one ever did. They've forgotten how."

The Death lifted her hands to the veils and let them fall. She was beautiful, pale of skin, with ebon hair and a blood-red stain of rubies at her brow. She held out hands to him, rising. And when she came to him he did not look away.

"Some change their minds," she said. "Even those who come of their own will."

The eyes were strange, constantly shifting in subtle tones ... the fires, perhaps, or all the souls she had drunk, all the torment. "I bring peace," she said. "If I did not exist, there would be no way out. And they would all go mad. I am their choice. I am possibility. I am change in the cycles."

He gazed into the flickerings, the all-too-tenanted eyes. "How is it done?" he asked, fearing to know.

She embraced him, and laid her head at his shoulder. He flinched from a tiny sharp pain at his throat, quickly done. A chill grew in his limbs, a slight giddiness like love.

"Go back," she said, releasing him. "Run away until your time."

He stumbled back, found the door, realized belatedly her words.

"Go," she said. "I'll come for you ... in my agreed time. I at least keep my word, Jade Alain."

And when he would have gone ...

"Jade Alain," she said. "I know you have moved to Onyx. I know most things in the City. Tell your wife ... I keep my promises."

"She fears you."

"She is nothing," the Death said. "Do you fear me?"

He considered. The question found him numb. And for all his numbness he walked back to her, faced the dreadful eyes. He tested his courage by it. He tested it further, took the Death's face between his hands and returned the kiss she had given three years before.

"Ah," she said. "That was kind."

"You are gentle," he said. "I shall not mind."

"Sad Jade prince. Go. Go away just now."

He turned away, walked out the grim doorway into the light, walked up the stairs, a long, long walk, in which there were few passersby, for it was what passed for night in the City now, and of that he was very glad, because of the shame which Onyx had dealt him and the anger he felt. Those who did see him stared, and muttered behind their hands and shrank away. So did those at the doors of Onyx, who blanched and began to bar his way.

But the doors opened, and Ermine's several friends stood with knives.

"Go away," they said.

"That was not the bargain," he replied.

"Your wife is the bargain," the oldest woman said. "Take Ermine back to Jade. Don't involve us."

"*No*," Ermine wailed from the hall beyond; but they brought her to him, and he took her by the hand and dragged her along to his own doors. She ceased struggling. They entered within the ornate halls of Jade Palace, and under the fearful eyes of his own kin, he drew her through the maze of corridors to his own apartments and sealed the door fast behind them.

She was there. There was no possible means that she could be . . . but there the Death stood, clothed in black, among the green draperies by the bed. Ermine flung about and cried aloud, stopped by his opposing arms.

"Go," the Death said. "I've nothing to do with you yet. Your wife and I have business."

He held Ermine still, she shivering and holding to him and burying her face against him. He shook his head. "No," he said, "I can't. I can't give her to you."

"I've been offended," the Death said. "How am I to be paid for such an offense against my dignity?"

He thought a moment. Smoothed Ermine's pale hair. "The year that I have left. What is that to me? Don't take Ermine's lives. She cares so much to save them."

"Does Ermine agree?" the Death asked.

"Yes," Ermine sobbed, refusing to look back.

He sighed, hurt at last, shook his head and put Ermine from him. The Death reached out her hand, and he came to her, embraced her, looked back as she put her black-robed arm about him. Ermine cowered in the corner, head upon her knees.

"Cousin," the Death whispered to him, for she was once of Jade. He looked into the shifting eyes, and she touched her finger first to her lips and to his; it bled, and left the blood on his lips. "Mine," she said. "As you are."

He was. He felt cold, and hungry for life, desired it more than ever he had desired in his youth.

"I also," the Death said, "am once-born . . . and never die. Nor shall you. Nor have a name again. Nor care."

"Ermine," he whispered, to have the sight of her face again. She looked.

And screamed, and hid her face in her hands.

"When the lives grow too many," the Death said, "and you grow weary, Ermine . . . we will be waiting."

"Whenever you wish," he said to Ermine, and slipped his hand within the Death's warm hand, and went with her, the hidden ways.

Pertito shook his head sadly, poured more wine, stroked the cheek of Legran, who was his lover this cycle, and Claudette's sister. Below their vantage, beyond the balcony, a pale figure wavered on the tenth level of stairs, where the Sin began its dizzying fall. "I'll wager she's on the verge again," he said. "Poor Ermine. Thousands of years and no invention left. Never more years than twenty-two. When she reaches that age . . . she's gone."

"Not this time," Legran said.

"Ah. Look. She's on the edge."

Legran stretched her neck to see, remained tranquil. "A wager?"

"Has she whispered things in your brother's ear, perhaps? Lovers' confidences?"

Legran sighed, smiled lazily, settling again. She sipped at her cup and her smoky eyes danced above the rim. A crowd was gathering to watch the impending leap.

"Do you know something?" Pertito asked.

"Ah, my tragic brother, to be in love with Ermine. Three lifetimes now he could not hold her . . . Wager on it, my love?"

Pertito hesitated. A hundred lifetimes without variance. It was a small crowd, observing the suicide indifferently, expecting no novelty from Ermine.

"This time," Legran said, eyes dancing more, "there is a rival."

"A second lover?"

The white figure poised delicately on the topmost step of the chute. There were sighs, a polite rippling of applause.

"A very old one," Legran said. "For some months now. Ah. There she goes."

There were gasps, a dazed silence from the crowd.

Past the falls, this time, and down and down the stairs, a gleam of white and pearls.

Michael Bishop

THE QUICKENING

Displaced persons are not unusual in today's world and probably never have been, even in prehistoric times. Suppose, however, that everyone in the world became a displaced person, waking up one morning in a strange place among strangers, most of them speaking languages strange to each other. What kind of society would arise as a result of this cosmic displacement? Michael Bishop examines the possibilities in this highly unusual tale.

i.

Lawson came out of his sleep feeling drugged and disoriented. Instead of the susurrus of traffic on Rivermont and the early-morning barking of dogs, he heard running feet and an unsettling orchestration of moans and cries. No curtains screened or softened the sun that beat down on his face, and an incandescent blueness had replaced their ceiling. "Marlena," Lawson said doubtfully. He wondered if one of the children was sick and told himself that he ought to get up to help.

But when he tried to rise, scraping the back of his hand on a stone set firmly in mortar, he found that his bed had become a parapet beside a river flowing through an unfamiliar city. He was wearing, instead of the green Chinese-peasant pajamas that Marlena had given him for Christmas, a suit of

The Quickening

khaki 1505s from his days in the Air Force and a pair of ragged Converse sneakers. Clumsily, as if deserting a mortuary slab, Lawson leapt away from the wall. In his sleep, the world had turned over. The forms of a bewildered anarchy had begun to assert themselves.

The city—and Lawson knew that it sure as hell wasn't Lynchburg, that the river running through it wasn't the James—was full of people. A few, their expressions terrified and their postures defensive, were padding past Lawson on the boulevard beside the parapet. Many shrieked or babbled as they ran. Other human shapes dressed not even remotely alike, were lifting themselves bemusedly from paving stones, or riverside benches, or the gutter beyond the sidewalk. Their grogginess and their swiftly congealing fear, Lawson realized, mirrored his own: like him, these people were awaking to nightmare.

Because the terrible fact of his displacement seemed more important than the myriad physical details confronting him, it was hard to take in everything at once—but Lawson tried to balance and integrate what he saw.

The city was foreign. Its architecture was a clash of the Gothic and the sterile, pseudoadobe Modern, one style to each side of the river. On this side, palm trees waved their dreamy fronds at precise intervals along the boulevard, and toward the city's interior an intricate cathedral tower defined by its great height nearly everything beneath it. Already the sun crackled off the rose-colored tower with an arid fierceness that struck Lawson, who had never been abroad, as Mediterranean. . . . Off to his left was a bridge leading into a more modern quarter of the city, where beige and brick-red highrises clustered like tombstones. On both sides of the bridge buses, taxicabs, and other sorts of motorized vehicles were stalled or abandoned in the thoroughfares.

Unfamiliar, Lawson reflected, but not unearthly—he recognized things, saw the imprint of a culture somewhat akin to his own. And, for a moment, he let the innanimate bulk of the city and the languor of its palms and bougainvillea crowd out of his vision the human horror show taking place in the streets.

A dark woman in a sari hurried past. Lawson lifted his hand to her. Dredging up a remnant of a high-school language course, he shouted, "*¿Habla Español?*" The woman quickened her pace, crossed the street, recrossed it, crossed it again; her movements were random, motivated, it seemed, by panic and the complicated need to *do* something.

At a black man in a loincloth farther down the parapet, Lawson shouted, "This is Spain! We're somewhere in Spain! That's all I know! Do you speak English? Spanish? Do you know what's happened to us?"

The black man, grimacing so that his skin went taut across his cheekbones, flattened himself atop the wall like a lizard. His elbows jutted, his eyes narrowed to slits. Watching him, Lawson perceived that the man was listening intently to a sound that had been steadily rising in volume ever since Lawson had opened his eyes: the city was wailing. From courtyards, apartment buildings, taverns, and plazas, an eerie and discordant wail was rising into the bland blue indifference of the day. It consisted of many strains. The Negro in the loincloth seemed determined to separate these and pick out the ones that spoke most directly to him. He tilted his head.

"Spain!" Lawson yelled against this uproar. "*¡España!*"

The black man looked at Lawson, but the hieroglyph of recognition was not among those that glinted in his eyes. As if to dislodge the wailing of the city, he shook his head. Then, still crouching lizard-fashion on the wall, he began methodically banging his head against its stones. Lawson, helplessly aghast, watched him until he had knocked himself insensible in a sickening, repetitive spattering of blood.

But Lawson was the only one who watched. When he approached the man to see if he had killed himself. Lawson's eyes were seduced away from the African by a movement in the river. A bundle of some sort was floating in the greasy waters below the wall—an infant, clad only in a shirt. The tie-strings on the shirt trailed out behind the child like the severed, wavering legs of a water-walker. Lawson wondered, if, in Spain, they even had water-walkers . . .

Meanwhile, still growing in volume, there crooned above the high-rises and Moorish gardens the impotent air-raid siren of 400,000 human voices. Lawson cursed the sound. Then he covered his face and wept.

ii.

The city was Seville. The river was the Guadalquivir. Lynchburg and the James River, around which Lawson had grown up as the eldest child of an itinerant fundamentalist preacher, were several thousand miles and one helluva big ocean away. You couldn't get there by swimming, and if you imagined that your loved ones would be waiting for you when you got back, you were probably fantasizing the nature of the world's changed reality. No one was where he or she belonged anymore, and Lawson knew himself lucky even to realize where he was. Most of the dispossessed, displaced people inhabiting Seville today *didn't* know that much; all they knew was the intolerable cruelty of their uprooting, the pain of separation from husbands, wives, children, lovers, friends. These things, and fear.

The bodies of infants floated in the Guadalquivir; and Lawson, from his early reconnoiterings of the city on a motor scooter that he had found near the Jardines de Cristina park, knew that thousands of adults already lay dead on streets and in apartment buildings—victims of panic-inspired beatings or their own traumatized hearts. Who knew exactly what was going on in the morning's chaos? Babel had come again and with it, as part of the package, the utter disolution of all family and societal ties. You couldn't go around a corner without encountering a child of some exotic ethnic caste, her face snot-glazed, sobbing loudly or maybe running through a crush of bodies calling names in an alien tongue.

What were you supposed to do? Wheeling by on his motor scooter, Lawson either ignored these children or searched their faces to see how much they resembled his daughters.

Where was Marlena now? Where were Karen and Hannah? Just as he played deaf to the cries of the children in the boulevards, Lawson had to harden himself against the implications of these questions. As dialects of German, Chinese, Bantu, Russian, Celtic, and a hundred other languages rattled in his ears, his scooter rattled past a host of cars and buses with uncertain-seeming drivers at their wheels. Probably he too should have chosen an enclosed vehicle. If these frustrated and angry drivers, raging in polyglot defiance, decided to run over him, they could do so with impunity. Who would stop them?

Maybe—in Istanbul, or La Paz, or Mangalore, or Jönköping, or Boise City, or Kaesŏng—his own wife and children had already lost their lives to people made murderous by fear or the absence of helmeted men with pistols and billy sticks. Maybe Marlena and his children were dead . . .

I'm in Seville, Lawson told himself, cruising. He had determined the name of the city soon after mounting the motor scooter and going by a sign that said *Plaza de Toros de Sevilla*. A circular stadium of considerable size near the river. The bullring. Lawson's Spanish was just good enough to decipher the signs and posters plastered on its walls. *Corrida a las cinco de la tarde.* (Garcia Lorca, he thought, unsure of where the name had come from.) *Sombra y sol.* That morning, then, he took the scooter around the stadium three or four times and then shot off toward the center of the city.

Lawson wanted nothing to do with the nondescript highrises across the Guadalquivir, but had no real idea what he was going to do on the Moorish and Gothic side of the river, either. All he knew was that the empty bullring, with its dormant potential for death, frightened him. On the other hand, how did you go about establishing order in a city whose population had not willingly chosen to be there?

Seville's population, Lawson felt sure, had been redistributed across the face of the globe, like chess pieces flung from a height. The population of every other human community on Earth had undergone similar displacements. The result, as if by malevolent design, was chaos and suffering. Your ears eventually tried to shut out the audible manifestations of this pain, but your eyes held you accountable and you hated yourself for ignoring the wailing Arab child, the assaulted Polynesian woman, the blue-eyed old man bleeding from the palms as he prayed in the shadow of a department-store awning. Very nearly, you hated yourself for surviving.

Early in the afternoon, at the entrance to the Calle de las Sierpes, Lawson got off his scooter and propped it against a wall. Then he waded into the crowd and lifted his right arm above his head.

"I speak English!" he called. "*Y hablo un poco Español!* Any who speak English or Spanish please come to me!"

A man who might have been Vietnamese or Kampuchean,

or even Malaysian, stole Lawson's motor scooter and rode it in a wobbling zigzag down the Street of the Serpents. A heavyset blonde woman with red cheeks glared at Lawson from a doorway, and a twelve-or-thirteen-year-old boy who appeared to be Italian clutched hungrily at Lawson's belt, seeking purchase on an adult, hoping for commiseration. Although he did not try to brush the boy's hand away. Lawson avoided his eyes.

"English! English here! *"¡Un poco Español también!"*

Farther down Sierpes, Lawson saw another man with his hand in the air; he was calling aloud in a crisp but melodic Slavic dialect, and already he had succeeded in attracting two or three other people to him. In fact, pockets of like-speaking people seemed to be forming in the crowded commercial avenue, causing Lawson to fear that he had put up his hand too late to end his own isolation. What if those who spoke either English or Spanish had already gathered into survival-conscious groups? What if they had already made their way into the countryside, where the competition for food and drink might be a little less predatory? If they had, he would be a lost, solitary Virginian in this Babel. Reduced to sign language and guttural noises to make his wants known, he would die a cipher....

"Signore," the boy hanging on his belt cried. *"Signore."*

Lawson let his eyes drift to the boy's face. *"Ciao,"* he said. It was the only word of Italian he knew, or the only word that came immediately to mind, and he spoke it much louder than he meant.

The boy shook his head vehemently, pulled harder on Lawson's belt. His words tumbled out like the contents of an unburdened closet into a darkened room, not a single one of them distinct or recognizable.

"English!" Lawson shouted. "English here!"

"English here, too, man!" a voice responded from the milling crush of people at the mouth of Sierpes. "Hang on a minute, I'm coming to you!"

A small muscular man with a large head and not much chin stepped daintily through an opening in the crowd and put out his hand to Lawson. His grip was firm. As he shook hands, he placed his left arm over the shoulder of the Italian boy hanging on to Lawson's belt. The boy stopped talking and gaped at the newcomer.

"Dai Secombe," the man said. "I went to bed in Aberystwyth, where I teach philosophy, and I wake up in Spain. Pleased to meet you, Mr.—"

"Lawson," Lawson said.

The boy began babbling again, his hand shifting from Lawson's belt to the Welshman's flannel shirt facing. Secombe took the boy's hands in his own. "I've got you, lad. There's a ragged crew of your compatriots in a pool-hall pub right down this lane. Come on, then, I'll take you." He glanced at Lawson. "Wait for me, sir. I'll be right back."

Secombe and the boy disappeared, but in less than five minutes the Welshman had returned. He introduced himself all over again. "To go to bed in Aberystwyth and to wake up in Seville," he said, "is pretty damn harrowing. I'm glad to be alive, sir."

"Do you have a family?"

"Only my father. He's eighty-four."

"You're lucky. Not to have anyone else to worry about, I mean."

"Perhaps," Dai Secombe said, a sudden trace of sharpness in his voice. "Yesterday I would not've thought so."

The two men stared at each other as the wail of the city modulated into a less hysterical but still inhuman drone. People surged around them, scrutinized them from foyers and balconies, took their measure. Out of the corner of his eye Lawson was aware of a moonfaced woman in summer deerskins slumping abruptly and probably painfully to the street. An Eskimo woman—the conceit was almost comic, but the woman herself was dying and a child with a Swedish-steel switchblade was already freeing a necklace of teeth and shells from her throat.

Lawson turned away from Secombe to watch the plundering of the Eskimo woman's body. Enraged, he took off his wristwatch and threw it at the boy's head, scoring a glancing sort of hit on his ear.

"You little jackal, get away from there!"

The red-cheeked woman who had been glaring at Lawson applied her foot to the rump of the boy with the switchblade and pushed him over. Then she retrieved the thrown watch, hoisted her skirts, and retreated into the dim interior of the café whose door she had been haunting.

"In this climate, in this environment," Dai Secombe told

Lawson, "an Eskimo is doomed. It's as much psychological and emotional as it is physical. There may be a few others who've already died for similar reasons. Not much we can do, sir."

Lawson turned back to the Welshman with a mixture of awe and disdain. How had this curly-haired lump of a man, in the space of no more than three or four hours, come to respond so lackadaisically to the deaths of his fellows? Was it merely because the sky was still blue and the edifices of another age still stood?

Pointedly, Secombe said, "That was a needless forfeiture of your watch, Lawson."

"How the hell did that poor woman get here?" Lawson demanded, his gesture taking in the entire city. "How the hell did any of us get here?" The stench of open wounds and the first sweet hints of decomposition mocked the luxury of his ardor.

"Good questions," the Welshman responded, taking Lawson's arm and leading him out of the Calle de las Sierpes. "It's a pity I can't answer 'em."

iii.

That night they ate fried fish and drank beer together in a dirty little apartment over a shop whose glass display cases were filled with a variety of latex contraceptives. They had obtained the fish from a *pescadería* voluntarily tended by men and women of Greek and Yugoslavian citizenship, people who had run similar shops in their own countries. The beer they had taken from one of the classier bars on the Street of the Serpents. Both the fish and the beer were at room temperature, but tasted none the worse for that.

With the fall of evening, however, the wail that during the day had subsided into a whine began to reverberate again with its first full burden of grief. If the noise was not quite so loud as it had been that morning, Lawson thought, it was probably because the city contained fewer people. Many had died, and a great many more, unmindful of the distances involved, had set out to return to their homelands.

Lawson chewed a piece of *adobo* and washed this down with a swig of the vaguely bitter *Cruz del Campo* beer.

"Isn't this fine?" Secombe said, his butt on the tiles of the room's one windowsill. "Dinner over a rubber shop. And this a Catholic country, too."

"I was raised a Baptist," Lawson said, realizing at once that his confession was a non sequitur.

"Oh," Secombe put in immediately. "Then I imagine you could get all the rubbers you wanted."

"Sure. For a quarter. In almost any gas-station restroom."

"Sorry," Secombe said.

They ate for a while in silence. Lawson's back was to a cool plaster wall; he leaned his head against it, too, and released a sharp moan from his chest. Then, sustaining the sound, he moaned again, adding his own strand of grief to the cacophonous harmonies already afloat over the city. He was no different from all the bereaved others who shared his pain by concentrating on their own.

"What did you do in . . . in Lynchburg?" Secombe suddenly asked.

"Campus liaison for the Veterans Administration. I traveled to four different colleges in the area straightening out people's problems with the GI Bill. I tried to see to it that— Sweet Jesus, Secombe, who cares? I miss my wife. I'm afraid my girls are dead."

"Karen and Hannah?"

"They're three and five. I've taught them to play chess. Karen's good enough to beat me occasionally if I spot her my queen. Hannah knows the moves, but she hasn't got her sister's patience—she's only three, you know. Yeah. Sometimes she sweeps the pieces off the board and folds her arms, and we play hell trying to find them all. There'll be pawns under the sofa, horsemen upside down in the shag—" Lawson stopped.

"She levels them," Secombe said. "As we've all been leveled. The knight's no more than the pawn, the king no more than the bishop."

Lawson could tell that the Welshman was trying to turn aside the ruinous thrust of his grief. But he brushed the metaphor aside: "I don't think we've been 'leveled,' Secombe."

"Certainly we have. Guess who I saw this morning near the cathedral when I first woke up."

"God only knows."

"God and Dai Secombe, sir. I saw the Marxist dictator of . . . oh, you know, that little African country where there's just been a coup. I recognized the bastard from the telly broadcasts during the purge trials there. There he was, though, in white ducks and a ribbed T-shirt—terrified, Lawson, and as powerless as you or I. He'd been quite decidedly leveled; you'd better believe he had."

"I'll bet he's alive tonight, Secombe."

The Welshman's eyes flickered with a sudden insight. He extended the greasy cone of newspaper from the *pescadería*. "Another piece of fish, Lawson? Come on, then, there's only one more."

"To be leveled, Secombe, is to be put on a par with everyone else. Your dictator, even deprived of office, is a grown man. What about infant children? Toddlers and preadolescents? And what about people like that Eskimo woman who haven't got a chance in an unfamiliar environment, even if its inhabitants don't happen to be hostile? . . . I saw a man knock his brains out on a stone wall this morning because he took a look around and knew he couldn't make it here. Maybe he thought he was in Hell, Secombe. I don't know. But his chance certainly wasn't ours."

"He knew he couldn't adjust."

"Of course he couldn't adjust. Don't give me that bullshit about leveling!"

Secombe turned the cone of newspaper around and withdrew the last piece of fish. "I'm going to eat this myself, if you don't mind." He ate. As he was chewing, he said, "I didn't think that Virginia Baptists were so free with their tongues, Lawson. Tsk, tsk. Undercuts my preconceptions."

"I've fallen away."

"Haven't we all."

Lawson took a final swig of warm beer. Then he hurled the bottle across the room. Fragments of amber glass went everywhere. "God!" he cried. "God, God, God!" Weeping, he was no different from three quarters of Seville's new citizens-by-chance. Why, then, as he sobbed, did he shoot such guilty and threatening glances at the Welshman?

"Go ahead," Secombe advised him, waving the empty cone of newspaper. "I feel a little that way myself."

iv.

In the morning an oddly blithe woman of forty-five or so

accosted them in the alley outside the contraceptive shop. A military pistol in a patent-leather holster was strapped about her skirt. Her seeming airiness, Lawson quickly realized, was a function of her appearance and her movements; her eyes were as grim and frightened as everyone else's. But, as soon as they came out of the shop onto the cobblestones, she approached them fearlessly, hailing Secombe almost as if he were an old friend.

"You left us yesterday, Mr. Secombe. Why?"

"I saw everything dissolving into cliques."

"Dissolving? Coming together, don't you mean?"

Secombe smiled noncommittally, then introduced the woman to Lawson as Mrs. Alexander. "She's one of your own, Lawson. She's from Wyoming or some such place. I met her outside the cathedral yesterday morning when the first self-appointed muezzins started calling their language-mates together. She didn't have a pistol then."

"I got it from one of the Guardia Civil stations," Mrs. Alexander said. "And I feel lots better just having it, let me tell you." She looked at Lawson. "Are you in the Air Force?"

"Not any more. These are the clothes I woke up in."

"My husband's in the Air Force. Or was. We were stationed at Warren in Cheyenne I'm originally from upstate New York. And these are the clothes *I* woke up in." A riding skirt, a blouse, low-cut rubber-soled shoes. "I think they tried to give us the most serviceable clothes we had in our wardrobes—but they succeeded better in some cases than others."

" 'They'?" Secombe asked.

"Whoever's done this. It's just a manner of speaking."

"What do you want?" Secombe asked Mrs. Alexander. His brusqueness of tone surprised Lawson.

Smiling, she replied, "The word for today is Exportadora. We're trying to get as many English-speaking people as we can to Exportadora. That's where the commercial center for American servicemen and their families in Seville is located, and it's just off one of the major boulevards to the south of here."

On a piece of paper sack Mrs. Alexander drew them a crude map and explained that her husband had once been stationed in Zaragoza in the north of Spain. Yesterday she had recalled that Seville was one of the four Spanish cities supporting the American military presence, and with persistence and a little luck a pair of carefully briefed English-speaking DPs (the abbreviation was Mrs. Alexander's) had discovered the site of the American PX and commissary just before nightfall. Looting the place when they arrived had been an impossibly mixed crew of foreigners, busily hauling American merchandise out of the ancient buildings. But Mrs. Alexander's DPs had run off the looters by the simple expedient of revving the engine of their comandeered taxicab and blowing its horn as if to announce Armageddon. In ten minutes the little American enclave had emptied of all human beings but the two men in the cab. After that, as English-speaking DPs all over the city learned of Exportadora's existence and sought to reach it, the place had begun to fill up again.

"Is there an air base in Seville?" Lawson asked the woman.

"No, not really. The base itself is near Morón de la Frontera, about thirty miles away, but Seville is where the real action is." After a brief pause, lifting her eyebrows, she corrected herself: "Was."

She thrust her map into Secombe's hands. "Here. Go on out to Exportadora. I'm going to look around for more of us. You're the first people I've found this morning. Others are looking, too, though. Maybe things'll soon start making some sense."

Secombe shook his head. "Us. Them. There isn't anybody now who isn't a 'DP,' you know. This regrouping on the basis of tired cultural affiliations is probably a mistake. I don't like it."

"You took up with Mr. Lawson, didn't you?"

"Out of pity only, I assure you. He looked lost. Moreover, you've got to have companionship of *some* sort—especially when you're in a strange place."

"Sure. That's why the word for today if Exportadora."

"It's a mistake, Mrs. Alexander."

"Why?"

"For the same reason your mysterious 'they' saw fit to displace us to begin with, I'd venture. It's a feeling I have."

"Old cultural affiliations are a source of stability," Mrs. Alexander said earnestly. As she talked, Lawson took the rumpled map out of Secombe's fingers. "This chaos around us won't go away until people have settled themselves into units—it's a natural process, it's beginning already. Why, walking along the river this morning, I saw several groups of like-speaking people burying yesterday's dead. The city's churches and chapels have begun to fill up, too. You can still hear the frightened and the heartbroken keening in solitary rooms, of course—but it can't go on forever. They'll either make connection or die. I'm not one of those who wish to die, Mr. Secombe."

"Who wishes that?" Lawson put in, annoyed by the shallow metaphysical drift of this exchange and by Secombe's irrationality. Although Mrs. Alexander was right, she didn't have to defend her position at such length. The map was her most important contribution to the return of order in their lives, and Lawson wanted her to let them use that map.

"Come on, Secombe." He said. "Let's get out to this Exportadora. It's probably the only chance we have of making it home."

"I don't think there's any chance of our making it home again, Lawson. Ever."

Perceiving that Mrs. Alexander was about to ask the Welshman why, Lawson turned on his heel and took several steps down the alley. "Come on, Secombe. We have to try. What the hell are you going to do in this flip-flopped city all by yourself?"

"Look for somebody else to talk to, I suppose."

But in a moment Secombe was at Lawson's side helping him decipher the smudged geometries of Mrs. Alexander's map, and the woman herself, before heading back to Sierpes to look for more of her own kind, called out, "It'll only take you twenty or so minutes, walking. Good luck. See you later."

Walking, they passed a white-skinned child lying in an alley doorway opening on to a courtyard festooned with two-day-old washing and populated by a pack of orphaned dogs. The child's head was covered by a coat, but she did appear to be breathing. Lawson was not even tempted to examine her more closely, however. He kept his eyes resolutely on the map.

v.

The newsstand in the small American enclave had not been looted. On Lawson's second day at Exportadora it still contained quality paperbacks, the most recent American news and entertainment magazines, and a variety of tabloids, including the military paper *The Stars and Stripes*. No one knew how old these publications were because no one knew over what length of time the redistribution of the world's population had taken place. How long had everyone slept? And what about the discrepancies among time zones and the differences among people's waking hours within the same time zones? These questions were academic now, it seemed to Lawson, because the agency of transfer had apparently encompassed every single human being alive on Earth.

Thumbing desultorily through a copy of *Stars and Stripes*, he encountered an article on the problems of military hospitals and wondered how many of the world's sick had awakened in the open, doomed to immediate death because the care they required was nowhere at hand. The smell of spilled tobacco and melted Life Savers made the newsstand a pleasant place to contemplate these horrors; and, even as his conscience nagged and a contingent of impatient DPs awaited him, Lawson perversely continued to flip through the newspaper.

Secombe's squat form appeared in the doorway. "I thought you were looking for a local roadmap."

"Found it already, just skimmin' the news."

"Come on, if you would. The folks're ready to be off."

Reluctantly, Lawson followed Secombe outside, where the raw Andalusian sunlight broke like invisible surf against the pavement and the fragile-seeming shell of the Air Force bus. It was of the Bluebird shuttle variety, and Lawson remembered summer camp at Eglin Air Force Base in Florida and bus rides from his squadron's minimum-maintenance ROTC barracks to the survival-training camps near the swamp. That had been a long time ago, but this Bluebird might have hailed from an even more distant era. It was as boxy and sheepish-looking as if it had come off a 1954 assembly line, and it appeared to be made out of warped tin rather than steel. The people inside the bus had opened all its windows, and many of those on the driver's side were watching Secombe and Lawson approach.

"Move your asses!" a man shouted at them. "Let's get some wind blowing through this thing before we all suffo-damn-cate."

"Just keep talking," Secombe advised him. "That should do fine."

Aboard the bus was a motley lot of Americans, Britishers, and Australians, with two or three English-speaking Europeans and an Oxford-educated native of India to lend the group ballast. Lawson took up a window seat over the hump of one of the bus's rear tires, and Secombe squeezed in beside him. A few people introduced themselves; others, lost in fitful reveries, ignored them altogether. The most unsettling thing about the contingent to Lawson was the absence of children. Although about equally divided between men and women, the group contained no boys or girls any younger than their early teens.

Lawson opened the map of southern Spain he had found in the newsstand and traced his finger along a highway route leading out of Seville to two small American enclaves outside the city, Santa Clara and San Pablo. Farther to the south were Jerez and the port city of Cádiz. Lawson's heart misgave him; the names were all so foreign, so formidable in what they evoked, and he felt this entire enterprise to be hopeless. . . .

About midway along the right-hand side of the bus a black woman was sobbing into the hem of her blouse, and a man perched on the Bluebird's long rear seat had his hands clasped to his ears and his head canted forward to touch his knees. Lawson folded up the map and stuck it into the crevice between the seat and the side of the bus.

"The bottom-line common denominator here isn't our all speaking English," Secombe whispered. "It's what we're suffering."

Driven by one of Mrs. Alexander's original explorers, a doctor from Ivanhoe, New South Wales, the Bluebird shuddered and lurched forward. In a moment it had left Exportadora and begun banging along one of the wide avenues that would lead it out of town.

"And our suffering," Secombe went on, still whispering, "unites us with all those poor souls raving in the streets and sleeping facedown in their own vomit. You felt that the other night above the condom shop, Lawson. I know you did, talking of your daughters. So why are you so quick to go looking for what you aren't likely to find? Why are you so ready to unite yourself with this artificial family born out of catastrophe? Do you really think you're going to catch a flight home to Lynchburg? Do you really think the bird driving this sardine can—who ought to be out in the streets plying his trade instead of running a shuttle service—d'you really think he's ever going to get back to Australia?"

"Secombe—"

"Do you, Lawson?"

Lawson clapped a hand over the Welshman's knee and wobbled it back and forth. "You wouldn't be badgering me like this if you had a family of your own. What the hell do you want us to do? Stay here forever?"

"I don't know, exactly." He removed Lawson's hand from his knee. "But I do have a father, sir, and I happen to be fond of him. . . . All I know for certain is that things are *supposed* to be different now. We shouldn't be rushing to restore what we already had."

"Shit," Lawson murmured. He leaned his head against the bottom edge of the open window beside him.

From deep within the city came the brittle noise of gunshots. The Bluebird's driver, in response in this sound and to the vegetable carts and automobiles that had been moved into the streets as obstacles, began wheeling and cornering like a stock-car jockey. The bus clanked and stuttered alarmingly. It growled through an intersection below a stone bridge, leapt over that bridge like something living, and roared down into a semi-industrial suburb of Seville where a Coca-Cola bottling factory and a local brewery lifted huge competing signs.

On top of one of these buildings Lawson saw a man with a rifle taking unhurried potshots at anyone who came into his sights. Several people already lay dead.

And a moment later the Bluebird's front window shattered, another bullet richocheted off its flank, and everyone in the bus was either shouting or weeping. The next time Lawson looked, the bus's front window appeared to have woven inside it a large and exceedingly intricate spider's web.

The Bluebird careened madly, but the doctor from Ivanhoe kept it upright and turned it with considerable skill onto the highway to San Pablo. Here the bus eased into a quiet and rhythmic cruising that made this final incident in Seville—except for the evidence of the front window—seem only the cottony aftertaste of nightmare. At last they were on their way. Maybe.

"Another good reason for trying to get home," Lawson said.

"What makes you think it's going to be different there?"

Irritably Lawson turned on the Welshman. "I thought your idea was that this change was some kind of *improvement*."

"Perhaps it will be. Eventually."

Lawson made a dismissive noise and looked at the olive orchard spinning by on his left. Who would harvest the crop? Who would set the aircraft factories, the distilleries, the chemical and textile plants running again? Who would see to it that seed was sown in the empty fields?

Maybe Secombe had something. Maybe, when you ran for home, you ran from the new reality at hand. The effects of this new reality's advent were not going to go away very soon, no matter what you did—but seeking to reestablish yesterday's order would probably create an even nastier entropic pattern than would accepting the present chaos and working to rein it in. How, though, did you best rein it in? Maybe by trying to get back home. . . .

Lawson shook his head and thought of Marlena, Karen, Hannah; of the distant, mist-softened cradle of the Blue Ridge. Lord. That was country much easier to get in tune with than the harsh, white-sky bleakness of this Andalusian valley. If you stay here, Lawson told himself, the pain will *never* go away.

They passed Santa Clara, which was a housing area for the officers and senior NCOs who had been stationed at Morón. With its neatly trimmed hedgerows, tall aluminum streetlamps, and low-roofed houses with carports and picture windows, Santa Clara resembled a middle-class exurbia in New Jersey or Ohio. Black smoke was curling over the area, however, and the people on the streets and lawns were definitely not Americans—they were transplanted Dutch South Africans, Amazonian tribesmen, Poles, Ethiopians, God-only-knew-what. All Lawson could accurately deduce was that a few of these people had moved into the vacant houses—maybe they had awakened in them—and that others had aimlessly set bonfires about the area's neighborhoods. These fires, because there was no wind, burned with a maddening slowness and lack of urgency.

"Little America," Secombe said aloud.

"That's in Antarctica," Lawson responded sarcastically.

"Right. No matter where it happens to be."
"Up yours."

Their destination was now San Pablo, where the Americans had hospital facilities, a library, a movie theater, a snackbar, a commissary, and, in conjunction with the Spaniards, a small commercial and military airfield. San Pablo lay only a few more miles down the road, and Lawson contemplated the idea of a flight to Portugal. What would be the chances, supposing you actually reached Lisbon, of crossing the Atlantic, either by sea or air, and reaching one of the United States's coastal cities? One in a hundred? One in a thousand? Less than that?

A couple of seats behind the driver, an Englishman with a crisp-looking moustache and an American woman with a distinct southwestern accent were arguing the merits of bypassing San Pablo and heading on to Gibraltar, a British possession. The Englishman seemed to feel that Gibraltar would have escaped the upheaval to which the remainder of the world had fallen victim, whereas the American woman thought he was crazy. A shouting match involving five or six other passengers ensued. Finally, his patience at an end, the Bluebird's driver put his elbow on the horn and held it there until everyone had shut up.

"It's San Pablo," he announced. "Not Gibraltar or anywhere else. There'll be a plane waitin' for us when we get there."

vi.

Two aircraft were waiting, a pair of patched-up DC-7s that had once belonged to the Spanish airline known as Iberia. Mrs. Alexander had recruited one of her pilots from the DPs who had shown up at Exportadora; the other, a retired TWA veteran from Riverside, California, had made it by himself to the airfield by virtue of a prior acquaintance with Seville and its American military installations. Both men were eager to carry passengers home, one via a stopover in Lisbon and the other by using Madrid as a stepping-stone to the British Isles. The hope was that they could transfer their passengers to jet aircraft at these cities' more cosmopolitan airports, but no one spoke very much about the real obstacles to success that had already begun stalking them: civil chaos, delay, inadequate communications, fuel shortages, mechanical hangups, doubt and ignorance, a thousand other things.

At twilight, then, Lawson stood next to Dai Secombe at the chain link fence fronting San Pablo's pothole-riven runway and watched the evening light glimmer off the wings of the DC-7s. Bathed in a muted dazzle, the two old airplanes were almost beautiful. Even though Mrs. Alexander had informed the DPs that they must spend the night in the installation's movie theater, so that the Bluebird could make several more shuttle runs to Exportadora, Lawson truly believed that he was bound for home.

"Good-bye," Secombe told him.

"Goodbye? . . . Oh, because you'll be on the other flight?"

"No, I'm telling you good-bye, Lawson, because I'm leaving. Right now, you see. This very minute."

"Where are you going?"

"Back into the city."

"How? What for?"

"I'll walk, I suppose. As for why, it has something to do with wanting to appease Mrs. Alexander's 'they,' also with finding out what's to become of us all. Seville's the place for that, I think."

"Then why'd you even come out here?"

"To say good-bye, you bloody imbecile." Secombe laughed, grabbed Lawson's hand, shook it heartily. "Since I couldn't manage to change your mind."

With that, he turned and walked along the chain link fence until he had found the roadway past the installation's commissary. Lawson watched him disappear behind that building's complicated system of loading ramps. After a time the Welshman reappeared on the other side, but, against the vast Spanish sky, his compact striding form rapidly dwindled to an imperceptible smudge. A smudge on the darkness.

"Good-bye," Lawson said.

That night, slumped in a lumpy theater chair, he slept with nearly sixty other people in San Pablo's movie house. A teen-age boy, over only a few objections, insisted on showing all the old movies still in tins in the projection room. As a result, Lawson awoke once in the middle of *Apocalypse Now* and another time near the end of Kubrick's *The Left Hand of Darkness*. The ice on the screen, dunelike *sastrugi* ranged from horizon to horizon, chilled him, touching a sensitive spot in his memory. "Little America," he murmured. Then he went back to sleep.

vii.

With the passengers bound for Lisbon, Lawson stood at the fence where he had stood with Secombe, and watched the silver pinwheeling of propellers as the aircraft's engines engaged. The DC-7 flying to Madrid would not leave until much later that day, primarily because it still had several vacant seats and Mrs. Alexander felt sure that more English-speaking DPs could still be found in the city.

The people at the gate with Lawson shifted uneasily and whispered among themselves. The engines of their savior airplane whined deafeningly, and the runway seemed to tremble. What woebegone eyes the women had, Lawson thought, and the men were as scraggly as railroad hoboes. Feeling his jaw, he understood that he was no more handsome or well-groomed than any of those he waited with. And, like them, he was impatient for the signal to board, for the thumbs-up sign indicating that their airplane had passed its latest rudimentary ground tests.

At least, he consoled himself, you're not eating potato chips at ten-thirty in the morning. Disgustedly, he turned aside from a jut-eared man who was doing just that.

"There're more people here than our plane's supposed to carry," the potato-chip cruncher said. "That could be dangerous."

"But it isn't really that far to Lisbon, is it?" a woman replied. "And none of us has any luggage."

"Yeah, but—" The man gagged on a chip, coughed, tried to speak again. Facing deliberately away, Lawson felt that the man's words would acquire eloquence only if he suddenly volunteered to ride in the DC-7s unpressurized baggage compartment.

As it was, the signal came to board and the jut-eared man had no chance to finish his remarks. He threw his cellophane sack to the ground, and Lawson heard it crackling underfoot as people crowded through the gate onto the grassy verge of the runway.

In order to fix the anomaly of San Pablo in his memory,

Lawson turned around and walked backward across the field. He saw that bringing up the rear were four men with automatic weapons—weapons procured, most likely, from the installation's Air Police station. These men, like Lawson, were walking backward, but with their guns as well as their eyes trained on the weirdly constituted band of people who had just appeared, seemingly out of nowhere, along the airfield's fence.

One of these people wore nothing but a ragged pair of shorts, another an ankle-length burnoose, another a pair of trousers belted with a rope. One of their number was a doe-eyed young woman with an exposed torso and a circlet of bright coral on her wrist. But there were others, too, and they all seemed to have been drawn to the runway by the airplane's engine whine; they moved along the fence like desperate ghosts. As the first members of Lawson's group mounted into the plane, even more of these people appeared—an assembly of nomads, hunters, hodcarriers, fishers, herdspeople. Apparently they all understood what an airplane was for, and one of the swarthiest men among them ventured out onto the runway with his arms thrown out imploringly.

"Where you go?" he shouted. "Where you go?"

"There's no more room!" responded a blue-jean-clad man with a machine gun. "Get back! You'll have to wait for another flight!"

Oh sure, Lawson thought, the one to Madrid. He was at the base of the airplane's mobile stairway. The jut-eared man who had been eating potato chips nodded brusquely at him.

"You'd better get on up there," he shouted over the robust hiccoughing of the airplane's engines, "before we have unwanted company breathing down our necks!"

"After you." Lawson stepped aside.

Behind the swarthy man importuning the armed guards for a seat on the airplane, there clamored thirty or more insistent people, their only real resemblance to one another their longing for a way out. "Where you go? Where you go?" the bravest and most desperate among them yelled, but they all wanted to board the airplane that Mrs. Alexander's charges had already laid claim to; and most of them could see that it was too late to accomplish their purpose without some kind of risk-taking. The man who had been shouting in English, along with four or five others, broke into an assertive dogtrot toward the plane. Although their cries continued to be modestly beseeching, Lawson could tell that the passengers' guards now believed themselves under direct attack.

A burst of machine-gun fire sounded above the field and echoed away like rain drumming on a tin roof. The man who had been asking, "Where you go?," pitched forward on his face. Others fell beside him, including the woman with the coral bracelet. Panicked or prodded by this evidence of their assailants' mortality, one of the guards raked the chain link fence with his weapon, bringing down some of those who had already begun to retreat and summoning forth both screams and the distressingly incongruous sound of popping wire. Then, eerily, it was quiet again.

"Get on that airplane!" a guard shouted at Lawson. He was the only passenger still left on the ground, and everyone wanted him inside the plane so that the mobile stairway could be rolled away.

"I don't think so," Lawson said to himself.

Hunching forward like a man under fire, he ran toward the gate and the crude mandala of bodies partially blocking it. The slaughter he had just witnessed struck him as abysmally repetitive of a great deal of recent history, and he did not wish to belong to that history anymore. Further, the airplane behind him was a gross iron-plated emblem of the burden he no longer cared to bear—even if it also seemed to represent the promise of passage home.

"Hey, where the hell you think you're goin'?"

Lawson did not answer. He stepped gingerly through the corpses on the runway's margin, halted on the other side of the fence, and, his eyes misted with glare and poignant bewilderment, turned to watch the DC-7 taxi down the scrub-lined length of concrete to the very end of the field. There the airplane negotiated a turn and started back the way it had come. Soon it was hurtling along like a colossal metal dragonfly, building speed. When it lifted from the ground, its tires screaming shrilly with the last series of bumps before take-off, Lawson held his breath.

Then the airplane's right wing dipped, dipped again, struck the ground, and broke off like a piece of balsa wood, splintering brilliantly. After that, the airplane went flipping, cartwheeling, across the end of the tarmac and into the desolate open field beyond, where its shell and remaining wing were suddenly engulfed in flames. You could hear people frying in that inferno; you could smell gasoline and burnt flesh.

"Jesus," Lawson said.

He loped away from the airfield's fence, hurried through the short grass behind the San Pablo library, and joined a group of those who had just fled the English-speaking guards' automatic-weapon fire. He met them on the highway going back to Seville and walked among them as merely another of their number. Although several people viewed his 1505 trousers with suspicion, no one argued that he did not belong, and no one threatened to cut his throat for him.

As hangdog and exotically nondescript as most of his companions, Lawson watched his tennis shoes track the pavement like the feet of a mechanical toy. He wondered what he was going to do back in Seville. Successfully dodge bullets and eat fried fish, if he was lucky. Talk with Secombe again, if he could find the man. And, if he had any sense, try to organize his life around some purpose other than the insane and hopeless one of returning to Lynchburg. What purpose, though? What purpose beyond the basic, animal purpose of staying alive?"

"Are any of you hungry?" Lawson asked.

He was regarded with suspicious curiosity.

"Hungry," he repeated. *"¿Tiene hambre?"*

English? Spanish? Neither worked. What languages did they have, these refugees from an enigma? It looked as if they had all tried to speak together before and found the task impossible—because, moving along the asphalt under the hot Andalusian sun, they now relied on gestures and easily interpretable noises to express themselves.

Perceiving this, Lawson brought the fingers of his right hand to his mouth and clacked his teeth to indicate chewing.

He was understood. A thin barefoot man in a capacious linen shirt and trousers led Lawson off the highway into an orchard of orange trees. The fruit was not yet completely ripe, and was sour because of its greenness, but all twelve or thirteen of Lawson's crew ate, letting the juice run down their arms. When they again took up the trek to Seville, Lawson's mind was almost absolutely blank with satiety. The only thing rattling about in it now was the fear that he would not know what to do once they arrived. He never did find out if the day's other scheduled flight, the one to Madrid, made it safely to its destination, but the matter struck him now as of little import. He wiped his sticky mouth and trudged along numbly.

viii.

He lived above the contraceptive shop. In the mornings he walked through the alley to a bakery that a woman with calm Mongolian features had taken over. In return for a daily allotment of bread and a percentage of the goods brought in for barter, Lawson swept the bakery's floor, washed the utensils that were dirtied each day, and kept the shop's front counter. His most rewarding skill, in fact, was communicating with those who entered to buy something. He had an uncanny grasp of several varieties of sign language, and, on occasion, he found himself speaking a monosyllabic patois whose derivation was a complete mystery to him. Sometimes he thought that he had invented it himself; sometimes he believed that he had learned it from the transplanted Sevillanos among whom he now lived.

English, on the other hand, seemed to leak slowly out of his mind, a thick, unrecoverable fluid.

The first three or four weeks of chaos following The Change had, by this time, run their course, a circumstance that surprised Lawson. Still, it was true. Now you could lie down at night on your pallet without hearing pistol reports or fearing that some benighted freak was going to set fire to your staircase. Most of the city's essential services—electricity, water, and sewerage—were working again, albeit uncertainly, and agricultural goods were coming in from the countryside. People had gone back to doing what they knew best, while those whose previous jobs had had little to do with the basics of day-to-day survival were now apprenticing as bricklayers, carpenters, bakers, fishers, water and power technicians. That men and women chose to live separately and that children were as rare as sapphires, no one seemed to find disturbing or unnatural. A new pattern was evolving. You lived among your fellows without tension or quarrel, and you formed no dangerously intimate relationships.

One night, standing at his window, Lawson's knee struck a loose tile below the casement. He removed the tile and set it on the floor. Every night for nearly two months he pried away at least one tile and, careful not to chip or break it, stacked it near an inner wall with those he had already removed.

After completing this task, as he lay on his pallet, he would often hear a man or a woman somewhere in the city singing a high, sweet song whose words had no significance for him. Sometimes a pair of voices would answer each other, always in different languages. Then, near the end of the summer, as Lawson stood staring at the lathing and the wall beams he had methodically exposed, he was moved to sing a melancholy song of his own. And he sang it without knowing what it meant.

The days grew cooler. Lawson took to leaving the bakery during its midafternoon closing and proceeding by way of the Calle de las Sierpes to a bodega across from the bullring. A crew of silent laborers, who worked very purposively in spite of their seeming to have no single boss, was dismantling the Plaza de Toros, and Lawson liked to watch as he drank his wine and ate the breadsticks he had brought with him.

Other crews about the city were carefully taking down the government buildings, banks, and barrio chapels that no one frequented anymore, preserving the bricks, tiles, and beams as if in the hope of some still unspecified future construction. By this time Lawson himself had knocked out the rear wall of his room over the contraceptive shop, and he felt a strong sense of identification with the laborers craftily gutting the bullring of its railings and barricades. Eventually, of course, everything would have to come down. Everything.

The rainy season began. The wind and the cold. Lawson continued to visit the sidewalk café near the ruins of the stadium; and because the bullring's destruction went forward even in wet weather, he wore an overcoat he had recently acquired and staked out a nicely sheltered table under the bodega's awning. This was where he customarily sat.

One particularly gusty day, rain pouring down, he shook out his umbrella and sat down at this table only to find another man sitting across from him. Upon the table was a wooden game board of some kind, divided into squares.

"Hello, Lawson," the interloper said.

Lawson blinked and licked his lips thoughtfully. Although he had not called his family to mind in some time, and wondered now if he had ever really married and fathered children, Dai Secombe's face had occasionally floated up before him in the dark of his room. But now Lawson could not remember the Welshman's name, or his nationality, and he had no notion of what to say to him. The first words he spoke, therefore, came out sounding like dream babble, or a voice played backward on the photograph. In order to say hello he was forced to the indignity, almost comic, of making a childlike motion with his hand.

Secombe, pointing to the game board, indicated that they should play. From a carved wooden box with a velvet lining he emptied the pieces onto the table, then arranged them on both sides of the board. Chess, Lawson thought vaguely, but he really did not recognize the pieces—they seemed changed from what he believed they should look like. And when it came his turn to move, Secombe had to demonstrate the capabilities of all the major pieces before he, Lawson, could essay even the most timid advance. The piece that most reminded him of a knight had to be moved according to two distinct sets of criteria, depending on whether it started from a black square or a white one; the "rooks," on the other hand, were able, at certain times, to *jump* an opponent's intervening pieces. The game boggled Lawson's understanding. After ten or twelve moves he pushed his chair back and took a long, bittersweet taste of wine. The rain continued to pour down like an endless curtain of deliquescent beads.

"That's all right," Secombe said. "I haven't got it all down yet myself, quite. A Bhutanese fellow near where I live made the pieces, you see, and just recently taught me how to play."

With difficulty Lawson managed to frame a question: "What work have you been doing?"

"I'm in demolition. As we all will be soon. It's the only really constructive occupation going." The Welshman chuckled mildly, finished his own wine, and rose. Lifting his umbrella, he bid Lawson farewell with a word that, when Lawson later tried to repeat and intellectually encompass it, had no meaning at all.

Every afternoon of that dismal, rainy winter Lawson came back to the same table, but Secombe never showed up there again. Nor did Lawson miss him terribly. He had grown accustomed to the strange richness of his own company. Besides, if he wanted people to talk to, all he needed to do was remain behind the counter at the bakery.

ix.

Spring came again. All of his room's interior walls were down, and it amused him to be able to see the porcelain chalice of the commode as he came up the stairs from the contraceptive shop.

The plaster that he had sledgehammered down would never be of use to anybody again, of course, but he had saved from the debris whatever was worth the salvage. With the return of good weather, men driving oxcarts were coming nowadays, probably because, over the winter, most of them through the city's backstreets and alleys to collect these items. You never saw anyone trying to drive a motorized vehicle had been hauled away. The scarcity of gasoline and replacement parts might well have been a factor, too—but, in truth, people seemed no longer to want to mess with internal-combustion engines. Ending pollution and noise had nothing to do with it, either. A person with dung on his shoes or front stoop was not very likely to be convinced of a vast improvement in the environment, and the clattering of wooden carts—the ringing of metal-rimmed wheels on cobblestone—could be as ear-wrenching as the hum and blare of motorized traffic. Still, Lawson liked to hear the oxcarts turn into his alley. More than once, called out by the noise, he had helped their drivers load them with masonry, doors, window sashes, even ornate carven mantles.

At the bakery the Mongolian woman with whom Lawson worked, and had worked for almost a year, caught the handle of his broom one day and told him her name. Speaking the odd, quicksilver monosyllables of the dialect that nearly everyone in Seville had by now mastered, she asked him to call her Tij. Lawson did not know whether this was her name from before The Change or one she had recently invented for herself. Pleased in either case, he responded by telling her his own Christian name. He stumbled saying it, and when Tij also had trouble pronouncing the name, they laughed together about its uncommon awkwardness on their tongues.

A week later he had moved into the tenement building where Tji lived. They slept in the same "room" three flights up from a courtyard filled with clambering wisteria. Because all but the supporting walls on this floor had been knocked out, Lawson often felt that he was living in an open-bay barracks. People stepped over his pallet to get to the stairwell and dressed in front of him as if he were not even there. Always a quick study, he emulated their casual behavior.

And when the ice in his loins finally began to thaw, he turned in the darkness to Tij—without in the least worrying about propriety. Their coupling was invariably silent, and the release Lawson experienced was always a serene rather than a shuddering one. Afterward, in the wisteria fragrance pervading their building, Tij and he lay beside each other like a pair of larval bumblebees as the moon rolled shadows over their naked, sweat-gleaming bodies.

Each day after they had finished making and trading away their bread, Tij and Lawson closed the bakery and took long walks. Often they strolled among the hedge-enclosed pathways and the small wrought-iron fences at the base of the city's cathedral. From these paths, so overwhelmed were they by buttresses of stones and arcaded balconies, they could not even see the bronze weathervane of Faith atop the Giralda. But, evening after evening, Lawson insisted on returning to that place, and at last his persistence and his sense of expectation were rewarded by the sound of jackhammers biting into marble in each one of the cathedral's five tremendous naves. He and Tij, holding hands, entered.

Inside, men and women were at work removing the altar screens, the metalwork grilles, the oil paintings, sections of stained-glass windows, religious relics. Twelve or more oxcarts were parked beneath the vault of the cathedral, and the noise of the jackhammers echoed shatteringly from nave to nave, from floor to cavernous ceiling. The oxen stood so complacently in their traces that Lawson wondered if the drivers of the carts had somehow contrived to deafen the animals. Tij released Lawson's hand to cover her ears. He covered his own ears. It did no good. You could remain in the cathedral only if you accepted the noise and resolved to be a participant in the building's destruction. Many people had already made that decision. They were swarming through its chambered stone belly like a spectacularly efficient variety of stone-eating termite.

An albino man of indeterminate race—a man as pale as a termite—thrust his pickax at Lawson. Lawson uncovered his ears and took the pickax by its handle. Tij, a moment later, found a crowbar hanging precariously from the side of one of the oxcarts. With these tools the pair of them crossed the nave they had entered and halted in front of an imposing mausoleum. Straining against the cathedral's poor light and the strange linguistic static in his head, Lawson painstakingly deciphered the plaque near the tomb.

"Christopher Columbus is buried here," he said.

Tij did not hear him. He made a motion indicating that this was the place where they should start. Tij nodded her understanding. Together, Lawson thought, they would dismantle the mausoleum of the discoverer of the New World and bring his corrupt remains out into the street. After all these centuries they would free the man.

Then the bronze statue of Faith atop the belltower would come down, followed by the lovely belltower itself. After that, the flying buttresses, the balconies, the walls; every beautiful, tainted stone.

It would hurt like hell to destroy the cathedral, and it would take a long, long time—but, considering everything, it was the only meaningful option they had. Lawson raised his pickax.

Jane Yolen

THE RIVER MAID

> *Mortals should consider carefully the consequences of becoming intimately involved with supernatural beings. Witness the fate of Jan, a rich farmer, who became enamored of a water spirit.*

There was once a rich farmer named Jan who decided to expand his holdings. He longed for the green meadow that abutted his farm with a passion that amazed him. But a swift river ran between the two. It was far too wide and far too deep for his cows to cross.

He stood on the river bank and watched the water hurtle over its rocky course.

"I could build a bridge," he said aloud. "But, then, any fool could do that. And I am no fool."

At his words the river growled, but Jan did not heed it.

"No!" Jan said with a laugh, "I shall build no bridge across this water. I shall make the river move aside for me." And so he planned how he would dam it up, digging a canal along the outer edge of the meadow, and so allow his cows the fresh green grass.

As if guessing Jan's thoughts, the river roared out, tumbling stones in its rush to be heard. But Jan did not understand it. Instead, he left at once to go to the town where he purchased the land and supplies.

The men Jan hired dug and dug for weeks until a deep ditch and a large dam had been built. Then they watched as the river slowly filled up behind the dam. And when, at Jan's signal, the gate to the canal was opened, the river was forced to move into its new course and leave its comfortable old bed behind.

At that, Jan was triumphant. He laughed and turned to the waiting men. "See!" he called out loudly, "I am not just Jan the Farmer. I am Jan the River Tamer. A wave of my hand, and the water must change its way."

His words troubled the other men. They spat between their fingers and made other signs against the evil eye. But Jan paid them no mind. He was the last to leave the river's side that evening and went home well after dark.

The next morning Jan's feeling of triumph had not faded and he went down again to the path of the old river which was now no more than mud and mire. He wanted to look at the desolation and dance over the newly dried stones.

But when he got to the river's old bed, he saw someone lying face-up in the center of the waterless course. It was a girl clothed only in a white shift that clung to her body like a skin.

Fearing her dead, Jan ran through the mud and knelt by her side. He put out his hand but could not touch her. He had never seen anyone so beautiful.

Fanned out about her head, her hair was a fleece of gold, each separate strand distinguishable. Fine gold hairs lay molded on her forearms and like wet down upon her legs. On each of her closed eyelids a drop of river water glistened and reflected back to him his own staring face.

At last Jan reached over and touched her cheek, and at his touch, her eyes opened wide. He nearly drowned in the blue of them.

He lifted the girl up in his arms, never noticing how cold her skin or how the mud stuck nowhere to her body or her shift, and he carried her up onto the bank. She gestured once toward the old river bank and let out a single mewling cry. Then she curled in towards his body, nestling and seemed to sleep.

Not daring to wake her again, Jan carried her home and put her down by the hearth. He lit the fire, though it was late spring and the house already quite warm. Then he sat by the sleeping girl and stared.

She lay in a curled position for some time. Only the slow pulsing of her back told him that she breathed. Then, as dusk settled about the house, bringing with it a half-light, the girl gave a sudden sigh and stretched. Then she sat up and stared. Her arms went out before her as if she were swimming in the air. Jan wondered for a moment if she were blind.

Then the girl leaped up in one fluid movement and began to sway, to dance upon the hearthstones. Her feet beat swiftly and she turned round and round in dizzying circles. She stopped so suddenly that Jan's head still spun. He saw that she was now perfectly dry except for one side of her shift; the left hem and skirt were still damp and remained molded against her.

"Turn again," Jan whispered hoarsely, suddenly afraid.

The girl looked at him and did not move.

When he saw that she did not understand his tongue, Jan walked over to her and led her back to the fire. Her hand was quite cold in his. But she smiled shyly up at him. She was small, only chest high, and Jan himself was not a large man. Her skin, even in the darkening house, was so white it glowed with a fierce light. Jan could see the rivulets of her veins where they ran close to the surface, at her wrists and temples.

He stayed with her by the fire until the heat made him sweat. But though she stood silently, letting the fire warm her first one side and then the other, her skin remained cold, and the left side of her shift would not dry.

Jan knelt down before her and touched the damp hem. He put his cheek against it.

"Huttah!" he cried at last. "I know you now. You are a river maid. A water spirit. I have heard of such. I believed in them when I was a child."

The water girl smiled steadily down at him and touched his hair with her fingers, twining the strands round and about as if weaving a spell.

Jan felt the touch, cold and hot, burn its way down the back of his head and along his spine. He remembered with dread all the old tales. To hold such a one against her will meant death. To love such a one meant despair.

He shook his head violently and her hand fell away. "How

foolish," Jan thought. "Old wives and children believe such things. I do not love her, beautiful as she is. And as for the other, how am I to know what is her will? If we cannot talk the same tongue, I can only guess her wants." He rose and went to the cupboard and took out bread and cheese and a bit of salt fish which he put before her.

The water maid ate nothing. Not then or later. She had only a few drops of water before the night settled in.

When the moon rose, the river maid began to pace restlessly about the house. Wall to wall, she walked. She went to the window and put her hand against the glass. She stood by the closed door and put her shoulder to the wood, but she would not touch the metal latch.

It was then that Jan was sure of her. "Cold iron will keep her in." He was determined she would stay at least until the morning.

The river maid cried all the night, a high keening that rose and fell like waves. But in the morning she seemed accommodated to the house and settled quietly to sleep by the fire. Once in a while, she would stretch and stand, the damp left side of her shift clinging to her thigh. In the half-light of the hearth she seemed even more beautiful than before.

Jan left a bowl of fresh water near the fire, with some cress by it, before he went to feed the cows. But he checked the latch on the windows and set a heavy iron bar across the outside of the door.

"I will let you go tonight," he promised slowly. *"Tonight,"* he said, as if speaking to a child. But she did not know his language and could not hold him to his vow.

By the next morning, he had forgotten making it.

For a year Jan kept her. He grew to like the wavering sounds she made as she cried each night. He loved the way her eyes turned a deep green when he touched her. He was fascinated by the blue veins that meandered at her throat, along the backs of her knees, and laced each small breast. Her mouth was always cold under his.

Fearing the girl might guess the working of window or gate, Jan fashioned iron chains for the glass and an ornate grillwork for the door. In that way, he could open them to let in air and let her look out at the sun and moon and seasons' changes. But he did not let her go. And as she never learned to speak with him in his tongue and thereby beg for release, Jan convinced himself that she was content.

Then it was spring again. Down from the mountains came the swollen streams, made big with melted snow. The river maid drank whole glasses of water now, and put on weight. Jan guessed that she carried his child, for her belly grew, she moved slowly and no longer tried to dance. She sat by the window at night with her arms raised and sang strange, wordless tunes, sometimes loud and sometimes soft as a cradle song. Her voice was as steady as the patter of the rain, and underneath Jan fancied he heard a growing strength. His nights became as restless as hers, his sleep full of watery dreams.

The night of the full moon, the rain beat angrily against the glass as if insisting on admission. The river maid put her head to one side, listening. Then she rose and left her window place. She stretched and put her hands to her back, then traced them slowly around her sides to the front. She moved heavily to the hearth and sat. Bracing both hands on the stones behind her, she spread her legs, crooked at the knees.

Jan watched as her belly rolled in great waves under the tight white shift.

She threw her head back, gasped at the air, and then, with a great cry of triumph, expelled the child. It rode a gush of water between her legs and came to rest at Jan's feet. It was small and fishlike, with a translucent tail. It looked up at him with blue eyes that were covered with a veil of skin. The skin lifted once, twice, then closed again as the child slept.

Jan cried because it was a beast.

At that very moment, the river outside gave a shout of release. With the added waters from the rain and snow, it had the strength to push through the earth dam. In a single wave, that gathered force as it rolled, it rushed across the meadow, through the farmyard and barn, and overwhelmed the house. It broke the iron gates and grilles as if they were brittle sticks, washing them away in its flood. Then it settled back into its old course, tumbling over familiar rocks and rounding the curves it had cut in its youth.

When the neighbors came the next day to assess the damage, they found no trace of the house or of Jan.

"Gone," said one.

"A bad end," said another.

"Never change a river," said a third.

They spat through their fingers and made other signs against evil. Then they went home to their own fires and gave it no more thought.

But a year later, in a pocket of the river, in a quiet place said to house a great fish with a translucent tail, an inquisitive boy found a jumble of white bones.

His father and the other men guessed the bones to be Jan's, and they left them to the river instead of burying them.

When the boy asked why, his father said, "Huttah! Hush, boy, and listen."

The boy listened and heard the river playing merrily over the bones. It was a high, sweet, bubbling song. And anyone with half an ear could hear that the song, though wordless, or at least in a language unknown to men, was full of freedom and a conquering joy.

Bob Leman

SKIRMISH ON BASTABLE STREET

A demon who has been entrapped in an inaccessible place by some form of enchantment must grant three wishes to any mortal who frees him, usually inadvertently. At least so the legends say. Fulfilling this requirement might not always be all that easy, as attested by the events one night on Bastable Street.

Quite recently, in a disreputable bar on Bastable Street in this city, a wino and an elderly couple fought a brisk little skirmish with a supernatural adversary and had the good fortune to prevail. None of the three ever grasped the magnitude of their accomplishment, and indeed they soon forgot what had actually happened, but they had in truth won a laudable small victory in an ancient war, and the facts of the affair deserve to be recorded.

These facts are not verifiable, for reasons that will be obvious, and it must be admitted that many of them have something of the flavor of the bedtime stories of our youth. You are therefore quite at liberty, if you are of a skeptical or cynical turn of mind, to view the following matter as nothing more than a fairy tale. Its beginning is, after all, one of the fairy tale cliches:

Once a poor woodcutter named Garft rescued a demon from the deep hole in which it had been confined by an enchantment, and the demon had no choice but to grant him three wishes as a reward. Garft wished first for a long and happy life, and second for a painless end when at last his time came round. Then he was stumped, and he thought about it for so long that the demon became impatient and displayed its true nature by threatening to eat him there and then.

"I'll tell you what," Garft said. "I'll give the other wish to my son, Garft. How would that be?"

"Done!" said the demon, and disappeared.

Garft's calling was chopping trees, not thinking, and so it was not until much later that he realized that the demon had left no instructions about how young Garft was to avail himself of his wish. No amount of shouting succeeded in causing the demon to reappear, and Garft finally concluded that the problem would have to be turned over to a wiser head. Unfortunately, there was no one in the village whom Garft conceded to be wiser than himself, and he very much doubted that any neighboring village had anyone better to offer.

He mulled over the matter for a considerable time, and the seasons came and went, and then the years. He felt no urgency. Indeed, nothing affected his tranquility and contentment. The demon had granted his wish for a happy life by the elegant expedient of making him somewhat simple-minded. No matter what misfortune befell him, he remained happy.

Because of this, his son Garft had to assume heavy responsibilities at a very early age. When he was seventeen, there was a winter of famine, and he killed one of the Earl's deer to feed his little brothers and sisters. The deer's hide was found by the Earl's men, and young Garft had to flee, an outlaw.

He fled south and west, living on what small game he could snare, until, in late summer, he found himself in a fat and prosperous countryside where the horses were enormous and the people small and dark. It was there that a petty lord elected, on a whim, to impress young Garft into his service

Skirmish on Bastable Street

instead of hanging him for a poacher, and a guardsman in the lord's service he remained for the rest of his life. He took a wife and had sons, and in the fullness of time he died, without ever having the wish that was his by birthright.

Now it is a fact that commerce between mortal men and supernatural creatures is regulated by a complex and immutable body of law, and that, once a bargain is struck, irresistible forces see to it that the letter of the law is fulfilled. The law holds, *stare decisis*, that the words of a contract mean what the mortal party to the contract understood them to mean. In Garft's language the word for "son" meant not only "son," but any male descendant, however remote. The third wish was there for the taking by any descendant of the woodcutter who bore the name Garft.

But young Garft's sons were named Guillaume and René, and their sons were Olivier and Robert and Jean. Jean's distant descendant Jean went to England with the Conqueror, and fathered a child upon a Saxon girl. She named the boy John, after Jean, his father. There followed many generations of villeins named John, and then one of the Johns rose in the world and acquired a little silver, and his grandson acquired a little land. In due course the Johnsons became a prosperous yeoman family in Devon.

Late in the seventeenth century a blacksheep son of the family ran off to the American colonies and settled in Boston, Massachusetts. His great-grandson Keble Johnson prospered in the rum trade and helped finance the War for Independence. In the nineteenth century another Keble Johnson lost most of the family fortune playing the railroad game with Jay Gould and J.P. Morgan. Just enough money remained to keep up appearances in a somewhat threadbare way and to send the eldest son to Harvard.

The money ran out in 1904, and the sixth Keble Johnson left Harvard at the end of his sophomore year, with no degree, no money, and no prospects, and no family: his father's liver had given out at about the same time as the money, and his mother died shortly thereafter. His two years of college secured him a job on the Boston *Transcript*, which he was unable to hold. He became an itinerant newspaperman, drifting westward. He ended his travels in Fowler, Illinois, where he edited *The Bedford County Chronicle*, married a local girl, and produced a son. This son grew up to manage the local creamery and cultivate a vegetable garden; he left absolutely nothing to show for his sixty years of life except his son George.

George was drafted into the army in 1940, and at the end of the war he brought back to Fowler a bride, a native of the distant northern kingdom where the woodcutter had labored centuries before. When their son was born, she selected for the child a name out of her own racial heritage; she named him Garft. And somewhere, on the boy's Christening day, an ancient record amended itself to show that there was now once more a mortal eligible to claim the outstanding wish.

George Johnson had not amounted to much before he went into the army, and after his return he was, if anything, even less useful. He worked intermittently as an auto mechanic, but most of his time was spent drinking beer at the Moose Club. When Garft was ten, his mother, having had as much as she could take of life in Fowler with George, disappeared. From that time on, Garft was largely on his own.

In high school he excelled in basketball, and upon graduation he was offered room, board, and pocket money to play for a small college in Missouri. After a semester and a half he was fired from the freshman squad, to widespread approbation. He had consistently broken training rules, had missed as many practice sessions as he had attended, and was loathed by every jock in the college. There was no possibility of his staying on as a student, as he had no more bothered to attend classes than basketball practice. He had, however, developed a circle of acquaintance among a set of hairy undergraduates with progressive political ideas and a fondness for rock music, and after his dismissal from the college he remained in the town, pretending to be a student and sponging. He felt that he was gaining an excellent education in rap sessions and was able to hold his own in conversations about Carlos Castenada and Kurt Vonnegut. He actually read most of one of the Vonnegut novels.

He liked to think that he was part of what the press called The Ferment On Campus, and he marched and demonstrated in the spirit of the times. The community was too small for the creation of really satisfactory disorder, however, and he moved on to a larger campus in a large city, living in a confused world he saw through a haze of pills and alcohol. As the sixties wore on to their end, he drifted away from the campus skid row and into the real thing: geographically the distance was not great.

And so here we have Garft Johnson at the age of thirty-five; a full-fledged bum, a dirty and emaciated scarecrow with bad teeth and shifty eyes, who sleeps on a pile of rags in an abandoned filling station and panhandles for enough wine to keep the shakes at bay. He is wholly untrustworthy and is capable of any nastiness he can find the courage to undertake. He deserves the contempt and scorn of every right-thinking citizen. He is the contingent recipient of absolutely anything at all that he may see fit to wish for.

But contingent recipient only; obviously he cannot be granted a wish until he has made a wish, and the wish cannot be made unless the demon is present. Since calling up a demon requires the performance of a complex ritual, involving a number of intricate and disgusting procedures, the likelihood of his ever realizing his good fortune would appear to be extremely remote. Certain events, however, have been evolving in such a way that they are militating in his behalf.

The realm of the supernatural lies outside of time and separate from space, and nothing about it is in any way comprehensible to the human understanding. It is thus necessary to use analogy in talking about it, rendering discourse among its beings as if it were human speech, and referring to their milieu in mundane terms. Using this method, we will transcribe a colloquy between two such beings. One of them might be called an efficiency expert or an expeditor, and the other could be labeled a middle executive. Call their topic the Obligations Backlog. Their conversation (we will call it a conversation) is taking place in the offices of the Fulfillment Section of the Contracts Division of the Mortal Relations Department of the Temporal Affairs Branch. Smith and Jones will do for their names.

"This is really appalling," Jones said. "I can't imagine what you people have been doing. It is the responsibility of this section to keep an account of our contractual obligations to mortal beings and to devise methods of keeping within the letter of the law without actually giving anything away. My audit shows that for five thousand years or so this office has simply been pushing the tough problems to the back of the drawer. But they all remain as charges on the books, and they've had a visible effect on the bottom line. The Chief himself has been asking about it. He was not pleased."

Smith turned pale, and sweat appeared on his face. "I—we don't have enough help," he said. "Every demon in the place has been working his tail off. Look at the time sheets. There's not a demon that doesn't log a century of overtime every millennium."

"Time sheets indeed," Jones said. "I'll tell you what the time sheets show. They show that the contact force has been hanging around headquarters keeping warm most of the time, instead of getting out in the field and taking care of our problems. Laxity, that's what it is. Inexcusable laxity. Now listen carefully, Smith. This thing has got to be cleared up without delay. If it isn't, somebody will have a few millennia on the griddle, and I promise you it won't be me. You have one century to clear your books, and not a day more. Do I make myself clear?"

"But—" said the hapless Smith. "But—"

"One century," Jones said with finality.

There almost immediately ensued a considerable stir in the Fulfillment Section, followed by a phenomenon much resembling a cloud of bats emerging from a cave at nightfall; it was a general exodus of demons on their way to undertake cleanup operations in the material worlds. A few thousand of them had, however, been kept at headquarters for individual admonishment. These were special offenders, demons whose logs showed extraordinary numbers of lapses. One by one they were brought before Smith, were questioned, lectured, and subjected to horrible punishments; they were then sent forth to rectify their errors. It was the kind of work that Smith usually enjoyed, but on this occasion he could take no pleasure in it; the threat that hung over him was too awful.

"Name?" he said to the trembling miscreant on the carpet.

"Robinson, sir," said the demon.

"Robinson, yes. Here we are. Current assignment, Earth, so-and-so galaxy, so-and-so sector—yes. B.C. 3,000 to A.D. 3,000—what's that mean, Robinson?"

"Local years before and after the granting of The Opportunity, sir."

"Humph. Now, let's see. What's this? What's this? Do you know how many delinquencies you have, Robinson? As the

Skirmish on Bastable Street

sands of the shore. Disgraceful. Inexcusable. I suppose you know the consequences."

Robinson did. He groveled and pled, but of course without result; he was subjected on the spot to the most abominable tortures. At their conclusion Smith said, "All right. Now get out there and straighten out your accounts. Otherwise, what you'll get will make what you just had seem like a delightful diversion. Understood?"

It was understood very well indeed, and Robinson departed without ceremony, disappearing from Smith's presence and instantly appearing in human form on earth. His delinquencies were, as Smith had pointed out, enormous in number, and he quailed at the thought of the work ahead. He was by nature indolent and slothful, and he remembered well the restful years he had spent in the hole before the officious woodchopper pulled him out. The memory of those years served to remind him that one of the items on his list was the woodchopper's third wish, and he caused himself to materialize in the city where Garft Johnson lived on skid row.

He popped into material existence on the sidewalk in front of Doyle's Shamrock Inn. Despite the establishment's name, the eponymous Doyle had been in his grave for more than forty years, and any Irish ambience his bar may have possessed was dead as Doyle. Now it was the very paradigm of skid-row saloon, shabby and soiled, a place where grimy defeated men (and a few women, who were in every way equal to the men, although they did not think of themselves as liberated) protracted the drinking of a beer or a glass of popskull wine for as long as the bartender would permit, because they had no other warm place to go.

At a table at the back of the room Garft Johnson was sitting with his friend, Billy. "Friend" is perhaps not the precise word to describe their relationship, but Garft and Billy had on a number of occasions combined their dimes and quarters to raise the price of a bottle, and that would do for friendship on Bastable Street. On this day Billy was standing treat. His wife had sent word that she was on her way down to see him, and Billy found himself in need of moral support. He was weak and his wife was strong, and she was resolutely determined that Billy was going to return to a respectable life, a prospect that filled him with terror.

"I stuck it out for thirty years," he told Garft. "Thirty

years of everything her way. Move to town so's we could have plumbing. Then move up here so's I could work in the tire factory. Then nags at me to try and make foreman. Thirty years. I ain't ambitious, Garfty. I would of been happy back there in Goster County, huntin' a mite, fishin' a mite, work once in a while at the canning factory if I needed a little cash money. Hell, I could of got on welfare with no sweat. But that there woman give me no peace, Garfty, no peace at all. So when I got my pension I says, 'I got to get me some peace, Lurlene. Let me take a hundert dollars a month,' I says, 'and you take the rest.' And I come down here, and it's peaceable. Except when she comes down to rescue me."

"Ah, screw her, Billy," Garft said. "Let's have another drink."

"Yeah, sure, Garfty," Billy said. "Hold my seat, I'll get 'em." He took the glasses to the bar for refills. Billy was not an alcoholic. He lived on skid row because he liked it. For thirty years he had hated almost every moment of his life; he disliked respectability, he resented keeping up appearances, he loathed responsibility. Here on Bastable Street, there were none of these. His hundred a month paid for his room and he worked as a casual from time to time for food and wine money. He drank the wine not out of need, but to be companionable. He was happy—or at any rate contented.

"Except for that damn woman," he said. "Keeps comin' down here, ever six months or so, hollers at me to come on home. Why, Lordamercy, Garfty, I can't live in that house no more. She's turned neat in her old age, keeps house like a demon. You drop anything on the floor, she screeches like a sireen. She's a witch, y'know."

"Yeah," Garft said. "They all are."

"No, I mean a real witch, knows spells and words of power. She's a Poecock, and all the women's witches in that tribe. Mother to daughter, ever since fur back."

"You believe that crap, Billy?"

"Can't say I believe it all, but there's something to it, all right. I seen her take off many a wart, and dry up cows, when we still lived up the valley. Them Poecocks been unto themselves on that ridge of theirn for anyhow two hundert years, moonshinin' and marryin' each other. They know some

Skirmish on Bastable Street

things. She's got a spell on me right now, tryin' to toll me home."

"Aw, come on, Billy," Garft said.

"It's a fact. It ain't much of a spell, Lord knows, for I've no intent of goin'. But I can feel the pull. Here she is, now."

Like a dumpy tugboat puffing through garbage-laden waters, Lurlene was advancing toward them, utterly oblivious of the disgruntled winos who muttered darkly in her wake. Wheezing, she sat down at the table. "Lordamercy," she said. "This street looks worse ever time I see it. Billy, get me a beer."

"This here's my friend, Garft," Billy said.

"Hoddy. Billy, get me that beer, will you?"

Billy went to the bar. Lurlene said to Garft, "He brought you to argue on his side, did he?"

Argument was the last thing Garft wanted. He was at the pleasantest point of the day's drinking, with his nerves calm and an easeful euphoria settling in. If nothing disturbing occurred, he might maintain this desirable state for several hours; but if strife or discord impinged upon his woolly contentment, he would instantly be plunged into quite another state of mind, a touchy, resentful irritation that was likely at any moment to turn to noisy, impotent rage. This would be followed by a deep depression, which ended only when he had drunk himself unconscious. These latter stages were not pleasant, and he liked to delay them for as long as possible. He by no means wanted an argument.

"Nah, Lurlene," he said. "I'm on your side. You're right. Billy don't belong down here." Only a few minutes previously he had been telling Billy that it was unreasonable of Lurlene to insist that he go home.

Billy came back with Lurlene's beer. "How about you drink this before we start, Lurlene," he said. "Let's be restful for a little." They sat and drank in a surprisingly companionable silence.

It was at this point that Robinson entered, creating something of a stir among the winos. He had not chosen wisely in selecting a model for his human appearance and costume. It is well known that demons have certain deficiencies in taste and intelligence, and it must be admitted that he was badly out of touch with twentieth-century Earth. So his error is perhaps understandable; but if his guise had been deliberately calculated to arouse suspicion and distrust in the human heart, it could not have been more successful. He was sharp, he was sleek: he was padded at the shoulders and pinched at the waist, he wore a tight vest and no tie, his shoes were square at the toe and lifted at the heel. Large gems flashed on his fingers, chains clinked on his wrists. The gaudy trendiness of the costume was, however, belied by his grooming: in an era of Pancho Villa mustaches and fluffy hair sprayed with fixative, he wore a thin black line on his upper lip, and his hair was greased down to a black shine. He carried himself with a sort of furtive jauntiness; he reeked fraudulence as an athlete reeks sweat.

The type was not unknown on Bastable Street, and the winos watched him with a mixture of disdain and fear. There was a faint collective sigh of relief when they saw that his destination was Billy's table, that he had no interest in them. They returned their attention to their glasses.

Robinson pulled a chair up to the table and sat down. "Hi, there, Garft," he said. "Lurlene. Billy."

"Oh, hi," Garft said. Billy said, suspiciously, "You know him, Garft?"

Garft made a vague noise. Robinson said, "He don't know me yet, but I got something for him."

No one in Doyle's had ever heard the caveat concerning Greeks bearing gifts, but every denizen of Bastable Street knew its meaning instinctively. All three pairs of eyes fixed themselves upon Robinson in deepest suspicion. He said, "Now I got to explain this like in detail. It's the law. I got to make you understand that this is for real. 'Cause it's going to seem like, you know, magic. And it is. Magic. But it's real."

If he had said that fire is hot or water is wet, he would have been unpersuasive. Garft said, "Look, buddy, we don't want any. We got things to talk about here. Private."

Lurlene sniffed at the air. She said, "There's something—I smell something."

"Well, sure," Billy said. "Naturally. You're in Doyle's."

"No, not that. Something wicked. Brimstone. I smell evil."

"Ah, witch stuff," Billy said.

Robinson shot a swift, covert glance at Lurlene. Something very ugly stared out of his eyes for a moment and then was gone. He said to Garft, "Listen, Garft, you got something coming to you. I brought it."

Skirmish on Bastable Street

"Let's see it, then."

"Why, it ain't something I can lay on the table. What it is, is a wish."

"Brimstone!" cried Lurlene. "Garft, be careful!"

"What you talking about, Lurlene?" Billy said.

"I smell hellfire. Garft, don't talk to him!"

"Oh, stop it, Lurlene," Billy said, and then, to Robinson: "What you mean, a wish?"

"Just what I said. He gets one wish to come true. I can do that."

"Wow, great!" Garft said. "I wish I had the whole bottle here on the table, instead of doing this one drink at a time."

"That's what I mean," Robinson said. "You got to understand that it's all real when you make your wish, or it don't work. You got to know what you're doing."

"Ah, come on," Garft said. "What's the scam?" He could feel cracks developing in his carapace of well-being, could feel acid drops of irritation dripping in through the cracks.

"No scam," Robinson said. "Your forty-times-great grandfather was granted three wishes, and only took two. You get the other one."

"Yeah, sure. Who the hell are you, anyhow?"

"I know him for sure, Garft," Lurlene said. "An imp of Satan. Lord Jesus, save us!"

"Shut up, old woman!" Robinson said, viciously.

Billy stirred uneasily. "Hey!" he said with weak indignation. "Watch how you talk, there."

Robinson ignored him. He said, "Okay, Garft. Watch right here." He pointed with his finger. In front of Garft on the table there was suddenly a snifter glass of delicate crystal, holding an inch of fluid.

Garft gave a startled twitch. "What—? How'd you do that?" he said. His voice was strained. His euphoria had wholly evaporated now, and his nerves were tuning themselves up for a bravura performance.

"I'm showing you I can do what I say," Robinson said. "Something you'll appreciate. Go ahead, drink it. You look like you could use it."

Garft shakily lifted the snifter. It contained three ounces of century-old *fine champagne,* a Cognac of such perfection and grandeur that it might have been the Platonic ideal of brandy. It was the distillation into amber droplets of a splendid summer long ago, so great and noble a Cognac that a connoisseur might have wept in gratitude upon inhaling its bouquet. Garft knocked it back in a single greedy swallow.

A second later he made a strangled sound, snatched up Lurlene's beer, and gulped noisily. "Whoo!" he said. "It's booze. I thought it was wine. What the hell *is* that stuff?" He looked suspiciously at Robinson. "You trying to poison me or something?"

Demons are not known for patience. For a moment the sulfurous smell became very strong. Lurlene made signs with her fingers and began to mumble. Robinson said, "You believe now I got the power to do it?"

"It's a good trick. Where was it, up your sleeve?"

"Up my sleeve, you lousy halfwit? Up my sleeve? It's magic, you putrid lump, magic. Can you understand that? You *will* understand that. You'll understand that, all right."

"Hey," said Garft. "I mean, hey, don't go calling no names. Nobody ast you to sit down here." He was by this time fully into stage two, full of resentment at the whole world and ripe for a quarrel. He was considerably intimidated by Robinson, but prepared to be belligerent until the altercation showed signs of graduating to a physical level. "Why don't you just get out of here?" he said. "We had about enough of you. Calling names. Goddamn street sharpy."

Robinson lost his temper entirely. It was not pleasant. Those traits which we hold to be most discreditable in a human being constitute a demon's entire personality, and the essential nastiness is in him never diluted by a decent impulse or a moral qualm. His is no proud and majestic wickedness; there is no Miltonic grandeur in him. It is not he, but his master who directs those enormous engines of evil that periodically afflict mortal beings; it is not he, but Milton's Satan (or something very like him) who inspires the great monsters, the Stalins and Maos and Hitlers. Robinson and his peers are otherwise. Theirs is a soiled and greasy wickedness, a wickedness of sly small peculations and furtive perversions, of gratuitous cruelties to the innocent, of moral cowardice and petulant selfishness, of willful squalor and mindless cynicism.

Such a being in a fit of rage evokes in bystanders approximately equal proportions of fear and disgust. It seemed to the three at the table that the atmosphere had suddenly taken on a dead, iron chill and an appalling fecal stench; a dreary sense of hopelessness and despair washed over them. They became aware that somewhere behind Robinson's ferrety sharpster's face was something toothed and purplish that squirmed and heaved.

Garft's belligerence vanished instantly. "Take it easy, buddy," he said, apprehensively. "Take it easy. No need to get mad. That's just the way I talk, y'know?"

Lurlene was made of sterner stuff. Terror and nausea chased each other across her face, and then there was a firming of her jaw. She took a deep breath and began to chant:

"By *Bee*vil and *Ash*kob and *Gnul:*
Git *back* in yer *hole*, beast.
Back whur ye *come* from.
Stay thar till *dooms*day,
Or *some*one sends *res*cue."

All parties, including Robinson, gaped at her. Garft recovered first. "Goddammit, Lurlene," he said, "don't get his goat any worse!"

Lurlene did not answer. She was staring at Robinson, the hopeful expression she had worn for a moment slowly fading from her face. Robinson smirked. "Whatta you know," he said. "The old girl thought she knew a spell. Make you feel better, grandma?"

Billy said, nervously, "What in blazes was you doing, Lurlene?"

"What he said. Casting a spell. I didn't really reckon it would work, but we got to do *something*."

"Now where'd you of got a spell for a creature like this, anyhow? Course it didn't work. What in the world was it?"

Lurlene looked embarrassed. "Well," she said, "it's for mice, really. Or rats or snakes. Maybe as big as groundhogs. Things in holes. It's all I could think of."

Robinson let out a bray of laughter. "Yeah, mice are about your speed, grandma. And it wouldn't even have worked with mice. You got the names all wrong." His expression became menacing again, and he turned to Garft. "All right, you slob," he said. "I've wasted about enough time here. *Now you make your lousy wish.*"

There was something monstrously offensive in his manner, something that went even beyond the offensiveness of the words. He was a bully, and a rather stupid one, but his power over his present company was an undeniable fact, and there was, behind the bullying, a cold, sneering arrogance. Only someone of saintly disposition could have remained unaffected. There were no saints in Doyle's.

No saints, and, to be blunt, not even standard human beings. Except perhaps for Billy, every habitué of Doyle's was in some degree deficient in those qualities that make it possible for the human race to cope with the world. These people had opted out. They had elected not to try any longer, and in making that election they had outraged some basic part of their natures. Uncountable generations of our ancestors were shaped by the unforgiving iron imperatives of ecology, and our genes know, even when our minds do not, that the failure to try is death. Deep in their hearts the people in Doyle's despised themselves, and their self-contempt made them in fact contemptible.

Thus Garft's behavior cannot be called courageous; it was not even the desperate valor of the cornered rat. It was, rather, simple failure to curb an access of spite and malice toward this creature who had had the effrontery to take him at his own evaluation. He was shaken by impotent rage, and for a brief moment his need to strike out at someone or something overrode his pusillanimity. But—all this having been said—he did, in the event, stand up to and prevail over a most repulsive and unquestionably powerful agent of darkness, and for that he deserves praise and thanks.

He pushed back his chair and rose to his feet, this unlikely David, sweating under his layers of ragged sweaters, trembling with equal parts of fear and rage, desperately winnowing his exiguous vocabulary for words that would flay and sear. The words simply were not there. It did not cross his mind that a gentle benediction might have caused Robinson at least a little discomfort, while the trite scatological and sexual imagery that made up his best effort at scathing words was, from Robinson's point of view, mild praise. He squeaked out his obscenities while Robinson grinned and his frustration grew, until at last Robinson said, "Okay, turkey, you've had your fun. Now make your wish. *Now*."

"My wish?" Garft said in a strangled voice. "My wish? I'll tell you my wish, you creepy little rat. I wish—" He stopped. He had nothing in mind except that he desperately wanted

Skirmish on Bastable Street 127

something very bad to happen to Robinson. There was, at that point, a distinct possibility that he might say, "I wish you'd go to hell"—or words to that effect. If he had done so, Robinson's mission would have been instantly and neatly completed: the wish would have been granted without actual benefit to Garft, and Robinson would have been back at headquarters to receive whatever plaudits are awarded by the likes of Smith and Jones.

But if that was Robinson's plan, it failed. The word "rat," which Garft had hurled only as a stock term of opprobrium, without thought of its literal meaning, had bred a sluggish activity in his brain, and he remembered Lurlene's abortive exorcism.

"You want my wish, I'll give you my wish, you—you lousy rat," he said. "I wish Lurlene's dumb poem worked, that's what I wish!"

And of course Robinson disappeared.

There was for a little time a bemused silence at the table. At length Lurlene said, "Kind of an ugly fella."

Billy nodded. "Yeah. Sure was. Glad he's gone. You want a drink, Garft?"

"Sure do, Billy. Say, what did that guy want, anyhow?"

The other two looked puzzled. The encounter was rapidly fading from all three memories, as invariably happens after such events.

"Why—I think he said he'd buy a drink," Billy said. "He never did, though. I'll do it." He went to the bar for the drinks, and all was as usual in Doyle's, and with that we reach the end of our fairy tale.

The question will of course be asked: Did they all live happily ever after? There is no answer at this time, because these things happened only recently. One can perhaps predict happiness—or at least reasonable contentment—for Lurlene and Billy. That was their state before they met Robinson, and there is no reason to think that anything may change for them. As for Garft, one would like to hope that some residual memory of his heroism lodged in his subconscious and will serve to spark a renascence of spirit in him, so that he will take a bath and find a job and perhaps have his teeth seen to. Such a beginning might lead him into the paths of productive respectability, where he would end with a wife and children and a lawn to rake. On the other hand (and this is no doubt more likely), he may simply continue his present life, which does, after all, bring him happiness of a kind. If he had thoughtfully considered his wish, instead of squandering it in a fit of temper, his highest aspiration would have been to spend the rest of his life in the condition we have described as stage one of his drinking day. It is probably safe to say that Garft will live happily for two or three hours of each day, and not so happily the rest of the time.

Last of all, Robinson. We know what happened to him. At the instant the wish was uttered he found himself without any sense of transition, at the bottom of a deep hole in a cold northern land. He did not even make an attempt to get out. He was well aware of where he was, and how he had come to be there, and he was resigned to his imprisonment. He knew that he was going to be there for nine hundred and forty years. At the end of that time a poor woodcutter named Garft was going to find the hole and pull him out, and he would have to grant the woodcutter three wishes as a reward.

Charles de Lint

A PATTERN OF SILVER STRINGS

Charles de Lint has produced several stories about Cerin Songweaver, a master harpist and songmaker of a mythic time and place, and his nonhuman wife Meran. Here is his latest—a wonderous tale of sorcery, music and the nature of pride.

For Mary Ann

Nagakaramu
Kokoro mo shirazu
Kurokami no
Midarete kesa wa
Mono wo koso omoe

Lady Horikawa

[Will he always love me?
I cannot read his heart.
This morning my thoughts
Are as disordered
As my hair.]

Meran Gwynder was the daughter of an oak king and the wife of a harper, though neither her royal green blood nor her marriage seemed very real to her just now. Loss filled her heart and she could find no way to deal with it. The sadness of what seemed a broken trust shared an uneasy rule with her unending questions. If she could know why...

"He left without a word," she said.

Bethowen the hillwife clicked her teeth in reply, though whether the sound was meant to be sympathetic or was only a habit, remained debatable. They sat on a hilltop, under the guardianship of an old longstone, with the stars glimmering pale in the night skies above and the fire between them throwing strange shadows that seemed to echo the whisper of the wind as it braided the hill's grasses. Stirring the fire with a short stick, Bethowen looked through the glitter of sparks at her guest.

Meran had nut-brown skin and brown-green hair. She was slim, but strong-limbed. Her eyes were the liquid brown of an otter's. The hillwife could see none of this in the poor light. Those images she drew up from her memory. What she saw was a troubled woman, her features strained and wan in the firelight. At the oakmaid's knee the striped head of Old Badger looked up to meet the hillwife's eyes.

"Men will do that," Bethowen said at last. "It's not a new thing, my dear."

"Not him."

"What makes me wonder," the hillwife continued as though she'd never been interrupted, "is what brings one of the treefolk so far from her tree." Ogwen Wood was a good two hours south and west across the dark hills, a long distance for an oakmaid.

"My tree fell in a storm years ago—you never heard? I should—*would* have died but for him. As the green blood spilled, he drew me back. With his harpmagic. With his love."

"And you have no more need of your tree?"

"He made me charms. Three talismans."

Meran could see his quick sure hands working the oakwood as surely as though he were beside her now. First he made a pendant, shaped like an oak leaf, and that she wore under her tunic, close to her heart. Then a comb, fine-toothed and decorated with acorn shapes, and that she wore in her hair to keep the unruly locks under control. Lastly a flute that she kept in a sheath hanging from her shoulder. Oak was not the best of woods for such an instrument, but his harpmagic had instilled in it a tone and timbre that the natural wood lacked.

"He built us a new home of sod and stone and thatch and there we lived as we had before. Until this morning . . ."

"When you awoke and found him gone," Bethowen finished for her. "But he journeys often, doesn't he, this husband of yours? Roadfaring and worldwalking from time to time. I have heard tales . . ."

"And well you might. But you don't understand. He left without a word. I woke and he was gone. Gone." She tugged at the edge of her cloak with unhappy fingers and looked up to meet the hillwife's bright eyes. "He left Telynros behind."

"Telynros?"

"His harp. The roseharp."

Telynros was a Tuathan gift, an enchanted instrument that plainly bore the touch of the old gods' workmanship. Silver-stringed and strangely carved, it had, growing from the wood where forepillar met the curving neck, a living blossom. A grey rose.

"Please," Meran asked, "tell me where he has gone."

Bethowen nodded. "I can try, my dear. I can only try."

From the unrolled cloth that lay at her knee, she chose a pinch of flaked alder bark and tossed it into the flames with a soft-spoken word. The fire's hue changed from red-gold to blue. Muttering under her breath, she added a second pinch and the blue dissolved into violet.

"Look into the flames," she said. "Look and tell me what you see."

"Only flames. No. I see . . ."

An oak tree strained at its roots, green-leafed boughs reaching for . . . something. There was a sense of loss about that tree, an incompleteness that reflected in the pattern of its boughs. Under the spread of its leafed canopy, half covered in autumn leaves, stood a harp.

"My tree," Meran whispered. "But it's . . ." She shook her head. "My tree standing in my father's wood as ever it did. And that is Telynros, his harp. Bethowen?"

"It is the present you see," the hillwife replied. "But a view of it that we already know, not what you seek."

Sighing, Bethowen closed her eyes. Deep inside, where the herenow curled around her thoughts, she drew on the heart of her strength. Her taw, the inner silence that is the basis for all magic, rose sure and firm like a well-remembered tune. When she spoke a word, the air crackled about her and a pale green rune hovered in the air above the fire. Sinking, it slowly became a part of the flames.

Meran leaned closer to the fire. The scent of wildflowers was strong in the air. The vision in the flames remained. Only its perspective changed. First the harp grew large and larger still, until all she could see was the silvery glisten of its strings, then between them, amidst eddying rivers of mist that hid more than they showed, she saw him, saw his face. Her heart grew tight in her breast.

"Cerin," she breathed. There was both hope and loss in her voice.

He stood on the ramparts of an old ruined fortress, the grey stoneworks stark against a spill of dusky hills and the tendrils of mist. Beside him was a tall man clad all in black—tunic, trousers, boots and jacket. The man in black had a strangely shaped lute hanging from a shoulder strap. Its shining wood was of the darkest ebony. Even the strings were black. Meran shivered and looked away.

"Who is he with?" she asked.

Bethowen shrugged.

"Where are they, then?"

"In this world, but not."

Bethowen passed her hands above the fire and the flames stirred the image into a new shape. The two men still stood on the ramparts, but now the fortress was changed. Gone were the ruined walls and tottering high towers. Stone was fashioned cunningly to stone, wall to towers to inner keep until the whole of it seemed the fashioning of master stoneworkers. Brave pennants fluttered in a breeze that blew across the sudden green hills.

"This is what he sees," the hillwife said.

She spoke a last word and the vision was lost in mists once

more. Harpstrings, silver and taut, took shape amidst the swirl of mist, then a harp, half covered with leaves, and above it a yearning oak keeping watch. Then there was only the fire and its red-gold flames.

"Where is that keep?" Meran asked.

"North of Abercorn and far from your father's wood. Across the Dolking Downs. Too far for an oakmaid. In the old days they named it Taencaer and it prospered. Now it is a nameless ruin where no one goes."

"I must go to him."

"Too far," Bethowen said.

"But still I must go." Meran bit at her lip, finding the next question, for all that it burned inside her, difficult to frame into words. It was not the question so much as what the answer to it might be.

"Is he . . . is he enspelled?" she asked.

Bethowen shrugged. "I have shown you all that the flames have to show, my dear. More I cannot do. For your sake, I hope . . ." The hillwife shut her mouth and entwined her knobby fingers together on her lap. She hoped what? That all was well? If all was well the oak king's daughter would not be here asking her questions.

"You must take care," she began, but stopped again. Hers was only the gift of farseeing and a few remedial cures. Advice had never been her province. To each their own wisdom. But this oakmaid, so determined, as stubborn as the badger that bided by her knee, as much a part of the Middle Kingdom as the ensorcered keep she meant to visit . . . what advice had the hills for her? None, save caution and, to one so headstrong, that would only be so much mouthing in the wind.

"He is enspelled," Meran said.

He had to be. He would never just leave her. But the fear, once having risen whisperingly inside her, couldn't be shunted aside. Like a serpent's insidious hiss it worried at all she'd ever held as certainty.

Is our love such a frail thing that I should question it like this? She demanded of herself.

He left, the whisperer replied slyly. Without a word.

He was enspelled! she insisted. He'd never be gone otherwise.

Men will do that, the inner voice replied, repeating Bethowen's earlier words, but mockingly, without the sense of comfort that one woman might offer to another.

Fiercely Meran shook her head. She thought of the roseharp's strings and the dead leaves entwined amidst them. She turned her gaze northward and followed the line of the hills with her eyes.

"Thank you," she murmured to the hillwife, her thoughts already far away, already planning her journey.

Fighting down the draw of her dead oak that still called to her for all the charms she carried with her, she left the hilltop. Old Badger trailed at her heels.

"Luck go with you," Bethowen said, but there was no one left to answer. Only the night remained, with its voiceless stars and the crackle of the flames.

Those same stars looked down on what was once named Taencaer, the old hillfort that straddled the border between Abercorn and Staynes. But where they saw the keep for the impoverished memory that it was, with leaning stone-cracked towers and debris rounding the once-straight planes of its walls, the two men who stood atop its ramparts saw it as it had been in longyears past, a bustling keep filled with the retainers of the old king's court, the last bastion of man before the grim wastes of the wild northlands. Where the hawk in the deserted west tower and the rodents that made their nests in the courtyards below heard only the wind and the stirrings of dead grasses as they rasped against the weathered stones, the two men heard music drifting lazily from the inner keep, the voices of stableboys and maids gossiping in the courtyard, horses stamping in the stables, the creak of the wooden pulley as water was drawn from the well, and the hundred other sounds of an occupied keep.

One of the men was a black-haired tinker, brown-skinned and dark-eyed. His name was Jeth Tewdol. He leaned against the old stone of the ramparts and eyed his prisoner with amusement, his lean fingers straying from time to time to the strings of his lute. The occasional snatch of music that answered had a sardonic quality to it that matched the dark cunning of his eyes for mood.

The other was Cerin called the Songweaver, the husband of Meran Gwynder and a harper, though he was far from his wife and had no instrument at hand to show his calling.

There was more grey than brown in his beard and his braided hair was greyer still. He was thin and his face seemed a map of lines, like the many roads he'd journeyed, but where the tinker's dark eyes reflected without depth, his were clear and tarn-deep, more the eyes of a young man for all his body's apparent age.

Staring across the darkened hills, Cerin worried at the why and where of his situation. It was a strange thing to go abed in your own house, with your wife at your side, and wake in a strange keep, who knew where, a prisoner. The sun had arisen and set once since then and still he was here. Try as he might, there was no way free of it. His captor's lutemagic bound him as surely as though he were chained, sapping his will, refusing him the chance to raise his own magics.

For he had magics, only they were denied him, here in this strangely familiar place. His taw, the inner quiet where his power had its birth, was silent, but silent with a silence of absence, not the silence that was like music, that was his strength. What he needed was his harp, but Telynros too was denied him.

Ordinarily there was a bond that joined them so that, no matter what the distance between them, he could call the roseharp to him, or him to it. But when he reached out to it, the lutemagic thickened about him and he heard no scatter of welcoming notes, no greeting. Nothing. With the roseharp in hand he could have surmounted his captor's spells, the clear notes cutting through his unseen fetters like an otter cutting through water. But as it was . . .

And Meran. What was she to think, waking and finding him gone?

As though reading Cerin's thoughts, Jeth Tewdol grinned. He pulled a flask from the pocket of his jacket and took a long swig before offering it to his prisoner.

Cerin shook his head. "I think not."

"Afraid it's a faery drink?" the tinker asked. "That if you take a sip you'll be bound here forever?"

"Something binds me already, tinker."

"Why, so it does."

Jeth Tewdol drew chords from his lute and Cerin's head swam with sharp pains that came like dagger blows on the heels of the dark music. He staggered and leaned against the stonework for balance, his lips drawn back as he fought the pain.

"A reminder," the tinker said with a smile. His hands fell away from his instrument.

As the last note failed, Cerin's breath returned to him in ragged gasps. The pains faded into a dull ache and were gone. All save the memory of them.

"You've only the one more night of my company, Songweaver," Jeth Tewdol added. "And then?" He grinned. "Why, then you're free to go as you will, where you will. Home to your woman of wood, if you want. If she'll still have you."

For all that he controlled the situation, the tinker took a step back at the sudden fire in his prisoner's eyes.

"No," he said, holding up his hands in a disarming manner. "You mistake me. I haven't harmed her, nor will I." His moment of unease dissolved as though it had never been and he made himself comfortable on the stoneworks, enjoying himself again. "This is the why of it," he explained. "Have you heard in your travels of Taencaer, the old king's keep?"

Cerin looked around with a new insight. The sharp edges of the keep wavered for a moment, as though the deepseeing of his magic had returned to him. The sounds that rose up from the courtyard and inner keep were now like the wind playing through ruined stonework. Then that moment was gone and all was as it had been, except that Cerin knew now where he was: in ruined Taencaer, where ghosts were said to play with the wind and the spirits of the dead slept lightly if they slept at all. The hillfort had been brought back to a semblance of life through the tinker's lutemagic, the same lutemagic that kept him from gathering his taw and putting an end to his captivity. Recognizing the fort and the hills beyond, he wondered how many he would know amongst the ghosts that the tinker had woken.

"What of it?" he asked. The where he was he understood now, but not the why.

"They had a contest here, in days long gone. Barden and musicians came from many lands to compete in it."

"I know," Cerin said. "Tasanin was the last to win it—a young fiddler from Yern."

The tinker regarded him strangely. Something in his prisoner's voice brought him up sharp, but Cerin, for all the furor of his thoughts, kept a bland expression on his face.

A Pattern of Silver Strings

"How could you know that?" Jeth Tewdol asked.

"I was here that day."

"But that was . . . long ago."

Cerin smiled, enjoying the tinker's disconcertment. "I know. But still I was here and remember it."

"Songweaver," Jeth Tewdol said. "That's your name? Not a title?" At Cerin's nod a queasy feeling went through the tinker. It had been one man through the centuries bearing that name, not wearing it as a title? For a long moment he said nothing, then a new gleam entered his eyes.

"That makes it even better," he said. "That contest will be held again tomorrow night—for the first time in many a year—and I mean to win it. It was for that reason that I raised the dead of Taencaer. I mean to win the contest and take the title of Songweaver from you. But now . . . now I take more than a title. I take your name and all the magic in it."

"Contests mean nothing," Cerin said. "They are for youths who have yet to prove something to themselves, not for men such as you and I. And my name, like the roseharp, was a gift of the Tuathan. You cannot take it from me."

Jeth Tewdol touched his lute and an eerie note sang forth. "You needn't sound so smug, Songweaver. I too have a god-gifted instrument, though mine was given to me by the Daketh."

Cerin looked from the lute that the tinker claimed came from the Tuathan's dark cousins, to the man's brown face.

"How so?" he asked. "Why were you gifted?"

"Through no special effort on my part," Jeth Tewdol said. "Would you know the tale? I can see by your eyes you would—for all that you shake your head. Then listen and marvel, you who have lived down through the longyears. We are more alike than I thought, for I see now that as you are, so must I be, for are we not both god-gifted?

"My instrument came to me in such a fashion: I was traveling through the Kierlands—do you know them? They're unfriendly dales in the best of times, but for a tinker there's none worse. It was winter and I sought lodgings, but was turned away from every inn until I took refuge in the one place no man could, or would, deny me—a ruined fane in the north marches. There was little enough there, but the walls that remained were enough to shelter me from the wind's cold bite, and what with this and that—a stolen haunch of a wild fowl from the last inn I'd tried, a small fire that spluttered and spat more than it gave off heat, and a threadbare cloak—I made do. A piteous picture, don't you think?

"I gave no thought to ghosts or the like—knew nothing of them save from my own people's roadtales. I fell asleep knowing nothing of the history of those ruins. That I found out later. Once it was a Tuathan fane, desecrated in years long gone, and now a place of dark shadows where the Daketh's power was strong. I slept and dreamt that they came to me, those dark gods, came to me who was nothing. I remember cowering from them, yet accepting their presence as we will do in a dream. They saw something in me—my bitterness, perhaps?—and fanned it to life with promises.

" 'What would you have?' they asked me.

"I remember thinking of the instrument my father had left me—a poor old flute that I sold for a week's lodgings and meals a year or so before. I'd never've done it, but I was desperate. The innkeeper had the city guard waiting at his door if I couldn't pay him something.

"Well, I thought of it, and remembered its warmth and comfort. You must know what I mean, Songweaver. When all's wrong in your world, a snatch of music can still lift your spirits. So I opened my mouth to ask for another like it, but when I spoke, all that came out was one word: 'Power.'

"The Daketh laughed—such a sound!

" 'Then power you shall have,' they said and were gone.

"When I woke, my fire was gone out and the wind was howling. I recalled my dream and found, lying next to me, this." The tinker tapped his lute. "They left me this instrument and its magics, yes, and the skill to use both. Why? Who can say? On a whim, perhaps? It makes little difference to me, for I'll tell you this, Songweaver. Innkeepers no longer look at my darkened skin and bid me begone. With the lutemagic I could tumble their walls down about their ears and they know it. They see it in my eyes, sense the lute's power. Ah, isn't she a beauty?"

Cerin nodded obligingly.

"And it's with it that I'll take your name."

"I do not engage in contests," Cerin replied.

"Are you afraid to lose?"

"Win or lose, it means nothing. I take my music as I find it. Whether you are the better musician or not, does not invalidate my own skill. And my name is still my name."

"And yet there will be a contest and you will play in it. And when the king's barden name me the winner, I will be the Songweaver and you will be nothing."

Cerin shrugged. If the tinker wished a contest, so be it. If he named himself Songweaver, there was little he could do about that either. A name was only a name. It had power, as all names must, but only if it was a true name. The tinker deluded himself if he thought otherwise.

"I have no instrument," he said.

Jeth Tewdol smiled. "I have one for you. A harp—the like of which you've never seen before."

And indeed he hadn't.

When the tinker brought the harp to him, Cerin could only stare. The soundbox was cracked. The supports, forepillar and curving neck both, were warped. The tuning pins had no hold in them so that a string wouldn't stay in tune, while the strings themselves were discolored with rust and buzzed when he tried one.

"Well?" the tinker asked.

Cerin looked from harp to man and answered softly. "A fine instrument, Jeth Tewdol, and I thank you for its use. If you will allow me to . . . accustom myself to it?"

"By all means." The tinker laughed. "I will leave you to your task. Only, Songweaver. Do us both a favour. Don't try to escape." He tapped his lute meaningfully, with all the subtlety of a bit actor in a mummer's play.

"I am yours to command," Cerin said.

"So you are. Why, so you are!"

Chuckling to himself, the tinker wandered off, plucking a tune from his lute. When he was gone, Cerin leaned against the stoneworks and eyed his borrowed harp for long moments. Then, sighing, he began to take out the tuning pins, one by one.

Rubbing dust and stone powder onto them, he fitted each back in place, testing them for give and how they'd hold for tuning. Some still fitted so loosely that he had to add slivers of wood to achieve the desired tightness. When he was done with them, he polished the strings themselves, working every fleck of rust out of them until they gleamed as bright as his roseharp's. He ignored the warpage and the soundbox's cracks. There was nothing he could do for them except rub the wood until it regained some of its lost luster.

He thought of Meran as he worked and wished there was some way he could get word to her so that she'd not think he was hurt or dead, or worse, that he'd left her. What *would* she think? The shock of waking alone and finding him gone . . . Frowning, he rubbed the wood all the harder, trying not to think of it.

At last he was done and he could test the instrument. The tuning pins held, for what it was worth, but the tone was abysmal, without projection. The bass strings still buzzed, though they could perhaps be fixed. Holding the harp on his lap, he closed his eyes and concentrated on Telynros, hoping that the tinker's guard might have dropped or the lutemagic fallen away enough for him to reach the roseharp with his need, but it was no use. He called up the grey rose and the silver strings, but only mists answered.

Weary, he went to find a place to sleep for the day. Finding it, he lay long awake, thinking of his wife and their home, and what the tinker would do with him when the contest was done. Surely he would not simply set him free? He would fear Cerin's reprisal, as well he might. But worry though he did, if there was a solution to his problem, Cerin couldn't see it.

Dawn found Meran many leagues north of Ogwen Wood and the longstone where Bethowen the hillwife kept her seeing-flames. Her legs ached, from ankle to calf especially, and she longed to rest. But there was still so far to go. And when she got there . . . What if he wasn't there? What if he was, but he'd gone of his own volition?

"I'm tired," she said, kneeling in the coarse grass. "Ah, but I'm tired."

Old Badger rubbed up against her and she ruffled his thick neck fur. She watched the sun rise, saw the hills unfolding for bleak miles north. Her dead oak called to her, stronger than before, for she'd never been this far from her father's wood. Rubbing her pendant, feeling the oak grain between her fingers, she tried to ignore the insistent summons to return, but it stayed with her, a constant need that sapped her determination, weakening her when she needed all her strength.

"I don't know if I can run that far, Old Badger. I don't know if it's in me."

But it had to be. As surely as though she felt Cerin's arm around her shoulders, she knew he needed her. Or was it her own need that drove her? She frowned, not liking this turn her thoughts kept taking. He was enspelled, she told herself yet again, and wished the voice inside her, whispering otherwise, would go away. She would continue. She'd run until her legs collapsed under her and then she'd run some more. Unless . . .

She smiled suddenly, wondering why she hadn't thought of it earlier. Drawing her flute from its sheath, she looked along its length, seeing Cerin's handiwork in its every curved inch. Then she lipped the instrument and, gazing skyward, began to play.

For a moment she thought she heard a harp answer, accompanying her as it had so many times before, then she knew that it was only her need that heard it. She shook off the feeling and concentrated on her playing. Her fingers moved in a slow dance across the wood and clear notes rang in the air. For a long time it was the only sound the hills heard. Then, far off in the distance, there was an answer—a deep-throated whistling call. A black speck grew larger in the sky and larger still, until a greatowl dropped groundward on silent wings.

Like calls to like, the old tales say. So an oakmaid's playing drew one of her skykin to her. The greatowl's wingspread spanned sixteen feet and his torso was as long as a man's. Landing, he ruffled his feathers and became a man, tall and round-eyed, with feathers streaming down to his shoulders in place of hair. Meran drew her flute back from her lips and laid it across her knees.

"Thairn," she said in greeting, her voice warm. They were old friends, these two.

"Your song was sad enough to make the wind weep, Meran. Why did you call me?"

Listening to her reply, he cocked his head like the great bird in whose shape he was more comfortable.

"I can bear one of you," Thairn said, looking from her to Old Badger when she was done.

Meran sheathed her flute and bent down to kiss Old Badger's brow.

"That will be enough," she said.

Thairn nodded and took his skyshape again. He lowered his neck to help her get a better purchase and she mounted awkwardly, afraid to pull the feathers too hard lest they loosen and come away in her hand. Once she was settled, Thairn rose effortlessly into the morning air and hovered.

"Goodbye, Old Badger!" Meran called down. "Wish me luck!"

Thairn's long wings plied the air and they were off, swifter than ever Meran's legs could have taken her. Behind, Old Badger whined, looking this way and that. Then he set off, doggedly following the bird and its rider. When they were only a speck in the distance and finally gone from sight, still he followed, his short legs churning, his body moving in a strange flowing motion that looked for all the world like a furry carpet come to life and floating a few inches off the ground as it followed the contours of the terrain.

The distance sped by under Thairn's tireless flight. Burrowing her face in his soft neck feathers, Meran stared ahead, northward, until just before the coming of twilight, she saw the fortress in the distance. By the time they reached its ruined walls, the night had fallen. Thairn coasted in and landed near the gates. Disembarking, Meran stretched, trying to work the stiffness out of her muscles.

"Thank you, Thairn," she said.

The greatowl took manshape again.

"I'll come with you," he said.

Meran shook her head. "Please. I have to go by myself." She didn't want to have to explain about the whisper that had kept up its constant nagging the whole of the journey north. All she knew was that she wanted to see Cerin on her own in case . . . in case. . . . She bit at her lip and savagely pushed the thought away.

"You're certain?" Thairn asked.

"I'm certain."

She waited until he'd changed back to a greatowl and his wings had lifted him into the dark skies again before she turned to make for the gate. As she reached it, the whole fortress seemed to waver in her sight. She blinked and rubbed at her eyes. In place of the ruin were solid walls, rearing high, lit by torchlight. Where the gateway had been empty, two guards now stood.

"Your business?" one of them demanded.

"I . . ."

The guard looked at the flute sheath hanging from her shoulder. "Are you here for the musician's contest?"

"The. . . ? Yes. Yes, I am!"

Musician's contest? Was it for this that her husband had left her? To take part in some mad contest? The whispering grew stronger in her mind and, feeling sick, she didn't have the strength to force it away.

"They're just finishing up," the guard said. "In the main hall. You'd better hurry."

Nodding her thanks, feeling more numb than real, Meran stepped through the gates and made her way across the inner courtyard. A musician's contest? Why had he come to it? Without his harp, even! As if he cared for such things in the first place. Contests were for people who needed titles, he'd told her often enough, not for anyone who cared about their music. Then she heard someone playing a harp, a strange harried sound as though the player were exhausted or drunk, and she recognized her husband's playing in the phrasing of the notes.

He *was* here! Part of this contest, and playing badly. Unsure if she was angry or sad, or perhaps some painful combination of the two emotions, she made for the door.

Disconcerting as the gathered dead were, what interested Cerin most was that there were more contestants than simply the tinker and himself. He wondered why. Long tables ran the length of the hall, except for the cleared space before the dais where the king and his retinue sat. And though he knew the people gathered here were only shades of the dead, he saw no mouldering corpses or gaunt bony shapes wrapped in their death palls. Instead they appeared as real as the tinker that walked at Cerin's side. They joined the other contestants, three men and a woman, at a table set aside for them to the left of the cleared space.

"The rules are simple," Jeth Tewdol told him. "Musicianship is judged by those three," he indicated the dais where the king's barden sat with fiddle, harp and flute respectively on their knees. Cerin didn't recognize any of them, though he knew the king. He looked away at the dead king's mocking smile. There had been no love between them when the king was alive.

"But the judging," the tinker was explaining, "is also measured on how well you appeal to the less tutored—those gathered here to listen. Thunderous applause is what you're seeking, Songweaver. If you wish to keep your name." He glanced down at Cerin's instrument and grinned. "I wish you the best of luck."

One by one the contestants played and, living or dead though they might be (Cerin was no longer sure), they were all skilled musicians. He found himself enjoying their strange tunes and tried to remember this flourish or that decoration for future reference. *If* Jeth Tewdol was going to allow him a future. Then it was the tinker's turn.

He bowed, first to the king's dais, then to the crowd that filled the hall to overflowing. Giving Cerin a wink, the tinker began to play.

There was no doubting his skill. Why on top of that he needed to be named the best, Cerin couldn't understand. He played with a dark grace. Moody tunes grew out of his fey instrument that sent shivers up the spines of his listeners and their feet to tapping the weird rhythms. When his last note died away, a long silence filled the hall. Then it was shattered as the people roared, clapping their hands and stamping their feet. They banged their mugs on the tables, whistled shrilly and generally raised a hullabaloo. Beaming, the tinker returned to the contestants' table.

"Now it is your turn," he said.

Cerin nodded, rising as his name was called.

"Lastly, Cerin called the Songweaver, Harper from Ogwen Wood."

As Cerin took his place, settling the tinker's harp on his lap, a murmur went through the crowd. There were faces he knew amongst them—the faces of folk long dead—and they recognized him and his name, though there wasn't one that had a friendly smile for him. Looking down at his instrument, he sighed. It's not the harp, it's the player, he told himself. And it matters not whether you win or lose, just let it be done.

He was tempted to play badly, just to let the tinker win, but knew he couldn't. Whatever he might think of contests or his present situation, he had the pride of his art to consider as well. When he played, he always played his best, whether it be for a king in his court or a shepherd in his cot. Tonight could be no different else he'd lost his name in truth, though not in the way that the tinker meant he should lose it. Turning so that he could watch Jeth Tewdol, he began to play.

He started with a familiar air, fingers curled like a hawk's talons as they plucked sweet notes from the shabby instrument on his lap. It was a simple piece but, in his hands, for all the drawbacks of the instrument, he breathed new life into it; gave it a deepness so that for all that his listeners had heard it played a thousand times before, in his hands it sounded like a newly-composed piece. He grinned at Jeth Tewdol as he began a second tune, enjoying despite himself the look on the tinker's face. But his amusement didn't last long.

Seven bars into the tune, he saw Jeth Tewdol caress a string of his lute and the harp Cerin played rang discordantly. He tried to remedy the turn his music had taken, but the more he tried, the worse it sounded. The damage was done. Titters started up at the back of the hall and his neck reddened, but try though he did, he could no longer control the instrument. For every true note he fingered, the lutemagic awoke a dozen discords. At last he let his hands fall from the strings and he bent his head under the laughter of the gathered dead. And laughing loudest of all was Jeth Tewdol.

"Ha!" he cried. "I've won! See him now, he who was once called the Songweaver!"

Cerin's face burned. He knew he could play better, knew the flaws heard by these people were none of his doing, but knew as well that as far as they were concerned, he was worse than a novice player. They had wanted to see him fail and cared not how that failure was brought about. He could hold the truth of his own skill in his heart, but it did little to diminish the weight of the ridicule he bore. This was like his worst nightmares as a fledgling harper come to life. How often hadn't he woken bolt upright in his bed, sticky with sweaty fear, the dregs of a dream thudding in his heart? He'd be before a crowd, playing his best, and then it would all go wrong, and instead of applause, he received jeering and laughter. Like now.

Slowly he rose to his feet and, clutching the harp tight

against his chest, made his way back to his seat. There was no use protesting, no use in doing anything except seeing this thing through to its end. And perhaps, in some measure, he deserved to be treated in this way, taken down a notch. He didn't believe in contests, no. But perhaps all his noble wordage as to why merely covered up the fact that he thought himself above them. Just as when he'd been playing and he'd mocked the tinker—something he'd never done to another musician no matter how good or bad his playing. Who was better? Was it because perhaps Jeth Tewdol *was* better? Why should it matter? It never had before. But just now, with the jeering and catcalls still loud in his ears and the tinker's grinning face so near his own, it seemed to matter more than anything else ever had before.

"We have little love for the living," the dead king said as the noise finally fell away. His voice boomed hollowly through the hall. "But, in truth, Jeth Tewdol, you have provided an entertainment this evening that we'll not soon forget. To see the Bright Gods' champion brought so low! Ha! Arise and accept from me now the winner's cup!"

"See?" the tinker said to Cerin. "It's done."

As he rose to collect his reward, Cerin caught at his arm.

"Am I free to go now?" he asked.

Jeth Tewdol shrugged. "Perhaps." He ran a finger along one of his lute's dark strings and Cerin shivered as the lutemagic bit at him. "There's still the matter of a name to settle between us. We can scarce have two Songweavers wandering the world, now can we?"

He laughed at the impotent rage in Cerin's eyes and turned away. Laying his instrument on the dais before the king, he went to where the king's harper held the winning cup. But before his hand touched it, the clear sound of flute-playing spoke across the hall.

As one, all heads turned to the door to see the woman with her green-brown hair and her cloak like leaves who lipped her flute. Her fingers fluttered across the holes of the instrument as though she were caressing a lover and there came forth such a sound! The low notes thrummed like a bear's honeyed breath, the high ones skirled and pierced the sky with sudden stars.

"Who?" the tinker cried, but none save Cerin and the

king's harper heard him. The rest were too entranced by her playing to heed him.

"At last contestant it seems," the king's harper said.

"Meran!" the Songweaver cried.

Her playing was like the woods in summer, full and merry, deep with old tree secrets, yet held an underpining sweet sorrow, for, like music, the seasons change, summer to autumn to winter and round again to spring. Her music told the tale of that cycle, now joyful, now sad. And, by the faces of those who listened, such a music had never been heard in that hall before.

Jeth Tewdol's features contorted with rage. He leapt for his lute to stop her music, but Cerin was there first. The harper's boot crushed the hellish instrument before ever the tinker could lay a hand on it. With the sound of a great wind, the glamour of Taencaer fled, ghosts and all. The three of them stood in a ruined hall, the stars showing through the roofless heights above them. And still Meran played. Jeth Tewdol spun away from Cerin's grasp and made for her.

But as the tinker scrabbled across the rubble, he forgot who his prisoner was, the power Cerin wielded that had been denied him. Still seething from the ridicule he'd undergone, concerned for his wife, no longer restrained, Cerin reached out to Telynros, his thoughts leaping the distance between the ruins of Taencaer and the cottage where his roseharp awoke with music as it stood by the hearth, though no hand touched its strings. A moment it played on its own, then the harp was in Cerin's hands and its music rushed forward to accompany the sound of Meran's flute.

Across the ruined hall, harper and flautist met each other's gaze. Meran brought her flute from her lips and held it at her side, her fingers whitening as she squeezed it. She tried to focus on her husband's face, but her vision swam.

She didn't know what had possessed her to play in the doorway as she had, unless it be that those people had mocked her love and she meant to show them that it was wrong to do so. She'd not played to be a part of the contest. Rather she'd only tried, through her music, to reach out and touch the audience, show them that ridicule was cruel, hoped to awaken some compassion in their dead hearts. Blinking now, she saw only the vision from Bethowen's seeing-flames—the pattern of silver strings and the dead leaves that half covered the instrument, the mists aswirl, and then, at last, her husband's face.

The sly whisperer inside her was laid to rest at last as she looked into his eyes. But a new fear rose to take its place. He played Telynros savagely and the dark-clothed man that was between them jerked to the music, helpless as a marionette. Cerin's eyes were dark with a wild anger, as though he didn't know what he was doing, or worse, that he knew all too well.

"Cerin!" she cried. "Cerin!"

His anger seemed to blind him, for there was no flicker of recognition in his eyes when she called his name, no lessening of that terrible harping. She opened her mouth to call again, then lifted her flute to her lips and sent her own music skirling through the maelstrom of the roseharp's notes, weaving and binding them. As their musics joined, she came to understand what drove him. It was not so much his ordeal that burned in him, as what he'd found in himself.

A new tone entered her playing and it pierced his anger with its reason.

No one can be perfect, love, it seemed to say. Yet remember that he drove you to it and learn the lesson of it. Don't become what he is. Where is the gentle man I love? Where is the Songweaver amid such anger?

Slowly his rage faded. Telynros's grim notes dissolved into echoes and Cerin slumped to his knees, hugging his roseharp to him. He stared at the tinker's still form, sick at what he'd done. But as he watched, Jeth Tewdol raised himself painfully and sat up against a block of weather-roughened stonework, lifted, it seemed, by the flute music that still rang sweetly through the hall, healing all hurts. Then it too died and Meran picked her way across. She paused by the tinker and looked down at him.

"Why?" she asked. "By my father's Oak, why?"

Jeth tewdol lifted his gaze. "I am a tinker," he said bitterly.

"That is not reason enough."

"The Dark Gods gave me an instrument that made me a prince of players—I who was nothing before they gifted me, a two-copper pretender of a musician, a tinker welcomed more often with a cuff in the face and a curse. The Daketh gave me power. They delight in torment, so should I not offer it to them in payment? Is that reason enough? They . . ." He shook his head. "How could you understand?"

Meran regarded him silently for long moments, then handed him her flute.

"Then I gift you with this," she said. "Will you now take delight in bringing joy to people?"

"I . . ." The tinker looked at the flute, remembering its sweet tone when she'd played it. His fingers trembled as he took it in his hands, running his fingers along the smooth length of its wood. For long moments, now he was silent. When he spoke again, his voice had a different tone to it. Gone was the mockery and self-assurance.

"I . . . I know it's the player, not the instrument that makes a musician. Your husband . . . even on that box with strings I gave him to use . . . he was still the better player. I can't accept this. I . . ." His eyes glistened with unshed tears. "I don't deserve it."

"Still you don't understand," Meran said softly. "It's the music that matters, not who's better or worse."

"But . . . I . . . What will you use?"

Meran looked to Cerin and smiled. "Perhaps my husband will make me another. There's still some of the old tree left."

Jeth Tewdol could find no more words. He simply leaned against the stone, holding the flute as though it were the greatest treasure the world had to offer. Watching them, hearing his wife speak, Cerin felt the tightness in his chest ease and he could breathe again. He thought to himself that he should still be angry, but searching inside, all he could find was pity. Shaking his head, he stood and then Meran came to him, lifting her face to be kissed.

"Such a spell you wove!" he said with a smile. "Who's the Songweaver now?"

She grinned. "You are, silly! Who else?"

"Perhaps," he said as he kissed her.

Meran looked at his harp and, remembering the pattern the strings had made in the seeing-flames, reached out to touch one. A tiny bell-like note rang forth.

"Maybe I'll take up the harp then," she said, "and maybe not. But right now there's an Old Badger stuck somewhere between here and home, and a night's sleep that we never saw completed."

"So there is." He looked over her shoulder to the tinker. Jeth Tewdol raised his gaze from the flute to meet Cerin's eyes.

"If I said I was sorry . . ." the tinker began, but Cerin shook his head.

"We both learned something tonight, Jeth. I as much as you. If you're ever 'round Ogwen Wood, visit us, will you? Only come when we're awake."

Cerin's smile awoke a tentative answer on the tinker's lips.

"If you'll have me," he said slowly, "I'd be honored to come."

"Good. Till then . . ."

Cerin set the roseharp to ringing with deep chords and an amber hue surrounded Meran and him.

"Thank you!" the tinker called.

From the amber glow he heard a chorus of farewells. When the harping died away and the amber hue was gone, Jeth Tewdol sat alone amidst the ruined stoneworks of Taencaer. Rising he went to the ramparts to watch the dawn pink the sky above the eastern hills. He thought for a moment of the Daketh instrument that lay broken below him, then shook his head and lifted Meran's flute to his lips. He was out of practice, so the sound that came forth was awkward and breathy, but the tinker smiled.

Lisa Tuttle

A FRIEND IN NEED

Having an imaginary playmate in one's childhood is not uncommon. Meeting that playmate years later as an adult is definitely not an everyday occurrence and could lead to some serious questions about the reality of one's own existence.

Photographs lie, like people, like memories. What would it prove if I found Jane's face and mine caught together in a picture snapped nearly twenty years ago? What does it mean that I can't find such a photograph?

I keep looking. My early life is so well documented by my father's industrious camera work that Jane's absence seems impossible. She was, after all, my best friend; and all my other friends—including one or two I can't, at this distance, identify—are there in black and white as they run, sit, stand, scowl, cry, laugh, grimace, and play around me. Page after page of birthday parties, dress-up games, bicycle riding, ice-cream eating, of me and my friends Shelly, Mary, Betty, Carl, Julie, Howard, Bubba, and Pam. But not Jane, who is there in all my memories.

Was she ever really there? Did I imagine her into existence? That's what I thought for twelve years, but I don't believe that anymore.

I saw her in the Houston airport today and I recognized

151

her, although not consciously. What I saw was a small woman of about my own age with dark, curly hair. Something about her drew my attention.

We were both waiting for a Braniff flight from New York, already five minutes late. A tired-looking man in uniform went behind the counter, made a throat-clearing noise into the microphone, and announced that the flight would be an hour late.

I swore and heard another voice beside me, like an echo. I turned my head and met her eyes. We laughed together.

"Are you meeting someone?" she asked.

"My mother."

"What a coincidence," she said flatly. "We've both got mothers coming to visit."

"No, actually my mother lives here. She went to New York on business. Your mother lives there?"

"Long Island," she said. It came out as one word; I recognized the New Yorker's pronunciation.

"That's where you're from?"

"Never west of the Hudson until two years ago." Her sharp eyes caught my change of expression. "You're surprised?"

"No." I smiled and shrugged, because the feeling of familiarity was becoming stronger. "I thought I knew you, that's all. Like from a long time ago. Grade school?"

"I'm Jane Renzo," she said, thrusting out her hand. "Graduate of Gertrude Folwell Elementary School and Elmont High, class of '73."

Jane, Jane Renzo, I thought. Had I known someone by that name? There were distant resonances, but I could not catch them. "Cecily Cloud," I said, taking her hand.

"What a great name!"

Our hands unclasped and fell apart. She was grinning; there was a hint of a joke in her eyes, but also something serious.

"But it doesn't ring any bells?" I asked.

"Oh, it does, it definitely does. Sets the bells a-ringing. It's the name I always wanted. A name like a poem. I hated always being plain Jane." She made a face.

"Better than Silly Cecily," I said. "The kids used to call me Silly until I got so used to it that it sounded like my real name. But I always hated it. I used to wish my parents had given me a strong, sensible name that couldn't be mispronounced or misspelled or made fun of—like Jane."

Jane. Memory stirred, but it was like something deep in a forest. I couldn't get a clear sight of it.

"We all have our own miseries, I guess," she said. She looked at her watch and then at me, a straightforward, friendly look. "We've got time to kill before this flight gets here. You want to go sit down somewhere and have some coffee?"

The rush of pleasure I felt at her suggestion was absurdly intense, inappropriate, as if she were a long-lost friend, returned to me when I had nearly given up hope of seeing her again. Trying to understand it, I said, "Are you sure we haven't met before?"

She laughed—a sharp, defensive sound.

Hastily, afraid of losing our easy rapport, I said, "It's only that I feel I know you. Or you remind me of someone. You never came to Houston when you were a kid?"

She shook her head.

"College?"

"Montclair State." We had begun to walk together in search of a coffee shop, down the long, windowless, carpeted, white-lit corridor. It was like being inside a spaceship, I thought, or in an underground city of the distant, sterile future. We were in Houston, but we might as easily have been in New York, Los Angeles, or Atlanta for all the cues our surroundings gave us. It was a place set apart from the real world, untouched by time or season, unfettered by the laws of nature.

"It's like the future," I said.

Jane looked at the curving walls and indirect lighting and gave me an appreciative smile. "It is kind of *Star Treky*," she said.

We came to rest in a small, dim, overpriced restaurant which was almost empty, in contrast to the bar on one side and the fast-food cafeteria on the other. I saw by my watch that it was too late for lunch and too early for dinner. We ordered coffee, causing the middle-aged waitress to sigh heavily and stump away.

"Actually, I'd rather have a shot of Tullamore Dew," said Jane. "Or a large snifter of brandy."

"Did you want—"

She shook her head. "No, no. Better not. It's just that the thought of seeing my mother again has me wanting reinforcement. But I'd be less capable of dealing with her drunk than I am sober."

I looked at her curiously, because she had struck me from the first as a capable, almost fearless person. "You don't get along with your mother?"

"Something like that. I moved out here to get away from her, and she still won't let me be. She calls me every night. Sometimes she cries. She won't believe that I'm grown up and that I have my own life to live, a life I've chosen. She's still waiting for me to give up this silliness and move back home. My sisters got away because they got married. But in her eyes I'm still a child."

The waitress returned, setting our coffees down before us with unnecessary emphasis. I watched the dark brown liquid slide over the rim of my cup, to be caught in the shallow white bowl of the saucer.

"You're lucky if you and your mother can relate to each other as people," Jane said.

I nodded, although I had never given the matter any thought; I'd simply taken it for granted. "We have disagreements, but we're pretty polite about them," I said.

This made Jane laugh. "Polite," she said. "Oh, my." She peeled the foil top off a plastic container of coffee whitener. "You're so lucky . . . to have had a happy childhood and a mother who knows how to let go."

It seemed at first acceptable, the way she so calmly passed judgment on my life, as if she knew it; then, suddenly, strange.

"I think I had a fairly normal childhood," I said. "Very ordinary. At least, it always seemed that way to me." It had been suburban, middle-class, and sheltered. I saw my experiences reflected in the lives of my friends, and I found it hard to believe that Jane had come from a background terribly dissimilar. "You were unhappy as a child?"

Jane hesitated, stirring her coffee from black to brown. Then she said, "I don't remember."

"What do you mean?"

"Just that. I don't remember my childhood. Most of it, anyway. It's as if I went to sleep when I was five and didn't wake up until I was twelve. The years in between are a blank."

I stared at her, trying to understand. I couldn't believe it. I didn't doubt that I had forgotten much of my own childhood, but there remained a satisfying large jumble of memories that I could rummage around in when the need arose. Some of the things that had happened to me remained as vivid in my imagination as if they had just happened: the day I had broken my bride doll, a rabbit-shaped cake my mother had baked one Easter, the taste of water warm from the garden hose at the height of summer, the Christmas when I had been sick, games of hide-and-seek, classroom embarrassments . . . I had only to let down the barriers to be flooded by memories, most of them far more intense than the recollections of anything that had happened to me as an adult. To be without such memories was to be without a childhood, to lack a certain identity.

"I can remember a few things from when I was very young," Jane said into my stunned silence. "None of them pleasant. And my sisters have told me things . . . it's just as well I don't remember. The things I've forgotten can't hurt me."

"But why? What happened to you? What was so terrible?"

"I'm sure other kids survived a lot worse. In fact, I know that for certain. There's no telling what will make one kid break and another survive, or what kind of defense mechanisms are needed. I work with emotionally disturbed children, and some of them have every right to be, given their backgrounds, while others come from loving families and just . . . crack over things that other kids take in stride. All I can say about the things that happened to me—well, I had my way of dealing with them, whether it was a good way or not. Forgetting, blotting it out, was part of it."

She sounded defensive and apologetic. I tried to look reassuring. "You don't have to—If it makes you uncomfortable, don't talk about it."

"No, that's it, I *do* want to talk about it. But I don't want to bore you. I don't want to burden you with my old stories."

"I don't mind at all," I said. "I'm happy to listen, if it helps you to talk."

"I think it might help. Well . . ." She cleared her throat and took a sip of coffee, looking at me self-consciously over the cup. "One of my earliest memories is when I was about four. My mother was forty-nine and menopausal. She was crazy that year, more than usual. Any little thing could set her off, and when she got angry, she got violent. I can't remember what it was I did, but it was probably something as minor as interrupting her while she was thinking—I got swatted for that more than once. At any rate, she started screaming. We were in the kitchen. She grabbed the carving knife and came for me, yelling that she'd cut off my hands so I couldn't make any more trouble."

"Jane!"

She shrugged, smiling wryly. "I'm sure I remember the knife as bigger than it really was. And maybe she wouldn't have hurt me at all. But what did I know? I was a little kid. And when somebody comes at you with a knife, the instinct is to get the hell away. She chased me all through the house. I finally hid in a cabinet and listened to her looking for me. One of my sisters got my father, and he managed to calm her down. But nobody knew where I was, and I was afraid to come out. I crouched there in the dark, beneath the bathroom sink, for hours, until I decided it was safe to come out. I hadn't heard her screaming for a long time, but I was afraid that she might be tricking me and that I'd open the door to find her on the other side, the knife in her hand and a horrible smile on her face."

"Was she insane?" I asked quietly.

"No." The denial came too quickly. Jane paused and shrugged. "I don't know. Define the term. Generally, she could cope. Was she really over the edge, or just trying to scare me into being good? It's hard to decide even now. She was very unhappy at that time in her life, and she's always been a very self-dramatizing person. We all have our own ways of dealing with life. What's insane?"

"I don't know," I said, although I thought I did. "Was she violent toward you most of the time? Did you go in fear of your life?"

"Sometimes. It was hard to know where you stood with her. That's the worst thing for a kid. I couldn't count on her, I didn't know how to get the right responses. Sometimes she would be very loving, sometimes what I did would make her laugh. At other times the same thing would have her screaming at me. But more often she turned her anger against herself. She must have tried to kill herself—or at least she pretended to—half a dozen times. I remember her lying on the floor in the living room with an empty bottle of pills and a half-full bottle of vodka. She told us she was going to die, and she forbade us to call for help. We were supposed to sit there and watch her die, so that she could die looking at the faces she loved most. We didn't dare move. Finally she seemed to have passed out, and Sue, my oldest sister, tried to call Dad. But the second her hand touched the telephone, my mother sat up and started screaming at her for being a disobedient bastard."

"Lord," I said, when Jane paused to sip coffee. I tried to imagine it, but could not quite achieve the child's point of view. "How did you survive?"

"Well, I blotted it out, mostly. I had my imaginary life." She smiled.

"How do you mean?"

"When you were a kid, weren't there some things which seemed just as real to you as real life, although you knew they were different? The things you didn't tell grown-ups about, although they were every bit as real and important—if not more so—as life at school and at home?"

"You mean like pretend games?" I asked. "I used to pretend—" And suddenly I remembered. "Of course. That's who you remind me of." I laughed, feeling silly. "Jane. I had an imaginary friend named Jane."

Jane's smile was somewhat wistful. "What was she like?"

"Oh, she was everything I wanted to be and wasn't. Practical and neat instead of dreamy and disorganized. Her hair was dark and curly instead of straight and mousy. She read a lot, like me, and knew all kinds of wonderful games. She had my favorite name, of course." I shrugged and then laughed. "She was like a real person. She didn't have any magical powers—except, of course, that she disappeared from time to time. She was actually rather like you, I guess. Isn't that funny, that my imaginary friend should remind me of you?"

Jane didn't look as if she found it particularly odd or amusing. She said, "I had imaginary friends, too. Except, at the time, they weren't in the least imaginary to me. The life I made up for myself was more important to me than my real life. It was my escape. It was how I survived the childhood I don't remember—the things that *really* happened to me." She paused to sip her coffee and then went on.

"I was six years old. I was wearing a brand-new brown velvet dress with a white lace collar. I'm not sure why, but I think I was going to a party later in the afternoon. I was feeling very special and happy, and I was sitting at the dining room table eating my lunch. My mother sat next to me and nagged me. She kept warning me to be careful. She kept telling me how expensive the dress was, and how difficult it would be to clean if I got it dirty. She told me not to be as clumsy as I usually was, and she warned me that I'd better not spill anything on myself. So of course, I did. I slopped a little bit of milk onto my dress. At that, she grabbed me and pulled me up out of my chair, screaming at me that I was messy, disobedient, and a complete disgrace. I didn't deserve to have nice clothes. I was an animal. I ate like a clumsy pig, and I didn't deserve the nice meals she fixed for me. I should never have been born. Nobody could stand to be around me. I should be kept in a cage where I could spill my food all over me to my heart's content. Screaming all the way, she dragged me up to the attic and left me there to meditate on my sins."

My stomach clenched with sympathy at Jane's level, matter-of-fact tone.

"But the odd thing," Jane went on, "the odd thing was that I *liked* the attic. I always had liked it. Being taken up there and left was no punishment at all. I was always begging to be allowed to play up there, but she would never let me. I could only go up there when my father went, to help him clean, or to get out the Christmas ornaments, or to store old clothes away. I suppose I liked the attic so much because it was outside her domain. She would send my father up for things instead of going herself. It was the only place in the house that didn't belong to her.

"And that was where she left me. Where I couldn't mess up any of her things. I was left all alone up there under the roof. It was cold and quiet and filled with cardboard boxes. I was very far away from the rest of the house. I couldn't hear my family downstairs—for all I knew, they might have gone out, or just disappeared. And I knew my mother couldn't hear me or see me, either. I could do anything I wanted and not be punished for it. I could think or say whatever I liked. For the first time in my life, it seemed, I was completely free.

"So I pretended that my family didn't exist—or at least that I didn't belong to it. I made up a family I liked a lot better. My new mother was pretty and young and understanding. She never lost her temper and she never shouted at me. I could talk to her. My new father was younger, too, and spent more time at home with us. My real sisters were so much older than me that they sometimes seemed to live in another world, so my new sisters, in my made-up family, were closer to my age. I had a younger sister who would look up to me and ask me for advice, and I had a sister exactly my age who would be my best friend. She was good at all the things I wasn't. And instead of being ugly, with kinky hair like mine, she was pretty with long, straight hair that she would let me braid and put up for her." She stopped short, as if on the verge of saying something else. Instead, she sipped her coffee. I waited, not saying a word.

"I know I invented them," she said. "I know it was all a game. But still it seemed—it still seems—that I didn't make them up but found them somewhere, and found a way of reaching them in that faraway, warm place where they lived. I lived with them for a long time—nearly seven years. When I remember my childhood, it's the time I spent with my make-believe family that I remember. Those people."

I wanted to ask her their names, but I said nothing, almost afraid to interrupt her. Jane was looking at me, but I don't think she saw me.

"I sat all alone in that cold, dusty attic, and I could feel the house changing below me. I was in the attic of another house. I could hear the voices of my new family drifting up to me. I could imagine every room, how each one was furnished. When I had it all clear in my mind, I went downstairs to see for myself. It was the same size as my real house, but completely different. There was a small chord organ in the living room that my make-believe mother played in the evenings, all of us gathered around to sing old-fashioned songs. The family room had a cork floor with woven Indian rugs on it. There was a deer head over the television set; my make-believe father liked to hunt. The wallpaper in the kitchen was gold and brown, and the cookie jar was shaped like a rabbit dressed in overalls. There was a big oak tree in the backyard that was perfect for climbing, perfect for playing pretend games in. It could be a pirate ship, or—"

My skin was crawling. It was my house she was describing. My parents. My childhood. "What about the front yard?" I asked.

"Another oak tree. We had lots of acorns in the fall. There was a magnolia tree on one side, and a big brick planter box built out of the front of the house. It was great to play in. I'm amazed those blue flowers managed to grow with us stomping on them all the time. Your mother—"

"It was you," I said.

She shut up and looked down into her coffee.

"Why didn't you say?" I asked. "Why this game? Why pretend you didn't know me? Did you think I'd forgotten? Jane?"

She gave me a wary look. "Of course I thought you'd forgotten. I wasn't sure myself that any of it had happened. I never thought I'd see you again. I thought I'd made you up."

"Made me up!" I laughed uneasily. "Come on, Jane! What are you talking about? What's the point of this whole story?"

"It's not a story," she said. Her voice was high and stubborn, like a child's. "I knew you wouldn't believe it."

"What is it you want me to believe? We were friends when we were children. We both remember that. But if you tell me that you grew up in New York, and I know that I—"

"Why did you say you had an *imaginary* friend called Jane?"

"Because I thought—" And I stopped and stared, feeling the little hairs prickling all over me as I remembered. "Because you disappeared," I said softly. "Whenever you left to go home, you just vanished. I saw you come and go out of nowhere, and I knew that real people didn't do that." I was suddenly afraid that I was sitting at a table with a ghost.

As if she read my thoughts, Jane reached across the table and gripped my hand. There was a sullen, challenging look on her face. Her hand was warm and firm and slightly damp. I remembered that, as a child, too, she had been solid and real. Once her firm grasp, just in time, had kept me from falling out of a tree. We had tickled each other and played

A Friend in Need

tag and helped each other into dress-up clothes. She had liked to braid my hair.

Jane took her hand away to look at her wristwatch. "We'd better go," she said.

I thought of the first time I had seen her, coming down the attic stairs. I was surprised to find a stranger in my house, but she had looked back at me, perfectly at ease, and asked me if I wanted to play. We were friends in that instant—although I couldn't remember, now, what we had said to each other or what we played. Only that first moment of surprise remains hard and clear and whole in my mind, like the last time I saw her disappear.

Usually when Jane left she simply walked away, and I did not see where she went. She was different from my other friends in that I never walked her home and we never played at her house. I didn't even know where her house was; I knew only, from things she had said, that it was in a different neighborhood.

But that last day, I remember, we had been playing Parcheesi on the floor of my bedroom. Jane said goodbye and walked out. A few seconds later I thought of something I had meant to ask or tell her, and I scrambled to my feet and went after her. She was just ahead of me in the hallway, and I saw her go into the living room. She was just ahead of me, in plain sight, in daylight—and then she wasn't. She was gone. I looked all through the living room, although I knew she hadn't hidden from me; there hadn't been time.

I couldn't believe what I had seen. Things like that didn't happen, except on *The Twilight Zone*. I was eleven and a half years old, too old to have imaginary friends. I never saw Jane again.

Until today.

And now she was standing, preparing to leave me.

Hastily I stood up, pushing my chair away from the table. "I don't get it," I said. "I don't understand what you're saying."

She looked at me and shrugged. "Why do you think I know? I thought I'd imagined you, and here you are. But I grew up in New York, you grew up in Texas. We *couldn't* have known each other as kids. But that's what we both remember."

"And now what?"

She smiled at me ironically. "And now the plane is coming in. Let's go."

We walked together through the featureless corridors in silence. It felt right and familiar for me to be at her side, as if we'd never been apart, as if we'd walked together many times before.

"I wish she wasn't coming," Jane said suddenly. "I wish I could have told her no. I wish I didn't have to deal with her. Will I be running away from my mother all my life?"

I touched her arm. She was real. She was real. She was there. I felt very close to her, and yet I knew, sadly, that she must be lying to me, or crazy. One of us must be. I said, "You'll be all right. You're strong. You're grown up now, and you've got your own life. Just tell yourself that. Your mother's just another woman. She can't make you do anything you don't want to do."

She looked at me. "You always thought I was braver than I really was. It's funny, but your thinking that made me try to live up to it. In order to be as brave and strong as you thought I was, I did things that terrified me. Like the time I climbed from a tree up onto the roof of the house—"

"I was terrified!" I said. Her words brought it back vividly, those moments when, from my own precarious treetop perch, I had seen her thin, small figure drop to the dark shingles of the roof, the breath catching in my throat as if I were the one in danger.

"So was I," she said. "But it was worth it for the way you looked at me. I'd always been a quiet little coward, but to you I was wild and daring."

Through the big window we saw a bright orange plane land and roll along the runway.

"Thank you," said Jane. "I needed a friend today."

"Not just today," I said. "Now that we've found each other, we'll get together again, often."

She smiled and looked away. I followed her gaze and saw the plane docking.

"That's ours," I said, turning my head to look at her. She was gone.

I whirled away from the window, scanning the crowds for her dark hair, her white blouse, her particular way of moving. She was nowhere to be seen.

There hadn't been time. I had turned my head only for a

moment. She had been right beside me; I could feel her presence. From one second to the next, she had simply vanished.

Feeling dizzy, I moved indecisively a few steps this way, a few steps that. There was no point in searching for her. I already knew I wouldn't find her. I wondered what airport she might be waiting in; I realized she had never said where she lived. Was she able to find me because our lives briefly intersected in the bland, anonymous limbo of an airport, or could she have come to me wherever I was, because of her need?

I am waiting, wondering if I will ever see her again. Jane is real; she exists; I know I didn't imagine her. But did she imagine me?

Gillian FitzGerald

POOKA'S BRIDGE

Irish folklore is replete with mischievous imps and goblins such as leprechauns, pookas and other fey creatures. Here, in an enchanting tale based on that folklore, Gillian FitzGerald tells us how a courageous and loving young woman charmed a pooka.

There was an old lord named Niall MacMahon O'Farrell who saw all of his sons die in battle, leaving him without an heir to his great riches. He knew he had but a handful of years left on earth, and he had no wish to see his land go to his cousin Cathal, who was a hard man. So he looked about for a wife, and his eyes fell upon Mairi Ni Rory, a woman whose temper was as sweet as her warm, green eyes. He'd not hoped to love his new wife, for he had thought his heart buried with Maeve, the woman who'd given him four fine sons and twenty years of her life. After the fierce passion of his love for Maeve, he felt he had no right to ask for more, but he could not help loving Mairi: she had the way about her. She was as gay and pretty as a bird, with long, dark hair falling like a river about a petal-pale face, and tilting green eyes that smiled as gaily as her wide, soft mouth. She sang often as she moved about his house, and her gentle ways won the hearts of everyone in the hall from the youngest kitchenmaid to the gruffest of Niall's soldiers. For all her soft answers, though, no one thought her weak; they knew her for a brave woman, as well as a sweet one.

She bore Niall a son, and three years later, a daughter, and their joy was complete. But the happiness was not to last, for Cathal grew angry at the news that he had lost the hall to a babe in arms. He kept hoping that the boy would die of some childhood illness, but instead Garrett grew strong. So, seeing no other chance, he led a troop against his cousin. Niall heard, and made his plans carefully, for he knew that his few men could not hope to win against the hired soldiers bought by Cathal's gold. He took Mairi aside, and told her to flee with their children. She protested that she had no wish to leave him, but he was firm.

"Mairi, my wife, you have given me more happiness these last years than I had any right to expect. I do not desire to be the cause of your death, and if you stay with me, you and our children will most surely die. So you must go, so that you can raise our son to manhood, and when he is grown he can reclaim what is his." He took her in his arms and kissed her tenderly, then smiled. "Now go to the stables, Mairi. You'll find Seumas waiting for you, and he will see you safe away."

She flung her arms around him, kissed him one last time, for she knew she would not see him again, but she did not allow her tears to fall for that was not her way. She found her children, packed a small bundle of clothes and food, then took them to the yard where old Seumas, Niall's trusted lieutenant, sat waiting with two horses. He took seven-year-old Garrett in front of him, and she held little Megeen in her arms as they rode out under the cover of darkness. Two hours' ride away they came to a forest, but to enter the wood they had to cross a deep stream. There was a bridge across it, and as they rode over Seumas said, "You and the little ones will be safe enough here, lady. They say the bridge is the haunt of a Pooka, and Cathal is one to stay clear of such things, so his men will not bother you."

They followed a narrow path deep into the dark and silent wood until they reached a clearing. There was a small cottage with a thatched roof, the kind that poor farmers lived in, and it was here that Seumas reined his horse to a halt. "This will be your home, lady. You will find food and turf for the fire, and all that you need. The people will know where to find you, and they will see to your needs. As for me, I go back to the hall. I have lived at Niall's side, and I will die there." He gave her a brief salute, then wheeled about and was lost in the darkness.

She found the cottage as he said it would be, and set about making a fire from the turf piled on the hearth, and when it had blazed high, she had a look about. It was a small place, with two small rooms. The main room, with a fireplace, was a kitchen, holding a rough table and a cupboard and some chairs. The other room was a bedchamber with a large bed for her and Megeen, and a little trundle bed that pulled out from it for Garrett. There was a chest for their clothes, and another small one with blankets against the cold of winter.

She put the children to sleep, then went back to the kitchen to kneel before the fire. She saw that someone had provided her with a spindle and a small loom, that she might spin thread and weave cloth for their needs, and there was a large sack of wool beside the spindle. It was Niall's doing, she thought, for he knew how much she hated idleness. And then she stared long and sadly into the fire, too unhappy for tears at the thought that she would never again see the good old man who had been her husband. Though he had not been the hero of a young girl's dreams, still he had been a kind companion and the father of her children, and his death left an empty place that ached and could not be filled. She fell asleep like that, and when she woke to the first light of dawn, she put aside her sorrow and began to live her new life.

Her days took on a sameness. She fed and cared for the children and kept the little house sparkling, and sometimes she gathered herbs and plants that she could use for healing, for she knew much about curing the sick. As the days grew colder, she spun her wool into thread, and then wove woolen cloth from it so that they might have warm clothes for the winter. It was a simple life, and a pleasant one. She had few cares, for her husband's people took it upon themselves to see that she and her little ones were fed; they would leave her cheese or milk or a slab of bacon. In return, she did what she could for the sick, but she felt ashamed that she could give back so little to her people who gave her so much.

There was little love lost for Cathal, for he was what Niall had called him; a hard man. He showed no mercy for a peasant whose rent was a day or two late, or who could not

Pooka's Bridge

meet the rents because of sickness or misfortune. Those who could not pay he turned out homeless, with no care for their families. Mairi heard the stories from those who came to see her in the evenings, and she remembered her promise to her husband. But how could a little boy like Garrett gain back his land? That was a job for a soldier, not a lad of seven years.

Garrett was growing into a fine boy, with his mother's dark hair and his father's grey eyes, and the courage of them both. He had a high heart, did the boy, and the curiosity of a cat. He loved best to be exploring the woods, and though his mother bade him stay close by, if the truth be told, he did not always obey. And so it was that one day he wandered away as far as the Pooka's bridge, and when it grew late he still had not come home. Mairi was nearly wild with worry, but she could not leave the house and Megeen all alone so that she could search for him.

When one of her husband's men came to leave her some food, she begged him, weeping (and she did not cry often), to find her son for her, and he promised to do what he could. He returned the next night, and his lined face was grave.

"Lady, the news is not good. I've asked about, and this is what I've heard: It seems some of Cathal's men came down to the pub for a drink or two, and they spoke long of what they'd seen. They were down at the bridge—the Pooka's bridge. They came upon young Garrett, and thought to make sport of him, for they thought he'd a look of the old lord about him—that he might be one of his by-blows—begging your pardon, lady, but they judge all by Cathal. When they went to cross the bridge to grab him and carry him to the hall, a huge, grey horse came out of the woods, and bent down to let the boy mount. And then the horse disappeared into the woods, and they could find no trace of it, not even a hoofprint in the dirt." He shook his head. "It must have been the Pooka, lady, that came for your son, and I don't know which could be worse, the Pooka taking him or Cathal."

"I've a better chance of getting Garrett back from the Sidhe, than from Cathal O'Farrell, for if he'd gotten his hands on my son, there'd be no hope at all. Cathal would know him for Niall's son as soon as he laid eyes upon him." She got to her feet and pulled her grey cloak from the hook by the door and wrapped it round her. "And if you will stay with Megeen, I will go fetch my son."

And though she sounded quite calm and unafraid, her heart was thudding quickly in her breast, for she was sorely troubled for Garrett. She hid her fear, however, and spoke calmly, for that was the way she was. "I shall return as soon as I have found him," she said, and told him where to find a loaf of bread, and the makings of the breakfast porridge and tea, in case she should not get back before Megeen woke.

Wrapped in her drab cloak, she made her way through the forest. She no longer feared the woods. All the creatures knew her, and would not have harmed her, and the night-noises were as reassuring to her as the soft sound of Megeen breathing in her sleep. But when she reached the bridge she no longer felt at ease. It was a wild, dark place, a stone bridge built so long ago that it was easy to believe that the Sidhe themselves had made it, and it glittered darkly in the wan light of the moon.

She crossed the bridge, till she stood in its exact center. Then she called softly in her clear, sweet voice, "Pooka! I have come for the boy you took yester night. Pooka!"

All was silent.

"Pooka! I have come for my son, the boy you carried away last night! Pooka, come to me."

There was no sound but her own breathing to disturb the quiet.

Shivering in the cold, more frightened by the silence than if she'd heard a banshee keening, Mairi tried a third time. "Pooka, it's tired of waiting for you I am. You've taken my son, and I've come for him. Show yourself to me now, or I'll think you a coward."

Then from the woods she heard a sound like distant thunder, and she trembled, for she knew it must be the Pooka coming in answer to her challenge. She was not a coward to tremble, for anyone with sense would think twice before angering a Pooka. They were said to be fiery of temper, wild spirits that could not be tamed, and with little love for humankind. They were shape-shifters, taking many forms, but most often that of a horse or an ass, and leading travelers astray.

The dim crashing of hoofbeats grew louder and louder as

the Pooka came closer and closer. At last it stood at the edge of the wood, a great grey horse with eyes that shone like flame and a mane and tail of silver, and silver hooves. It looked at her and spoke.

"Who is it who calls me so late at night?" It had a wild, fearsome voice, like the wind, but there was an undertone of sweetness in it, like the clean quiet after a summer storm, and the huge, glowing eyes had the warmth of flame as well as its brightness.

"Tis Mairi O'Farrell, and I've come to fetch my son. He's the boy you stole last night," she said boldly.

"And what use would I have for a boy, silly mortal woman? Why should I steal a boy?"

"As for that, I'm sure I don't know, but the old tales say the Sidhe sometimes do so, and it's you that Cathal's men saw carry off my boy last night."

"Oh, is it the dark-haired lad you're after? I did not steal him at all, I just carried him away to safety before that villain's men did harm to him. That will teach you not to heed the gossip of old women," he said reproachfully.

"Then I thank you for saving my son, for Cathal would have had him killed, and I'll thank you doubly for bringing the boy back to me."

Then the Pooka pawed the ground three times with his silver hoof, and shook his silver-maned head. "That I cannot do, mortal woman, for he dwells with the Sidhe now, and only our king, Finvarra, can let him go."

At that Mairi threw back her hood and raised her pale face to the sky, and whispered, "God in heaven, what's to become of me? I've lost my husband, and now I must lose my son as well." Her white cheeks were wet with tears that shone like diamonds in the moonlight, and even in her sorrow she was beautiful.

"If you ask Finvarra, it is possible that he will send the boy back to you," said the Pooka.

"But how shall I find him?"

"In his sid, under the earth."

"And how should I know where that is?" asked Mairi. "It is not marked on any map I've ever seen."

"And why should it be? Such maps are for men, and what have men to do with the Good Folk? But I can carry you there on my back, as I carried your son."

Then he stood quietly so that she might climb onto his back. "Catch hold of my mane, for the ride will be long and swift, and you must not fall off for I will not be able to save you if you do."

"Pooka," said Mairi, clutching tightly around his neck, "what can I give you for this favor?"

"You have given me your tears, and that's more than any other human has done. Now hold fast, for we go!"

It seemed to Mairi that they took to the air, though the Pooka had no wings. The only sounds were the rushing whoosh of the wind, the distant roaring of the sea, and the occasional hoot of an owl. At first she kept her face buried in the Pooka's mane, which was soft as silk against her cheek, so that she could see nothing, but at last she looked about her and saw that the ground seemed very far away, the trees and road and houses like a toy village. Then the mist swirled up around them, and the dark night clouds enwrapped them like a cloak of black velvet and there was nothing but the wind and the darkness.

"Pooka," whispered Mairi, "if the Sidhe do not steal children, why are the stories told?"

"And how would I know that, Mairi O'Farrell? Who tells these stories?"

"The minstrels sing them, and the seannachies tell them at the hearth. One of the old stories says that the Good Folk pay a tax to hell of a living man," said Mairi.

"Not the Sidhe!" roared the Pooka. "We are the children of Danu, who came to Ireland long before your race thought of it, and we owe allegiance only to our king, and to no other—not even Hell would dare to stand against us. So if you hear this story again, tell them the truth of it."

"Well," conceded Mairi, "they say it happened over the sea, and not in Ireland."

The mists of darkness began to thin, and once more Mairi could see the earth spread out below her, but it was not the countryside she knew. It was a strange and wondrous place, an island set in the middle of a lake like a jewel, and on the island was a great castle all of shining glass. Through the crystal walls she could see the light of torches and richly-garbed figures moving gracefully through the halls.

"You see the castle of Finvarra."

And the Pooka glided down to the smooth grass. Then he stamped his silver hooves three times, and suddenly there stood in the place of the great grey horse, a man.

He was tall and slim, garbed in shimmering grey velvet and silk, embroidered all over with silver thread. His hair, falling to his shoulder, was so pale that it had a silver sheen to it, and his light grey eyes sparkled with silver lights. He had the merry face of one who has never known fear or pain, only joy, with a wide, mischievous mouth made for laughter. He bowed to her with an elegant grace.

"My lady, shall I bring you to the king?"

"Are you my Pooka?" asked Mairi, a little breathless from the swiftness of it all.

"And who else should I be? But this is my real shape, if any shape is real. Now come, you must see to your son." He took her hand and led her through the crystal doors and into the great hall of the palace.

The crowd of dancers, all beautiful, all richly dressed, parted before them, and they walked straight from the door to the dais on which sat Finvarra and his lady on two thrones of silver and gold. Behind them hung tapestries shining with gems, and the torches burned bright in jeweled holders. The floors were marble, whiter than new snow, but the dais on which the two thrones rested was of pure gold. Finvarra, the King of the Sidhe, was a man as golden as the sun, and his flame-haired queen was as glorious as a summer sunset.

The Pooka bowed low before them. "My lord and lady, I ask your pardon for this, but I have brought a mortal to your hall."

"This is the second time you have done so," said the King sternly. "Do you plan to make a habit of it?"

"You told me I had done well to bring the boy, and now I come with his mother, who would speak to you about her son."

Mairi curtsied. "I am most grateful for what you have done for my son, but I have come to fetch him home."

Finvarra said, "No one leaves this land once they have come."

"My son is mortal, and he belongs at home, not here. He and his sister are all I have left, and I promised his dead father I would raise him to claim his heritage that Cathal O'Farrell stole."

Then the queen spoke. "The Pooka told us he saved the boy from those who would do him harm. Would you take the boy away from here, where he is safe and will never grow old—would you take him from this, back to the world, where he will know toil and pain and death, where an enemy waits who might kill him if he had the chance?"

Mairi shut her eyes against the magnificence of it all, for what mother could wish her child to trade such beauty for a poor cottage and the hope of gaining back a timbered hall? But at last she met the king's gaze squarely, and this was her answer: "My lord king, it is not my choice to make. I made a vow to my dear husband Niall, and I must keep that vow. Now where is my son?"

The king made a gesture, and one of his lords came forward, leading Garrett by the hand. He ran to his mother and put his arms about her, and she held him tight for a moment, then said over his shoulder, "Thank you, my lord, for what you have done for me."

"Mairi O'Farrell, you are no ordinary woman. Not since the days of Finn and the Fianna has one of your kind come freely to this land, seeking nothing from us. You have the heart of Emer when she came to Tir N'an Og searching for Cuchulain, and for your courage I grant you this: if ever you have great need, you have only to send us word by the Pooka and we will aid you. Go now, and take your son with you."

So Mairi and her son left the castle with the Pooka, and when they reached the lawn, the Pooka resumed his horse shape. Mairi mounted him, with Garrett before her.

"The trip back will go easier—it's easier to go than to come," said the Pooka.

"Why is that?" asked Mairi.

"And how would I know that? I only know that it is."

The ride was swift as a bird's flight, and it seemed scarcely a moment before Miari stood again on the old stone bridge, with the pale moonlight glinting silver on the Pooka's mane.

"I have done what you asked, woman," said the Pooka. "I hope you are satisfied."

"I am that, Pooka. Is there nothing I can do to show you my thanks?"

"Nothing."

Then, as quickly as the moon vanishing behind a cloud,

she bent and kissed the Pooka on his forehead, between his great, glowing eyes. "My thanks for your help, then."

And she took Garrett home to the little cottage where Megeen slept peacefully, guarded by the old soldier.

For a time all went well for the three of them. They did not grow rich, but they did not want for much either. Mairi's fine weaving and needlework brought them a little money, and she used this to pay back the people who had helped her. Winter came, and on most days she and the children huddled around the warm fire, while she sang and told them stories of the old days. Garrett especially loved to hear of the Sidhe, and he would often talk of the wonders he had seen in Finvarra's land—and Mairi would remember how the Pooka looked in human form, with those large grey eyes smiling down at her.

Then one day, a young farmer came to Mairi and begged her to help his wife, who was having their first child, and the midwife could not come because of the snow. Mairi had no wish to leave her children alone, but she saw the fear in the young husband's face, and so she told Garrett to stay with his sister and let no one in. Then she drew on her cloak and went out. The birth was a long, hard one, but at last the mother lay with her new babe in her arms, and Mairi could go home.

As she walked through the woods at the young man's side, she was suddenly overcome by foreboding. The woods were too quiet, as if all the animals were hiding, and the snow looked as if many feet had trampled it flat. When she saw smoke, she broke into a run, and although she half-expected what she saw, it was still a shock.

The little cottage was only a smoking ruin. Her children were nowhere to be seen, and there was no sign of them, though she searched the charred remains of her home.

"It is Cathal who has done this, may the devil take his black heart," she whispered. "He has killed my husband, and now he has taken my children. I will have him for this. I will have him."

"Lady!" The young man caught her arm, but she shook free of him.

"I go to seek my vengeance for this. Go, and bring together all of my husband's men who still live. We will meet together at the Pooka's bridge at dawn."

She strode away from him, and made her way to the bridge.

"Pooka!" she called. "Pooka, I have come to claim my boon from Finvarra."

With a thudding of hooves, the Pooka came galloping, then stopped stock-still before her. "What do you want of me, Mairi O'Farrell?"

"Vengeance," she said.

"For what?"

"For my husband, who is slain, and my children who will die at Cathal's hands. He came this night, and burned my house and carried away my children. I have called together my husband's men, and we will attack at dawn."

"And what do you want me to do?"

"Bear my message to Finvarra, and tell him that I ask his aid in my trouble. He will know what is the best way to help me. I have faith in his wisdom."

He bent his head, as if to bow. "I am gone, my lady."

She waited through the night at the bridge, and one by one the men gathered there. When the first light of dawn lit the sky, there were only a score of men with her, all that remained of her husband's once-proud troops. When the sun began to rise in the sky against the crimson clouds, the Pooka appeared.

"What news from Finvarra?"

"He bids you climb on my back, and ride against Cathal. His aid will come when you most need it."

So she did as Finvarra bade her, and led her men against Cathal's troops at the hall. And as the dawn flamed brightly, they charged forward across the snow.

"And what do you think to do with those old men at your back, woman? Surely you don't mean to do battle? If so we'll have to arm ourselves with brooms, for fear we'll break their aged bones."

She ignored the taunts of the sentries. "Tell Cathal I've come for my children, and to reclaim the hall in my son's name."

The sentries laughed, but a moment or two later Cathal himself appeared on the walls. "Go away, woman. Your children will be safe with me."

"As safe as their father, Cathal O'Farrell?"

But what answer he might have made to that the world will never know, for at that moment, as the sun glowed golden in the dawn sky, turning the icicles to diamonds, a cloud of glimmering gold and silver and bronze appeared on the horizon, and thunder was heard, and lightning flashed, though there was not a storm cloud in the sky. And as the great, shining mass moved closer, it could be seen to be a host of riders in armor of silver and bronze, and at their head was a rider all in gold, holding aloft a golden spear, and he was Finvarra himself.

"Do you dare to stand before the host of the Sidhe?" cried the Pooka. "Can a mortal man hope to withstand the might and glory of the Tuatha de Danann? Surrender, Cathal, if you've a grain of sense."

It was not up to Cathal to order his men to do anything, for they were so terrified at the sight of the great troop that they dropped their weapons and fell to their knees, too afraid to lift their heads. Then Finvarra threw his golden spear, and it struck Cathal in the breast, killing him instantly. When its work was done, the spear returned to his hand.

"Take warning, mortal men, that you do not interfere again with those I have chosen to protect, for I may not spare the rest of you next time."

Then the host left as swiftly as they had come, and there was not even a hoofprint left behind to show that they had ever been there.

The men went in to set the hall to rights, and Mairi turned to thank the Pooka, and found that he had taken human form again.

"Mairi O'Farrell, you have done as you promised your husband. The hall belongs to your son, to rule when he comes of age. Your life is your own now. Spend it with me in Finvarra's land."

She leaned her head against his shoulder. "Would that I could, but I am not yet free, Pooka. I have still to raise my son to manhood, before my vow is fulfilled."

"And how long will that take, woman?"

"When he takes a wife, my duty will be over. Then I will be mistress of my own life again."

"When that day comes, you need only call for me, and I will be there."

"Pooka, Pooka, how can I thank you for your kindness?"

He bent his head and kissed her lips. "You have given me your tears, and you have given me your kiss. For now that is enough."

Then he was gone as well, leaving her alone.

She whispered softly, so that no one would hear, "I give you my love, Pooka, and my heart."

The years passed, and Garrett grew into a handsome young man. He ruled wisely and well with Mairi's advice, and never acted rashly or harshly, remembering how his people had cared for the three of them after his father's death. Megeen found a kind and handsome husband, and Garrett saw her wed with great ceremony and joy. At last his own eyes fell upon the lovely daughter of a lord of the West, and so they were married. Mairi, still lovely though her long, dark braids now glinted with silver, smiled as she saw her son lead his new wife to the place of honor.

While the hall feasted, she dressed herself in her finest gown of green silk sewn with a design of leaves and knotwork, and donned a cloak of white wool bordered in green and embroidered all over with green and gold, so that she looked like a bride herself. Then she crept out of the hall and rode to the bridge, where she called in her clear, sweet voice, "Pooka!"

This time, when she heard the sound like distant thunder, she still trembled, but not from fear. As the dim crashing of hoofbeats grew louder and louder, her heart thudded in her breast. At last the Pooka stood before her, a great grey horse with eyes that shone like flame and a mane and tail of silver and silver hooves.

"Who is it that calls me so late at night?" And its voice was wild and fearsome like the wind, but with an undertone of sweetness like the clean quiet after a summer storm.

"Tis I, Mairi O'Farrell."

"And what do you want of me?"

Before her eyes, he changed into the smiling young lord with pale hair that shone like silver, and she turned away from him, suddenly seeing herself as he must see her. Her dark hair was streaked with gray, her pale skin lined, her green eyes set about with wrinkles. She had grown old, old, while he, through the magic of Finvarra's land, was still young. How could she ask for his love?

"There is nothing I want from you, Pooka," she said dully, her heart aching with sadness.

"Then I will tell you what I will give you, Mairi, my heart's treasure. You have my love, for as long as you want it."

"You can look at me and say that? Pooka, do not mock me. I know I have grown old. Do not laugh at me."

"I look at you and see the fairest of women, with hair as dark as the night sky, and cheeks smooth as rose petals, and whiter than seafoam, and a heart brave enough to dare to tame a wild thing like a Pooka. You have tamed me, Mairi. Will you leave me alone to grieve for all my days?"

He turned her about and took her in his two arms and kissed her gently as a summer rain. "See yourself through my eyes, lady."

And when she looked down she saw that her thick braids were indeed dark as the night sky, with no silver at all, and when she reached up a hand to her cheek, her skin was soft as a girl's.

And they went away together to Finvarra's land, and there they may be living still, for no one ever dies or grows old there. And that is how a lady once tamed a Pooka, with nothing but a brave and loving heart.

John Shirley and William Gibson

THE BELONGING KIND

Anyone who has ever dropped into a bar cannot have failed to notice that among the customers are some who appear to be so thoroughly a part of the scene that they actually belong there along with the fixtures. Some of these habitues might be stranger than we imagine, or so the authors of "The Belonging Kind" speculate.

It might have been in Club Justine, or Jimbo's, or Sad Jack's, or The Rafters; Coretti could never be sure where he'd first seen her. At any time, she might have been in any one of those bars. She swam through the submarine half-life of bottles and glassware and the slow swirl of cigarette smoke ... she moved through her natural element, one bar after another.

Now, Coretti remembered their first meeting as if he saw it through the wrong end of a powerful telescope, small and clear and very far away.

He noticed her first in The Backdoor Lounge. It was called The Backdoor because you entered through a narrow back alley. The alley's walls crawled with graffiti, its caged lights ticked with moths. Flakes from its white-painted bricks crunched underfoot. And then you pushed through into a dim space inhabited by a faintly confusing sense of the half-dozen other bars that had tried and failed in the same room under different managements. Coretti sometimes went there because he liked the weary smile of the black bartender, and because the few customers rarely tried to get chummy.

He wasn't very good at conversation with strangers, not at parties and not at bars.

He was fine at the community college where he lectured in introductory linguistics; he could talk with the head of his department about sequencing and options in conversational openings. But he could never talk to strangers in bars or at parties. He didn't go to many parties. He went to a lot of bars.

Coretti didn't know how to dress. Clothing was a language and Coretti a sartorial stutterer, unable to make the kind of basic coherent fashion statement that would put strangers at their ease. His ex-wife told him he dressed like a Martian; that he didn't look as though he belonged anywhere in the city. He hadn't liked her saying that, because it was true.

He hadn't ever had a girl like the one who sat with her back arched slightly in the undersea light that splashed along the bar in The Backdoor. The same light was screwed into the lenses of the bartender's glasses, wound into the necks of the rows of bottles, splashed dully across the mirror. In that light her dress was the green of young corn, like a husk half stripped away, showing back and cleavage and lots of thigh through the slits up the side. Her hair was coppery that night. And, that night, her eyes were green.

He pushed resolutely between the empty chrome-and-formica tables until he reached the bar, where he ordered a straight bourbon. He took off his duffelcoat, and wound up holding it on his lap when he sat down one stool away from her. Great, he screamed to himself, she'll think you're hiding an erection. And he was startled to realize that he had one to hide. He studied himself in the mirror behind the bar, a thirtyish man with thinning dark hair and a pale, narrow face bobbling on a long neck, too long for the open collar of the nylon shirt printed with engravings of 1910 automobiles in three vivid colors. He wore a tie with broad maroon and black diagonals, too narrow, he supposed, for what he now saw as the grotesquely long points of his collar. Or it was the wrong color. Something.

Beside him, in the dark clarity of the mirror, the green-eyed woman looked like *Irma La Douce*. But looking closer, studying her face, he shivered. A face like an animal's. A beautiful face, but simple, cunning, two-dimensional. When she senses you're looking at her, Coretti thought, she'll give you the smile, disdainful amusement—or whatever you'd expect.

Coretti blurted, "May I, um, buy you a drink?"

At moments like these, Coretti was possessed by an agonizingly stiff, schoolmasterish linguistic tic. *Um*. He winced. *Um*.

"You would, um, like to buy me a drink? Why, how kind of you," she said, astonishing him. "That would be very nice." Distantly, he noticed that her reply was as stilted and insecure as his own. She added, "A tom collins, on this occasion, would be lovely."

On this occasion? Lovely? Rattled, Coretti ordered two drinks and paid.

A big woman in jeans and an embroidered cowboy shirt bellied up to the bar beside him and asked the bartender for change. "Well hey," she said. Then she strutted to the jukebox and punched for Conway and Loretta's, "You're the Reason Our Kids Are Ugly." Coretti turned to the woman in green, and murmured haltingly:

"Do you enjoy country and western music?" *Do you enjoy* ... ? He groaned secretly at his phrasing, and tried to smile.

"Yes indeed," she answered, the faintest twang edging her voice, "I sure do."

The cowgirl sat down beside him and asked her, winking, "This li'l terror here givin' you a hard time?"

And the animal-eyed lady in green replied, "Oh hell no, honey, I got my eye on 'im." And laughed. Just the right amount of laugh. The part of Coretti that was dialectologist stirred uneasily; too perfect a shift in phrasing and inflection. An actress? A talented mimic? The word "mimetic" rose suddenly in his mind, but he pushed it aside to study her reflection in the mirror; the rows of bottles occluded her breasts like a gown of glass.

"The name's Coretti," he said, his verbal poltergeist shifting abruptly to a totally unconvincing tough-guy mode, "Michael Coretti."

"A pleasure," she said, too softly for the other woman to hear, and again she had slipped into the lame parody of Emily Post.

"Conway and Loretta," said the cowgirl, to no one in particular.

"Antoinette," said the woman in green, and inclined her head. She finished her drink, pretended to glance at a watch, said thank-you-for-the-drink too damn politely, and left.

Ten minutes later Coretti was following her down Third Avenue. He had never followed anyone in his life and it both frightened and excited him. Forty feet seemed a discreet distance, but what should he do if she happened to glance over her shoulder?

Third Avenue isn't a dark street, and it was there, in the light of a streetlamp, like a stage light, that she began to change. The street was deserted.

She was crossing the street. She stepped off the curb and it began. It began with tints in her hair—at first he thought they were reflections. But there was no neon there to cast the blobs of color that appeared, color sliding and merging like oil slicks. Then the colors bled away and in three seconds she was white-blond. He was sure it was a trick of the light until her dress began to writhe, twisting across her body like shrink-wrap plastic. Part of it fell away entirely and lay in curling shreds on the pavement, shed like the skin of some fabulous animal. When Coretti passed, it was green foam, fizzing, dissolving, gone. He looked back up at her and the dress was another dress, green satin, shifting with reflections. Her shoes had changed too. Her shoulders were bare except for thin straps that crossed at the small of her back. Her hair had become short, spiky.

He found that he was leaning against a jeweler's plate-glass window, his breath coming ragged and harsh with the damp of the autumn evening. He heard the disco's heartbeat from two blocks away. As she neared it, her movements began subtly to take on a new rhythm—a shift in emphasis in the sway of her hips, in the way she put her heels down on the sidewalk. The doorman let her pass with a vague nod. He stopped Coretti and stared at his driver's license and frowned at his duffelcoat. Coretti anxiously scanned the wash of lights at the top of a milky plastic stairway beyond the doorman. She had vanished there, into robotic flashing and redundant thunder.

Grudgingly the man let him pass, and he pounded up the stairs, his haste disturbing the lights beneath the translucent plastic steps.

Coretti had never been in a disco before; he found himself in an environment designed for complete satisfaction-in-distraction. He waded nervously through the motion and the fashions and the mechanical urban chants booming from the huge speakers. He sought her almost blindly on the pose-clotted dance floor, amid strobe lightning.

And found her at the bar, drinking a tall, lurid cooler and listening to a young man who wore a loose shirt of pale silk and very tight black pants. She nodded at what Coretti took to be appropriate intervals. Coretti ordered by pointing at a bottle of bourbon. She drank five of the tall drinks and then followed the young man to the dance floor.

She moved in perfect accord with the music, striking a series of poses; she went through the entire prescribed sequence, gracefully but not artfully, fitting in perfectly. Always, always fitting in perfectly. Her companion danced mechanically, moving through the ritual with effort.

When the dance ended, she turned abruptly and dived into the thick of the crowd. The shifting throng closed about her like something molten.

Coretti plunged in after her, his eyes never leaving her—and he was the only one to follow her change. By the time she reached the stair she was auburn-haired and wore a long blue dress. A white flower blossomed in her hair, behind her right ear; her hair was longer and straighter now. Her breasts had become slightly larger, and her hips a shade heavier. She took the stairs two at a time, and he was afraid for her then. All those drinks.

But the alcohol seemed to have had no effect on her at all.

Never taking his eyes from her, Coretti followed, his heartbeat outspeeding the disco-throb at his back, sure that at any moment she would turn, glare at him, call for help.

Two blocks down Third she turned in at Lothario's. There was something different in her step now. Lothario's was a

The Belonging Kind

quiet complex of rooms hung with ferns and Art Deco mirrors. There were fake Tiffany lamps hanging from the ceiling, alternating with wooden-bladed fans that rotated too slowly to stir the wisps of smoke drifting through the consciously mellow drone of conversation. After the disco, Lothario's was familiar and comforting. A jazz pianist in pinstriped shirt sleeves and loosely knotted tie competed softly with talk and laughter from a dozen tables.

She was at the bar; the stools were only half taken, but Coretti chose a wall table, in the shadow of a miniature palm, and ordered bourbon.

He drank the bourbon and ordered another. He couldn't feel the alcohol much, tonight.

She sat beside a young man, yet another young man with the usual set of bland, regular features. He wore a yellow golf shirt and pressed jeans. Her hip was touching his, just a little. They didn't seem to be speaking, but Coretti felt they were somehow communing. They were leaning toward one another slightly, silent. Coretti felt odd. He went to the rest room and splashed his face with water. Coming back, he managed to pass within three feet of them. Their lips didn't move till he was within earshot.

They took turns murmuring realistic palaver:

"—saw his earlier films, but—"

"But he's rather self-indulgent, don't you think?"

"Sure, but in the sense that—"

And, for the first time, Coretti knew what they were, what they must be. They were the kind you see in bars who seem to have grown there, who seem genuinely at home there. Not drunks, but human fixtures. Functions of the bar. The belonging kind.

Something in him yearned for a confrontation. He reached his table, but found himself unable to sit down. He turned, took a deep breath, and walked woodenly toward the bar. He wanted to tap her on her smooth shoulder and ask who she was, and exactly what she was, and point out the cold irony of the fact that it was he, Coretti, the Martian dresser, the eavesdropper, the outsider, the one whose clothes and conversation never fit, who had at last guessed their secret.

But his nerve broke and he merely took a seat beside her and ordered bourbon.

"But don't you think," she asked her companion, "that it's all relative?"

The two seats beyond her companion were quickly taken by a couple who were talking politics. Antoinette and Golf Shirt took up the political theme seamlessly, recycling, speaking just loudly enough to be overheard. Her face, as she spoke, was expressionless. A bird trilling on a limb.

She sat so easily on her stool, as if it were a nest. Golf Shirt paid for the drinks. He always had the exact change, unless he wanted to leave a tip. Coretti watched them work their way methodically through six cocktails each, like insects feeding on nectar. But their voices never grew louder, their cheeks didn't redden, and when at last they stood, they moved without a trace of drunkenness—a weakness, thought Coretti, a gap in their camouflage.

They paid him absolutely no attention while he followed them through three successive bars.

As they entered Waylon's, they metamorphosed so quickly that Coretti had trouble following the stages of the change. It was one of those places with toilet doors marked Pointers and Setters, and a little imitation pine plaque over the jars of beef jerky and pickled sausages: *We've got a deal with the bank. They don't serve beer and we don't cash checks.*

She was plump in Waylon's, and there were dark hollows under her eyes. There were coffee stains on her polyester pantsuit. Her companion wore jeans, a T-shirt, and a red baseball cap with a red-and-white Peterbilt patch. Coretti risked losing them when he spent a frantic minute in "Pointers," blinking in confusion at a hand-lettered cardboard sign that said, *We aim to please—You aim too, please.*

Third Avenue lost itself near the waterfront in a petrified snarl of brickwork. In the last block, bright vomit marked the pavement at intervals, and the old men dozed in front of black-and-white TVs, sealed forever behind the fogged plate-glass of faded hotels.

The bar they found there had no name. An ace of diamonds was gradually flaking away on the unwashed window, and the bartender had a face like a closed fist. An FM transistor in ivory plastic keened easy-listening rock to the uneven ranks of deserted tables. They drank beer and shots. They were old now, two ciphers who drank and smoked in the light of bare bulbs, coughing over a pack of crumpled Camels she produced from the pocket of a dirty tan raincoat.

At 2:25 they were in the rooftop lounge of the new hotel complex that rose above the waterfront. She wore an evening dress and he wore a dark suit. They drank cognac and pretended to admire the city lights. They each had three cognacs while Coretti watched them over two ounces of Wild Turkey in a Waterford crystal highball glass.

They drank until last call. Coretti followed them into the elevator. They smiled politely but otherwise ignored him. There were two cabs in front of the hotel; they took one, Coretti the other.

"Follow that cab," said Coretti huskily, thrusting his last twenty at the aging hippie driver.

"Sure, man, sure. . . ." The driver dogged the other cab for six blocks, to another, more modest hotel. They got out and went in. Coretti slowly climbed out of his cab, breathing hard.

He ached with jealousy: for the personification of conformity, this woman who was not a woman, this human wallpaper. Coretti gazed at the hotel—and lost his nerve. He turned away.

He walked home. Sixteen blocks. At some point he realized that he wasn't drunk. Not drunk at all.

In the morning he phoned in to cancel his early class. But his hangover never quite came. His mouth wasn't desiccated, and staring at himself in the bathroom mirror he saw that his eyes weren't bloodshot.

In the afternoon he slept, and dreamed of sheep-faced people reflected in mirrors behind rows of bottles.

That night he went out to dinner, alone—and ate nothing. The food looked back at him, somehow. He stirred it about to make it look as if he'd eaten a little, paid, and went to a bar. And another. And another bar, looking for her. He was using his credit card now, though he was already badly in the hole under VISA. If he saw her, he didn't recognize her.

Sometimes he watched the hotel he'd seen her go into. He looked carefully at each of the couples who came and went. Not that he'd be able to spot her from her looks alone—but there should be a *feeling*, some kind of intuitive recognition. He watched the couples and he was never sure.

In the following weeks he systematically visited every boozy watering hole in the city. Armed at first with a city map and five torn Yellow Pages, he gradually progressed to the more obscure establishments, places with unlisted numbers. Some had no phone at all. He joined dubious private clubs, discovered unlicensed after-hours retreats where you brought your own, and sat nervously in dark rooms devoted to areas of fringe sexuality he had not known existed.

But he continued on what became his nightly circuit. He always began at The Backdoor. She was never there, or in the next place, or the next. The bartenders knew him and they liked to see him come in, because he bought drinks continuously, and never seemed to get drunk. So he stared at the other customers a bit—so what?

Coretti lost his job.

He'd missed classes too many times. He'd taken to watching the hotel when he could, even in the daytime. He'd been seen in too many bars. He never seemed to change his clothes. He refused night classes. He would let a lecture trail off in the middle as he turned to gaze vacantly out the window.

He was secretly pleased at being fired. They had looked at him oddly at faculty lunches when he couldn't eat his food. And now he had more time for the search.

Coretti found her at 2:15 on a Wednesday morning, in a gay bar called The Barn. Paneled in rough wood and hung with halters and rusting farm equipment, the place was shrill with perfume and laughter and beer. She was everyone's giggling sister, in a blue-sequined dress, a green feather in her coiffed brown hair. Through a sweeping sense of almost cellular relief, Coretti was aware of a kind of admiration, a strange pride he now felt in her—and her kind. Here, too, she belonged. She was a representative type, a fag-hag who posed no threat to the queens or their butchboys. Her companion had become an ageless man with carefully silvered temples, an angora sweater and a trenchcoat.

They drank and drank, and went laughing—laughing just the right sort of laughter—out into the rain. A cab was waiting, its wipers duplicating the beat of Coretti's heart.

Jockeying clumsily across the wet sidewalk, Coretti scurried into the cab, dreading their reaction.

Coretti was in the back seat, beside her.

The man with silver temples spoke to the driver. The driver muttered into his hand mike, changed gears, and they flowed away into the rain and the darkened streets. The cityscape made no impression on Coretti who, looking inwardly, was seeing the cab stop, the gray man and the laughing woman pushing him out and pointing, smiling, to the gate of a mental hospital. Or: the cab stopping, the couple turning, sadly shaking their heads. And a dozen times he seemed to see the cab stopping in an empty sidestreet where they methodically throttled him. Coretti left dead in the rain. Because he was an outsider.

But they arrived at Coretti's hotel.

In the dim glow of the cab's dome light he watched closely as the man reached into his coat for the fare. Coretti could see the coat's lining clearly and it was one piece with the angora sweater. No wallet bulged there, and no pocket. But a kind of slit widened. It opened as the man's fingers poised over it, and it disgorged money. Three bills, folded, were extruded smoothly from the slit. The money was slightly damp. It dried, as the man unfolded it, like the wings of a moth just emerging from the chrysalis.

"Keep the change," said the belonging man, climbing out of the cab. Antoinette slid out and Coretti followed, his mind seeing only the slit. The slit wet, edged with red, like a gill.

The lobby was deserted and the desk clerk bent over a crossword. The couple drifted silently across the lobby and into the elevator, Coretti close behind. Once he tried to catch her eye, but she ignored him. And once, as the elevator rose seven floors above Coretti's own, she bent over and sniffed at the chrome wall ashtray, like a dog snuffling at the ground.

Hotels, late at night, are never still. The corridors are never entirely silent. There are countless barely audible sighs, the rustling of sheets, and muffled voices speaking fragments out of sleep. But in the ninth-floor corridor, Coretti seemed to move through a perfect vacuum, soundless, his shoes making no sound at all on the colorless carpet and even the beating of his outsider's heart sucked away into the vague pattern that decorated the wallpaper.

He tried to count the small plastic ovals screwed on the doors, each with its own three figures, but the corridor seemed to go on forever. At last the man halted before a door, a door veneered like all the rest with imitation rosewood, and put his hand over the lock, his palm flat against the metal. Something scraped softly and then the mechanism clicked and the door swung open. As the man withdrew his hand, Coretti saw a grayish-pink, key-shaped sliver of bone retract wetly into the pale flesh.

No lights burned in that room, but the city's dim neon aura filtered in through venetian blinds and allowed him to see the faces of the dozen or more people who sat perched on the bed and the couch and the armchairs and the stools in the kitchenette. At first he thought that their eyes were open, but then he realized that the dull pupils were sealed beneath nicitating membranes, third eyelids that reflected the faint shades of neon from the window. They wore whatever the last bar had called for; shapeless Salvation Army overcoats sat beside bright suburban leisurewear, eyening gowns beside dusty factory clothes, biker's leather by brushed Harris tweed. With sleep, all spurious humanity had vanished.

They were roosting.

His couple seated themselves on the edge of the formica countertop in the kitchenette, and Coretti hesitated in the middle of the empty carpet. Light-years of that carpet seemed to separate him from the others, but something called to him across the distance, promising rest and peace and belonging. And still he hesitated, shaking with an indecision that seemed to rise from the genetic core of his body's every cell.

Until they opened their eyes, all of them simultaneously, the membranes sliding sideways to reveal the alien calm of dwellers in the ocean's darkest trench.

Coretti screamed, and ran away, and fled along corridors and down echoing concrete stairwells to cool rain and the nearly empty streets.

Coretti never returned to his room on the third floor of that hotel. A bored house detective collected the linguistics texts, the single suitcase of clothing, and they were eventually sold at auction. Coretti took a room in a boardinghouse run by a grim Baptist teetotaler who led her roomers in prayer at the start of every overcooked evening meal. She didn't mind

The Belonging Kind

that Coretti never joined them for those meals; he explained that he was given free meals at work. He lied freely and skillfully. He never drank at the boardinghouse, and he never came home drunk. Mr. Coretti was a little odd, but always paid his rent on time. And he was very quiet.

Coretti stopped looking for her. He stopped going to bars. He drank out of a paper bag while going to and from his job at a publisher's warehouse, in an area whose industrial zoning permitted few bars.

He worked nights.

Sometimes, at dawn, perched on the edge of his unmade bed, drifting into sleep—he never slept lying down, now—he thought about her. Antoinette. And them. The belonging kind. Sometimes he speculated dreamily. . . . Perhaps they were like house mice, the sort of small animal evolved to live only in the walls of man-made structures.

A kind of animal that lives only on alcoholic beverages. With peculiar metabolisms they convert the alcohol and the various proteins from mixed drinks and wine and beers into everything they need. And they can change outwardly, like a chameleon or a rockfish, for protection. So they can live among us. And maybe, Coretti thought, they grow in stages. In the early stages seeming like humans, eating the food humans eat, sensing their difference only in a vague disquiet of being an outsider.

A kind of animal with its own cunning, its own special set of urban instincts. And the ability to know its own kind when they're near. Maybe.

And maybe not.

Coretti drifted into sleep.

On a Wednesday three weeks into his new job, his landlady opened his door—she never knocked—and told him that he was wanted on the phone. Her voice was tight with habitual suspicion, and Coretti followed her along the dark hallway to the second-floor sitting room and the telephone.

Lifting the old-fashioned black instrument to his ear, he heard only music at first, and then a wall of sound resolving into a fragmented amalgam of conversations. Laughter. No one spoke to him over the sound of the bar, but the song in the background was "You're the Reason Our Kids are Ugly."

And then the dial tone, when the caller hung up.

Later, alone in his room, listening to the landlady's firm tread in the room below, Coretti realized that there was no need to remain where he was. The summons had come. But the landlady demanded three weeks' notice if anyone wanted to leave. That meant that Coretti owed her money. Instinct told him to leave it for her.

A Christian workingman in the next room coughed in his sleep as Coretti got up and went down the hall to the telephone. Coretti told the evening shift foreman that he was quitting his job. He hung up and went back to his room, locked the door behind him, and slowly removed his clothing until he stood naked before the garish framed lithograph of Jesus above the brown steel bureau.

And then he counted out nine tens. He placed them carefully beside the praying-hands plaque decorating the bureau top.

It was nice-looking money. It was perfectly good money. He made it himself.

This time, he didn't feel like making small talk. She'd been drinking a margarita, and he ordered the same. She paid, producing the money with a deft movement of her hand between the breasts bobbling in her low-cut dress. He glimpsed the gill closing there. An excitement rose in him—but somehow, this time, it didn't center in an erection.

After the third margarita their hips were touching, and something was spreading through him in slow orgasmic waves. It was sticky where they were touching; an area the size of the heel of his thumb where the cloth had parted. He was two men: the one inside fusing with her in total cellular communion, and the shell who sat casually on a stool at the bar, elbows on either side of his drink, fingers toying with a swizzle stick. Smiling benignly into space. Calm in the cool dimness.

And once, but only once, some distant worrisome part of him made Coretti glance down to where soft-ruby tubes pulsed, tendrils tipped with sharp lips worked in the shadows between them. Like the joining tentacles of two strange anemones.

They were mating, and no one knew.

And the bartender, when he brought the next drink, offered

his tired smile and said, "Rainin' out now, innit? Just won't let up."

"Been like that all goddamn week," Coretti answered. "Rainin' to beat the band."

And he said it right. Like a real human being.

Don't miss any of these SF winners:

By JOHN BRUNNER
- ☐ POLYMATH (#UE1766—$2.25)
- ☐ INTERSTELLAR EMPIRE (#UE1668—$2.50)
- ☐ THE REPAIRMEN OF CYCLOPS (#UE1638—$2.25)

By M. A. FOSTER
- ☐ THE MORPHODITE (#UE1669—$2.75)
- ☐ THE GAMEPLAYERS OF ZAN (#UE1497—$2.25)
- ☐ THE WARRIORS OF DAWN (#UE1751—$2.50)

By PHILIP JOSÉ FARMER
- ☐ HADON OF ANCIENT OPAR (#UE1637—$2.50)
- ☐ FLIGHT TO OPAR (#UE1718—$2.50)

By SHARON GREEN
- ☐ THE WARRIOR WITHIN (#UE1707—$2.50)
- ☐ THE CRYSTALS OF MIDA (#UE1735—$2.95)

By PHILIP K. DICK
- ☐ FLOW MY TEARS (#UE1624—$2.25)
- ☐ NOW WAIT FOR LAST YEAR (#UE1654—$2.50)

By CLIFFORD D. SIMAK
- ☐ THE WEREWOLF PRINCIPLE (#UE1708—$2.50)
- ☐ THE GOBLIN RESERVATION (#UE1730—$2.25)

THE NEW AMERICAN LIBRARY, INC.,
P.O. Box 999, Bergenfield, New Jersey 07621

Please send me the DAW BOOKS I have checked above. I am enclosing
$_____ (check or money order—no currency or C.O.D.'s).
Please include the list price plus $1.00 per order to cover handling costs.

Name _____

Address _____

City _____ State _____ Zip Code _____